MW00584262

Current Impressions

Kelly Risser

Clean Teen Publishing

THIS book is a work of fiction. Names, characters, places and incidents are the product of the authors' imagination or are used factiously. Any resemblance to actual persons, living or dead, business establishments, events or locales is entirely coincidental.

NO part of this book may be reproduced, scanned, or distributed in any printed or electronic form without permission. Please do not participate in or encourage piracy of copyrighted materials in violation of the author's rights. Purchase only authorized editions.

Current Impressions
Copyright ©2014 Kelly Risser
All rights reserved.

CLEAN TEEN
PUBLISHING

Cover Design by: Marya Heiman
Typography by: Courtney Nuckels
Editing by: Cynthia Shepp

Content Disclosure

For more information about our content disclosure, please
utilize the QR code above with your
smart phone or visit us at

www.cleanteenpublishing.com.

Chapter 1

Two days ago, I left my human life behind.

I missed my boyfriend, Evan, who I loved and I knew loved me. I had felt his eyes on me when I dove into the ocean, but I refused to look back.

I Changed.

My Selkie fur flowed over my body, and my eyesight sharpened to that of a seal. Before the icy cold could register, the water felt comfortable, warm even. When I broke the surface, I discovered my other senses were enhanced as well. The sky was vibrant. The ocean glistened in a myriad of blues like a sapphire. Words whispered on the wind reached my ears, and the ocean sang. Then, there were the smells. I couldn't identify all of the scents in the bouquet, but I picked up the floral, tangy sea, and the woodsy, spicy scent that was Evan.

Evan. My heart ached. Without turning, I knew he stood guard. It broke my heart to leave him. I'd already lost my mother only months ago. Now I had to leave the man I loved, too. With a sigh that was more of a soft snort in this form, I slid back under the water to follow my father. His home was an island near Scotland. We swam with little rest until we reached it.

"Meara, aren't you coming out?"

Dad stood on the shore, wearing a faded, black T-shirt that bordered on gray and worn blue jeans. His feet were bare. I marveled how I could hear him, clear as if he were standing next to me. He was far away on the shore and not shouting. Would my developed senses stay with me when I switched back to human form?

Treading water, I tried to remember what he told me on the way over about shifting back. At the time, we were passing a whale and her offspring. The tenderness between mother and child distracted me. He said something about needing to choose a form for my Selkie skin. Whatever I chose the first time would be permanent. I studied my dad again. He held his leather jacket casually draped over his right shoulder. I knew it was his Selkie skin, and my aunt Ula's was her backpack. Both were too conspicuous for me. I wanted something small, something easy to carry, like a piece of jewelry. Aunt Brigid's was a choker, but an obvious piece of jewelry like that might not go with all of my outfits. I needed something even less noticeable.

Anklet, I thought.

The deep cold of the ocean seeped into my bones. I wrapped my arms around myself and shivered. Gooseflesh covered my body. My very naked, exposed body. Oh no! How could I get out of the water now? My dad was standing right there.

"Meara?" Dad's voice held the slight clip of impatience.

"I'm naked." It came out as a squeak, no more than a whisper. He bent forward, his hands on his knees, and his shoulders shook. Was he crying? Maybe he was exhausted from our long journey across the Atlantic. I felt strangely exhilarated, but I hadn't spent the last six months trying to keep my mother pain free and alive. During that time, my dad drained himself keeping her comfortable and buying her a few more days to be with us. I would be forever grateful to him.

"Are you okay?" I asked, uncertain. My teeth chattered. I needed to get out or change back. Soon. The water was freezing.

He raised his head and wiped his eyes. "I'm sorry." Dad coughed, but his grin told me he was covering a laugh. He was laughing at me!

"If you think this is so funny—" I scowled and sunk lower into the surf. Let me die of hypothermia and see how much he laughed then! There was no way I was getting out of the ocean and standing before him naked.

"Come out of the water, Meara." He cleared his throat a few times before continuing, his voice steadier. "I'll turn around if that will make you more comfortable." Before I could answer, he spun around and left me staring at his back. After waiting a beat, he asked, "Are you coming?"

"Yes," I mumbled. Straightening my shoulders, I walked toward him and prayed no one else could see me.

"Let's try a simple exercise," he said with his back still to me. "Visualize clothes."

"O-kay." Since when did my dad become Obi-Wan Kenobi? How in the world was I supposed to visualize clothes?

"Close your eyes and picture your favorite outfit. Can you see it?"

I thought about the dress I wore for my high school graduation, a sundress made of pearlescent fabric with thin spaghetti straps. It was so beautiful, and I loved how Evan looked at me in it. I swear I could feel his fingers as he slid the strap from my shoulder... I shivered and stopped that line of thought. Now was not the time. "Okay, I've got it," I said.

"Open your eyes," he said. I looked down and saw my dress. It was dry and like new. After a moment, Dad asked, "Can I turn around now?"

"Yes." I laughed and spun in a circle, watching the dress flare. When I stopped and faced him, he smiled at me proudly.

"I was wearing this when I dove into the ocean," I said. "How—?"

"That's not the actual dress," he interrupted to explain. "It's your visualization of your dress. A very accurate one at that."

I twirled again and felt the fabric grace my legs, my bare feet gliding across the smooth pebbles that made up the shoreline. "So I can change my outfit whenever I want?" The idea absurdly thrilled me.

He shrugged. "Try it."

I pictured something more practical for the rough terrain—jeans, Evan's hockey jersey, and tennis shoes. I didn't need to look to feel the tight jeans encase my legs, the jersey slide over my fingers—it was always a bit too long—and the shoes cover my feet. I laughed. How excellent was that?

"You're good at this." My dad smiled. He reached into his pocket and pulled out my charm bracelet, offering it to me.

"Is this an illusion too?" I held out my wrist and watched him fasten it.

"Visualization," he corrected. "An illusion is not real, but visualization is something you create with your mind. This it is quite real, believe me."

I could make anything I wanted by thinking about it? How unbelievably cool was that? I wished I could call my best friend Kim and tell her. I pictured her face in my mind, her mouth open in surprise, her eyes sparkling as she dared me to visualize one Oscar gown after another.

Dad tapped the bracelet on my wrist, bringing me back to the present. "I conjured that for you from your box."

"Conjured?" I didn't recognize the word. It sounded like witchcraft. "Unlike visualizing something, conjuring is when you call an item to yourself that already exists. Visualization doesn't use much energy; it's limited to clothes and personal items." I tried not to appear disappointed. I should've figured as much. If stories in books were true, then all magic had limitations. Dad continued, "Conjuring takes vast amounts of energy. It's best done with small objects, like your bracelet." He lifted the gold chain with one finger. "It will still protect you until you learn your powers."

Dad charmed the bracelet to protect me from Selkie persuasion. I asked him to after that a Selkie named Kieran manipulated my emotions at the dance club, and Ula and my dad realized my mind was vulnerable to Selkie powers.

"Do I need protection here?" We were in a small cove, surrounded by an embankment. The walls were steep and rocky, the tops covered in springy green moss that looked like hair. It reminded me of those Chia pets they advertised around the holidays. I turned in a slow circle. I didn't see another living creature. The roll of waves breaking on the shore was the only sound.

"I'd rather not take chances," he said, which really didn't answer my question. He added. "You should be safe. Humans cannot find us here."

I wasn't sure why he was worried about humans finding me. The threat had been another Selkie, not a human. It didn't keep me from asking, "Why not?" After all, we passed Scotland and many small islands to get here. The last one, I recalled, was only a short swim away, maybe five miles. I'm sure humans inhabited those places.

"This island is warded. It does not show on human maps or their fancy navigational equipment. Our magic is stronger." He offered me his hand. "Are you ready to see your new home?" When I nodded, he whispered, "Close your eyes."

No sooner had my eyes closed than the earth tilted, and a strong breeze lifted my hair. Jolted, my eyes flew open. We stood on top of the cliff, facing a large fortress. It was not pretty enough to be called a castle, but it was fierce. Weathered, gray stone blended into the hillside, making it appear to be one with the environment. A lookout tower on each corner and a spiked gate completed the striking façade. "I thought you said we were safe here," I murmured in awe.

"Better safe than sorry." His lips quirked. "At any rate, Ronac stood long before I was born."

"Ronac?"

His face softened when he turned toward me. "Our home."

Home. I tasted the word on my tongue even as my eyes drank in the endless green of the land. The brilliant emerald was broken only by the occasional jut of rock, and its beauty astounded me.

I tilted my head and studied my dad. The lines that appeared around his eyes and mouth in the final days of my mom's life had softened. He still looked older than when I first met him, early thirties now instead of mid-twenties, but he appeared healthy and happy. It must have been hard for him to leave his people and stay with us. He had been willing to give this all up.

He squeezed my hand. "Are you ready to go in?"

"Does everyone in the clan live here?" I asked. "I didn't expect you to live in something so—"

"Imposing? Grand?" His eyes sparkled. I shrugged, at a loss for words. Dad's mouth twitched. Was he laughing at me again? "I suppose you thought we slept on the shore like actual seals?"

"I guess... I hadn't really thought about it." I fell in step beside him, and we walked through the raised gate. "Do a lot of Selkies live here?"

"In our clan, yes, but of course, there are other clans all over the world."

"Clans?" I immediately thought of Celts, Highlanders, and other more barbaric communities. Clans sounded medieval.

"That is how we refer to ourselves, yes. You met Kieran. He hails from a clan near Southern California."

Figures, a surfer boy.

Dad cleared his throat. "I'm friends with his father, Stephen."

Confused, I glanced up at my dad. "I thought you told me to stay away from Kieran. That he was dangerous."

"Yes, well." Dad shifted uncomfortably. "You see, I confronted Kieran. He swears that he didn't use magic on you."

"You believe him?"

Dad shrugged. After I danced with Kieran at the club, we kissed. My emotions were such a mess that night, sorting them out was impossible. Maybe I couldn't blame Kieran for what happened. My pulse jumped when I pictured his deep brown eyes and gorgeous, tan body. I was attracted to him, magic or not. "Do clans interact?"

"Sometimes," Dad said. "Usually through marriage unions."

"Marriages are arranged?"

Please say no, I thought. *I love you, but I don't want you picking my future husband.*

"They used to be, but that hasn't occurred in the last century. We've modernized." He gestured for me to follow him down a stone hallway. It was cool and dry. Openings carved in the outer wall let in sunlight and fresh air. The walls were undecorated, not a tapestry in sight. The clean, smooth, gray stone was beautiful in its own way.

The hall emptied into a large chamber. A heavy, wooden table ran the length of one side, while comfortable chairs gathered around a large fireplace on the other. The room was empty save for one small, curly-haired figure, her nose in a book, her feet tucked up underneath her.

"Ula!" I cried.

She ran over and hugged me before pulling back to kiss both of my cheeks. "I'm so glad to see you." She took my hands in hers. "How was your journey?"

"Good," I said. "Uneventful."

Ula looked over my shoulder at my dad and smiled. "You made good time."

"She's a natural," he said from behind me, his voice full of pride.

Ula pulled me to the chair next to hers. "Sit and warm yourself. I'm sure you're tired."

I didn't think so, but once she said it, my muscles quivered and my eyelids grew heavy. Maybe I could rest for a while. I sank into the chair, kicking off my shoes and tucking my legs under me. It was very comfortable.

"Perhaps Meara would like some food and a drink?" Ula looked at my dad expectantly. He raised an eyebrow in reply, waited a moment, then sighed and left the room.

"Boys," Ula whispered once he was gone, and then added louder. "I sent the others away for now. I thought you might need a few minutes to yourself before you meet them all."

I nodded sleepily. "How many live here?"

Ula tilted her head and considered. "With the birth of the triplets—"

"Triplets?"

"Mmm... yes. They're quite a handful. Um, that would make it, ninety-seven."

"That many people live here?" I straightened in my chair and took in the room. "And they all fit?"

"It's a big castle," Ula said. "It's built into the rock, so it appears smaller than it is. This is one of three gathering halls. The smallest."

I was tempted to explore, but my eyes wouldn't cooperate. They were barely slits. Ula laughed.

"Stop fighting it, Meara." She patted my knee. "Rest. I'll stay right by your side and when you wake, we'll explore together."

That was the last thing I heard before I surrendered to sleep.

I stretched the stiffness out of my muscles. Considering we crossed the Atlantic, keeping a steady swimming pace, I wasn't too sore. The fireplace cast the room in dancing shadows. How long had Ula let me sleep? Her chair was empty, but I heard footsteps in the hall. A moment later, she peeked around the corner, eyes full of mischief and hair a riot of curls like always. It was good to see her again; I missed her. My dad had told me she returned home after my mom's funeral, and the months that passed afterwards were difficult without her. She'd become one of my closest friends and understood me better than most.

"Feel better?" She carried a tray into the room and set it on the table before me. My stomach rumbled in reply. "David brought food earlier, but I didn't want to wake you and it grew cold." She uncovered the plate. "I hope you like salmon."

My mouth watered as the savory scent hit my nose. The grilled salmon rested on a bed of wilted greens. I picked up subtle notes of basil and lemon. It was something I'd expect from a fancy restaurant, not a stone fortress on an island in the middle of nowhere.

"You made this?" I asked between mouthfuls. Being a vegetarian, I was surprised she cooked fish, but this was fantastic. The texture of the salmon was delicate, but the flavor intense. I tasted the fresh green of basil, the tang of citrus, velvety butter, and a spice I couldn't identify. Would all food seem richer to me now? If so, I hoped being a Selkie meant a fast metabolism.

"No. My brother, Padraic." She laughed. "Paddy's the chef of the family."

"He cooks for everyone here?" I wondered if my uncle would be able to show me a trick or two. I couldn't even heat spaghetti sauce without burning it. My grandma learned early last summer to keep me out of the kitchen unless it was time to eat.

Ula shrugged and settled into her chair. "He has a staff, and we all pitch in at times. No one is solely responsible for meals, although David is in charge of Ronac as a whole."

"In charge—?" I let my question hang unspoken.

Ula nodded. "Of everything. He's like our leader, I suppose you'd say."

I knew my dad was the oldest in his family, but I had no idea he was in charge of everyone, almost one hundred people. No wonder Ula said he was powerful.

"Who handled things while he was gone?" A year was a long time to be without your leader.

"Angus took over," Ula said. "He's our great-great uncle. He led the clan before my dad, and before David." Under her breath, she mumbled something. I thought I caught "crotchety" and "goat".

"What did you say?"

Her cheeks flushed slightly. "Oh, nothing."

I ate the rest in silence, noting the texture variations between the fish and vegetables. It was a new experience to be so aware while eating. This was a sensory feast. I was almost disappointed when I ate the last bite. It didn't feel right to ask for seconds.

Ula glanced at my empty plate, and then sprang from her chair. "Ready for that tour?"

"Sure. Let's go." I uncurled my legs and stood, taking a moment to stretch and assess. My muscles were sore, but no worse than a good workout. I had no idea what to expect, but I didn't think I would feel so much like me. Except calmer, much calmer. The pull of the ocean was one of comfort now, not anxiety.

Ula led me through a doorway in the back of the room. It was hidden behind a partial stone wall, and I hadn't noticed it before. It emptied into a hallway, and she turned to the right.

"We'll start in our family wing," Ula explained. "It's on the second floor."

We passed several closed doors before the hallway ended. To the immediate left was a stairwell, and I realized it was one of the towers I'd seen from the outside. I followed her up the stairs, which emptied into another stone hallway. This one was dimly lit by sconces, not windows. Doors lined the hall.

"Bedrooms," Ula said when she saw me looking. Halfway down the hall, she stopped at a door and opened it. She stood back to let me in. "This is my room."

Her room was bright and colorful. Scattered throughout were beanbag chairs in red, blue, and yellow, each covered in a soft, fuzzy fabric. Tie-dyed material draped along one wall to hide the gray stones. A large, shag carpet covered the floor, and a bookcase full of well-worn novels stood beneath the two large windows.

"It's great," I said. She had a wonderful view of the rocky shore. When I looked at her books, I saw many of my favorites.

"Feel free to borrow any that you like." She smiled at me. "There's a study upstairs with more books. You're welcome to those as well."

"Thank you."

She hesitated a moment before asking, "Would you like to see your room now?"

"I have a room?" My heart surged with a sudden sureness that I belonged here. This was family, more than I'd ever known.

Ula grinned. "Of course you do. David asked Brigid and me to get it ready for you. I hope you don't mind."

I thought of my aunt Brigid and her cold, violet eyes. "Brigid helped decorate my room?"

Now, Ula laughed. "As if I'd let her. Do you like the Goth look?"

"Um—"

"I didn't think so." Ula shut her door behind us, and we continued down the hall. "She was more than happy to let me take care of it." She paused outside the last door in the same hall. Just past it was another stairwell. Another tower.

"The end rooms are slightly bigger," Ula said. "David insisted you have this one. It was his as a child."

She opened the door, and I gasped. The room was beautiful, all soft greens and blues. It reminded me of the sea on a calm day. A bed covered in pillows of all shapes and sizes was centered on the long wall. A small dresser had my picture frame and other personal items already on it. A bookshelf, the twin of Ula's, sat under the windows. Its top was covered with fat candles, casting the air with the light scent of vanilla, though they were unlit. The shelves held a few books.

Ula saw me looking at the titles. "I added some that I remembered from your room," she said. "Though you can certainly expand your collection." When I looked at her, my eyes filled with tears. She frowned. "You hate it."

17

I shook my head and sobbed harder. "I love it," I finally managed. "It's one of the nicest things anyone has ever done for me."

Ula crossed to me and pulled me into her arms. She was slightly shorter than I was, but I still felt comforted. Who knew I had such a great aunt?

"We want you to feel welcome here," she said as she stepped back.

"I do," I answered honestly. "Thank you."

She wiped her eyes, and I realized she was just as affected by all of this as I was. She tugged my hand. "Come on, we still have lots to see."

We finished the tour of the second floor. The halls connected, resulting in a floor plan that made a large square. Each corner emptied into a stairwell, the inner portion of the floor contained the second of the common rooms.

"This one is exclusive to our family," Ula said. "There are two more areas for the rest of the clan in the cliffs." When I asked how much family we had, Ula told me not to worry. I'd meet them all later, and I'd already met the scariest of the bunch, which was Brigid. I laughed and wondered at Ula's ability to make me feel so at ease.

"We'll go up now," she said. "The top floor belongs to David and Angus, but that's where the study is, too."

"Is my dad in his room?" I hadn't seen him since he brought me to Ula. Judging by the darkening sky, that was several hours ago.

"Probably not," she said. "I'm sure he went to see the others. We'll go there next."

I nodded and tried to calm my jumpy stomach. I was nervous about meeting everyone. I had no idea that so many Selkies existed, let alone would live together on this island. How would the others feel about me? Would they accept me as one of their own? Ula didn't seem worried, and for that reason, I thought maybe I should just let it go. She'd tell me if I had a reason to be scared.

We didn't go into David's quarters, but I could see they took up half the third floor. Angus' quarters were about half the size of David's, and the remainder of the floor was the study, which we did go into.

My eyes widened when I entered the room. The last time I'd seen that many books was in a library. Books, maps, and globes crowded the floor-to-ceiling bookshelves that surrounded the room. There were no windows in here, but it was well lit nonetheless. Throughout the center area were comfortable chairs and side tables.

"I spend a lot of time here," Ula said. "By your reaction, I'm guessing you will, too."

"It's amazing," I said, running my finger along the spines of several books. The collection was vast and eclectic.

"While I'd love to stay here now," Ula said, "it's time I take you to meet the others. Are you ready?"

I took a deep breath. Was I?

"They'll love you, Meara." Ula's confidence reassured me. "Just like we do."

I braced my shoulders. I could do this. "Lead the way."

Chapter 2

*E*van watched Meara dive in, fighting every muscle in his body that wanted to follow her. *Less than two months*, he thought. In six weeks, he'd be in Scotland with Professor Nolan, and he'd find her. No matter what it took, he would find her.

A seal's head broke the surface. He didn't know if it was David or Meara, but when a second seal popped up, it reassured him. She'd done it. She'd Changed. How much the transformation changed her remained to be seen. Still, he took comfort in knowing that she wouldn't drown or freeze to death in the Atlantic. For the moment, she was safe.

He walked slowly back to his car, in no hurry to drive home. He already knew what he'd tell everyone. That he dropped David and Meara off at the airport and, right now, they were on their way to Scotland. It wasn't too far from the truth.

He wished school wasn't over. It would be nice to go back to the privacy of his dorm room. His mom was great, but she smothered with her concern, and his sister, Katie, usually meant well, but she was often just a brat. Professor Nolan offered to help him get one of the few exclusive apartments on campus, but Evan declined. His mom would be heartbroken if he didn't come home, at least for this summer. Next year, maybe he could finagle it.

It surprised him how quickly his parents agreed to the internship. He hadn't expected it, and he'd prepared a list of reasons why he should be able to go. He didn't even need to use the list once. They both agreed almost immediately that it was a great opportunity for him, and he should take it. He wasn't sure if they realized he planned to see Meara or not, and if that factored into their decision, but he didn't really care. In the end, he got what he wanted, and that was all that mattered.

He parked the car and moved to get out, but a flash of white on the backseat caught his eye. Meara's sweater. He didn't remember her taking it off. Reaching between the seats, he picked it up. Evan held it to his nose and closed his eyes. Sunshine and fresh air—she always smelled like that to him. She didn't wear perfume, but she didn't need to. Her scent was mesmerizing enough.

He took the sweater with him and shoved it in the picnic basket before going into the house. He didn't want Katie to see it and tease him, but he also didn't want to let it go. It was all he had of Meara now.

Ebb and Flow, his springer spaniels, greeted him at the door, tails wagging and tongues hanging happily. He scratched them both generously before heading toward the staircase. He'd drop his things off in his room first.

The house was quiet. The graduation party must have ended, and Meara's grandparents already gone home. He knew his dad was leaving for a business meeting in Toronto, and more than likely, his mom was in the kitchen baking for tomorrow's breakfast. Evan's family ran a bed and breakfast. With his dad's sales job and travel schedule, his mom handled most of the day-to-day responsibilities. Thinking of it made him feel guilty. Most summers, he and Katie helped when they could. This summer, Mom would only have Katie most of the time, and she wasn't that much help.

"What's in the basket?" Katie stood in her doorway, arms crossed.

No such luck avoiding her, Evan thought as he shrugged his shoulders. "Nothing really, just some dirty glasses and a picnic blanket."

Katie's eyes filled with sympathy. She knew Meara left with David, but she didn't know the real story. "I'm sorry, Evan. I know you'll miss her."

"Yeah. Thanks." He was anxious to put the basket in his room before she asked to take a look, but he didn't want to show it. "Where's Mom?"

Katie lifted her shoulder. "I dunno. I was on the phone with Brian."

Nodding, Evan tried not to let his irritation show. Sure, Brian was Katie's boyfriend, but he was also Evan's teammate. Evan liked Brian as a friend, and even better as a hockey player. He'd hate to deal with the fallout if they broke up. He never talked with Brian about his sister, though. That would be too weird.

"I'm just going to go in my room for a bit..." Evan stalled. He really didn't want Katie to follow him.

Katie studied him, and then nodded. "Yeah, okay. I'll go down and help Mom."

Once Evan closed his door, he sagged against it. He hadn't realized how hard he avoided fighting with Katie. She was always asking about what Meara's secret was, and he refused to say. It wasn't his secret to tell, but he was growing tired of her questions. He certainly didn't have the energy for it now. A nagging headache thrummed behind his right eye. He'd noticed it on and off over the last month. Painkillers didn't seem to help. He wasn't worried, though. Probably wasn't anything more than stress.

He put the basket on his desk and pulled out Meara's sweater. Tucking it under his pillow, he sprawled across his bed and promptly fell asleep.

Chapter 3

I could only stare in shock at the bodies crowded below me. We'd walked through the tunnel that connected the fortress to the cliff. It emptied onto the balcony where Ula and I stood. The cavern was filled with my father's people. My people now, too.

Ula waved. A few people in the crowd waved back or raised their hands in greeting. Most watched me with caution.

"Meara!" My dad surged forward, climbed the stairs, and embraced me. Moving behind me, he announced, "Clan of Ronac, meet my daughter, Meara."

"All hail Meara! Long live Ronac!" came the immediate reply. It reminded me of something I'd only seen in movies. Once again, I felt like I was in the midst of a medieval ritual, not the twenty-first century. I looked to my dad for guidance, and he took my hand.

"Come," he said, "and let everyone meet you. They have planned a feast in your honor."

Until that moment, I hadn't noticed the smoky smell of roast meat or the sweet tang of wine, but now the scents mingled enticingly. Although I'd recently eaten, my stomach growled. The journey had been long, and my body was not yet recovered. I could eat more. No problem.

The crowd parted, and families sought to sit together. The room was set for a banquet. Long tables were piled high with platters of carved meats, steamed vegetables, and sweet fruits. Children snuck rolls from covered baskets. Three young boys in particular tossed them back and forth across the table, their mother scolding to no avail.

"The triplets?" I asked Ula, remembering how she had told me about them earlier. I already knew the answer. They were identical.

The boys, as if they heard me, ran over. Ula grabbed the first in a hug and spun him around. "This one's grown a foot in the last month." She ruffled another's hair. "And you, Thomas, have you lost another tooth?"

As he grinned like a jack-o'-lantern, I leaned close to her and whispered, "How can you tell them apart?"

She shook her head and laughed. "Give it time, and you'll be able to, too." She turned her attention back to the boys. "Owen, Thomas, William." She nodded to each in turn. "Meet my niece, Meara."

"Pleased to meet you, Meara." They said it unison as though rehearsed. One boy lagged slightly behind, and the one with the missing teeth elbowed him. They couldn't be more than five years old, and they were all elbows and bony knees.

"Nice to meet you, too," I said. They openly stared at me as only little kids can do. Finally, Thomas assessed, "She's not bad. For a girl." The other two nodded, and they took off, running back to their mother.

"Imps," my dad said. I sensed he loved them like his own. He looked at me. "Are you hungry, Meara? I know you slept through lunch."

"Ula brought me more food when I woke up," I said. "But I can always eat."

I followed my dad to a table that was elevated on a platform. Most of the chairs were positioned to face the hall. We were going to eat on a stage?

"Don't worry," Ula whispered in my ear. "It's not so bad once you get used to it."

Dad took the furthest seat and motioned for me to sit next to him. Ula sat on my other side. Brigid walked toward us, her arm in the crook of an old man's elbow. He was old, but not frail. Tall with heavily muscled arms, I could only assume this was Angus. When I caught my aunt's eye, she nodded at me. I saw her lean in and say something to the old man. His eyes rose until he held mine. Was it my imagination, or did he seem pleased to see me?

As they took two of the remaining empty seats, I asked Ula who else would be joining us.

"Paddy." She shrugged. "If he ever takes the time to join us and eat. Most days, he just has his meal back in the kitchen."

"Why?"

"He's not too comfortable being the center of attention."

I looked out at the crowd. Although parents were busy restraining children and some small conversations blossomed, for the most part, all eyes were on us. I squirmed and realized I had something in common with my uncle. I wondered if I could escape to the kitchen, too.

"My brother, Ren, is visiting right now, too, with his wife and son." Ula shrugged, unconcerned that they weren't here. "Nico might still be napping."

Before I could say anything, my dad stood and addressed the crowd. "Tonight, we celebrate a family member coming home. My daughter, Meara. May you welcome her with open arms and open hearts. May this celebration be the first of many that we have together. Let the feast begin!"

After a round of applause, the attention in the room turned from the stage to the food. Platters were passed and glasses lifted in toasts. Laughter rang throughout the cavern. I filled my plate and ate with delight. Like the salmon at lunch, the food was prepared with expertise, and flavors burst in my mouth.

My dad poured me a glass of wine, which made me think of Mom, who never let me drink. I missed her. She would've loved it here. This was a side of my dad that she never knew. I was only beginning to see who he really was. I took a sip of wine and relished the taste of ripe summer berries. Setting down my glass, I caught my dad's eye. He looked happy and proud. My heart surged, and I was glad that he found us, that I had him in my life.

The hall buzzed with conversation. As families finished eating, they cleared their tables. Children and adults alike carried plates and platters out of the room. I moved to clear my own spot, but my dad covered my hand.

"Not tonight," he said. "This is in your honor. It would be disrespectful if you worked."

I sat back into my chair but, within minutes, started to fidget. To get here, Dad and I had to swim for two days straight. If I sat still long enough, I'd fall asleep at the table. I rubbed my eyes and wondered if I got sand in them on the way here. They felt gritty and sore.

"Come." Ula stood. "I'll walk you to your room."

I checked with Dad first. He nodded and stood to offer me his hand. Once I rose, he kissed my cheek. "Rest well, Meara. You've had a long journey."

As we walked back to my room, Ula chatted easily. She told me about some of the larger families and the antics of the triplets. I wasn't sure I'd remember what she said, but she didn't seem to care. It was Ula's nature to be easygoing and friendly.

We stopped outside my door, and she hugged me tight. "I'm so glad you're here, Meara."

"Me, too." I realized I meant it. This felt like home.

"Rest up." She turned to leave, but not before I saw her face. Why were her eyes filled with sympathy?

I caught her arm. "What's that look for?"

"Your first lesson is tomorrow," she said, as if that explained it all.

"And?"

"It's with Brigid."

She slipped out of my grasp and hurried down the hall. My dad chose Aunt Brigid for my first lesson? What was she going to teach me? How to stop an enemy with a death glare? I swallowed the lump that formed in my throat. Morning would come much too quickly.

Chapter 4

"How's your girlfriend? What's her name? Mary?"

"Meara," Evan automatically corrected. He ground his teeth and bit back a sharp reply. For some reason, Professor Nolan never remembered Meara's name. He got the M right, but every name followed except Meara.

"Meara." He said the name as if trying it out on his tongue. "That's right. Sorry. You haven't mentioned her much lately. Is everything okay?"

"She's in Scotland visiting her dad's family, remember?" Evan knew that he told Professor Nolan about Meara leaving several times already.

"Right. Right," he muttered. His eyes were currently glued to the microscope before him. "Hand me that tray by the sink. I'll need the other specimen, too. Hurry!"

After working with Professor Nolan for the last two semesters, Evan thought that he'd be used to his personality. The professor's quick mood changes still startled him. Theodore Nolan was nothing if not meticulous. His mind was brilliant, but scattered at times. Evan struggled to keep up with the orders barked at him in quick succession. Professor Nolan might be quiet and timid amongst strangers, but get him alone and he was a drill sergeant.

"Did you feed the animals?" Professor Nolan asked. He held his hand out for the other tray. Evan gave it to him.

"Yes." The animals Professor Nolan referred to were the seals and sea lions in the large pool, part of the aquarium section of the lab. The animals, retired entertainers, were used to putting on a show. Their antics amused Evan, but now he couldn't help looking at them and seeing Meara as a Selkie. There was something eerie about your girlfriend turning into a seal. He tried not to let it bother him. She couldn't help what she was, and in some ways, she would have better insight into marine biology than he would.

"And you've made arrangements for their care as I requested?"

"All set." He'd called the small group of students that Professor Nolan trusted, creating a schedule for the tanks to be cleaned and the fish and mammals fed. They were going to be gone for a month on the research project in Scotland. He tried to be fair and assign the chores evenly. The other students didn't seem to mind, and they'd be compensated for their work.

The professor looked up from the microscope. For a moment, Evan thought his eyes flashed a brilliant turquoise. When he looked closer, they were their normal slate blue. The professor raised his eyebrow. Too late, Evan realized he was staring.

"Is something wrong?" Professor Nolan asked.

"No." It must have been the light from the microscope causing a strange reflection. That, or Evan was just tired. He hadn't slept well for weeks.

Professor Nolan patted his shoulder. "Go home, Evan. You're exhausted. I'm almost done here, and we can continue in the morning."

Evan nodded. He knew the professor was right. He wasn't looking forward to the drive back to Peggy's Cove. As if he could read his mind, the professor asked, "Are you okay to drive?"

Evan shrugged. He wasn't really sure. Every muscle cried out in exhaustion. Professor Nolan snapped off the microscope, grabbing his coat and keys.

"Come on," he said. "Call your parents. You're crashing on my couch tonight."

"But—"

"I will not have you falling asleep behind the wheel." The professor's brows lowered, and he gave Evan a stern look. "You're coming with me, and that's final."

Evan called home while Professor Nolan closed up the lab. His mom answered on the first ring.

"Where are you?" She sounded worried.

"Still at the lab, Mom." He knew his tone was defensive, but he was almost twenty years old. When was she going to stop worrying about him? "I'm going to crash at Professor Nolan's house tonight."

"You sure? I can come get you."

"It's fine." Evan softened his voice. Of course she would offer to make a forty-minute trip just to bring him home. That was the kind of mother she was. "He invited me. I'll be home for dinner tomorrow." He'd just work in the same clothes again. It wasn't like it really mattered.

"Well, if you're sure..." Her voice trailed off.

"I love you, Mom."

He heard her soft sigh of resignation before she responded. "Love you, too, honey."

After she hung up, he pocketed his phone and looked at the professor, who was testing the handle on the door after locking it. He always ensured no one could enter his lab after hours.

"All set?" the professor asked. Evan nodded and followed him out of the building. Some of the faculty lived on the far end of campus in an apartment complex that was far away from the student dorms. Evan wasn't surprised to see that was where they headed. The professor led him into the long, brick building and started up the stairs. They went up three flights and stopped in the middle of the hall. Professor Nolan unlocked the door and stood back to let Evan pass. "Feel free to make yourself at home."

"Thanks." From the doorway, Evan could see that although no lights were on, the apartment was not dark. Reflections on the wall gave the effect of being underwater. When Evan passed the professor and gazed in the living room, he saw the source. A narrow fish tank ran the length of the room. Exotic fish of all sizes and colors swam inside. "Wow. Great tank."

Professor Nolan rubbed the back of his neck and gave Evan a sheepish smile. "Thanks. My job is also my hobby. I guess you could call it an obsession. There are few things more important to me."

Evan could understand. He lost himself in his studies all the time. He was thrilled when Professor Nolan took him on as his intern. He continued to study the room, which was sparsely furnished at best. There was no TV. No radio or sound system. No source of entertainment besides the tank. The room held a sleek, leather couch and a matching chair and ottoman. A glass coffee table completed the ensemble. The walls were bare.

"Are you hungry? Thirsty?" Professor Nolan asked as he went into the kitchen.

"A drink would be great." Evan didn't necessarily mean alcoholic, but when he was handed a cold beer, he didn't complain. "Thanks, Professor."

Professor Nolan laughed and shook his head. "Call me Ted." He drew a long drink, emptying half his beer at once. "If we're going to be working together all summer and traveling abroad, 'Professor' is going to get old." Evan didn't say anything, so he continued. "Sorry I don't have a TV. Never did like those things, but you're tired anyway, right?"

Evan nodded. "I appreciate you letting me stay, Ted." He tried the name out. It felt strange on his tongue, but he'd get used to it.

"No need to thank me. I'm the one making you work these crazy hours." He set his empty bottle on the table. "I'll get you a pillow and blanket. The couch actually isn't too bad to sleep on. I've done it many times myself."

While Ted went to get the bedding, Evan took a closer look at the tank. These fish were much more exotic than any in the lab, their colors vibrant. The tank was meticulously maintained. Not only were the fish thriving, but also plants of all varieties bloomed in complementary colors and abundant textures.

"Who needs entertainment when you have a fish tank, right?" The professor's voice came from behind him. Evan jumped slightly. "Sorry, didn't mean to startle you." Ted set the blanket and pillow on the couch. "Bathroom is the first door past the kitchen. Only other door here is to my room. It's a pretty small place."

"It's nice." Evan didn't know what else to say, but he figured he was expected to comment. Considering the professor was a single guy, it seemed big enough. He wondered if Ted ever married, if he had kids. He was so married to his work, it didn't seem like there was room in his life for more.

"Do you need anything else?" Ted asked. Evan shook his head. "Then I'll see you in the morning."

After Ted left the room, Evan unfolded the blanket and stretched out on the couch. It was comfortable. As tired as he was an hour ago, he found himself wide-awake now. He watched the fish in the tank and thought of Meara. He made it a week without her. He wondered what she was doing now. Was she learning about her new powers? Did she like her uncles and the rest of David's family? He hoped she was happy. He couldn't wait to see her again, but he wished it wasn't over a month away. Would he make it that long? Losing himself in his job helped some, but the ache in his heart was always present.

The fish glided around the tank as Evan watched, and his eyes eventually grew heavy. Finally, he slept, and when he did, he dreamed of the ocean.

He was following a seal. Though the water should have been frigid, it was not. He swam with strong, sure strokes. They passed coral and schools of fish, not unlike what was in his professor's tank. They swam for long stretches before Evan realized he was breathing underwater, wearing only his boxers. Why wasn't he in a diving suit?

How was he breathing underwater?

The seal sensed his hesitation and stopped to look back at him. He stared into its eyes and realized something else. This wasn't just any seal. It was Meara.

She jerked her head in the direction they were swimming, and her body shook impatiently. Without words, Evan knew she wanted him to follow her. He picked up his pace to match hers. He was so intent on keeping up with her that he almost slammed into her back when she stopped short.

He peered around her, and his mouth fell open in shock. A few feet in front of them, a fissure spewed foul, bitter liquid into the clear water. Along the length of the fissure was death—skeletons of plants and fish alike.

Meara watched him. Her eyes were filled with sadness and something else. She was trying to give him a message, but what? What was she trying to say?

Chapter 5

Ula told me that I'd find Brigid by the cove and sure enough, she was there. She stood with her back to me. Her long, black hair swayed in the breeze, her arms wrapped around her waist. She looked vulnerable until she turned, and her purple eyes pierced mine.

"You're late."

"Sorry." Although I apologized, I couldn't see how I was late. There were no clocks here, and my phone was in storage in Halifax along with my other belongings. My dad told me to leave it, so I did, even though I was hoping it could be a link to Evan. I missed our daily text exchanges. I missed hearing his voice. I'd asked my dad how I would reach my friends without my phone, and he laughed. He told me there was no reception on the island. When I said that I couldn't go all summer without talking to Evan and my best friend, Kim, he relented. I could travel to Scotland and call them from there, but not until I had my powers and could protect myself. I didn't see why I was in need of all this protection. It seemed safe here so far.

Brigid broke my reverie. "Are you ready to get started?"

"What are you teaching me?" I asked. Ula said nothing except that my first lesson was with Brigid.

"To shield your mind from other Selkies." She said it like I should know this already. "We are born with this ability, but you, it seems, must learn it."

"How—?"

"Ula told me about her experiment in Canada." Brigid smiled at me, but there was nothing friendly about it. "She was able to influence you."

It annoyed me that Ula told her. A few months ago, I met another Selkie named Kieran. We kissed in a dance club. It was something I never intended to happen, so I worried that he seduced me. To test whether I was susceptible to Selkies, Ula entered my mind and projected an image of glowing orbs. Because she was able to do this, it confirmed I was vulnerable. After that, I wore the charm bracelet my dad enchanted to keep my thoughts and feelings protected.

"Could I have gained the ability to shield once I Changed?" I felt different now. Stronger and more attuned to my environment, and I'd only been a Selkie for a little over three days.

She lifted one slim, black eyebrow. "Hand me your bracelet."

I unclasped the bracelet, and she took it. That was the last thing I saw before darkness closed around me. I was blind, deaf, and dumb. I couldn't even feel the ground beneath my feet. I floated in nothingness. Panic rose in my throat, and I felt myself scream. In a blink, I was back on the cliff, standing next to my aunt. She crossed her arms and asked in a voice filled with triumph, "Now, are you ready to begin?"

Humbled, I could only nod.

She seemed pleased by my response. She brushed her hands down the length of her midnight blue, velvet dress, cleared her throat, and then held her hands out, palms up. "Place your hands on mine."

I did as she said. Her hands were cool and dry. My skin tingled where it touched hers. For the first time, she gave me a real smile. "You have great power, Meara. I can feel so much untapped potential."

"Uh. Thanks?"

Her smile vanished. She must have realized that she paid me a compliment. Her brows knit together. "Do you know why I'm the first one to teach you? Why I was chosen to show you protection?"

"No."

"I am the strongest shielder here. No one can enter my mind unless I want them to, and I never do. I can show you how to block your thoughts. I can show you how to read another's. It's simply a matter of reversing the process. Do you want to learn?"

I was scared, but it didn't stop me from responding. "Yes."

"Good. Close your eyes and picture your brain. Picture the fluid in your head that coats your brain and runs down your spine, protecting your thoughts. Now, imagine that fluid becoming liquid metal, a flowing shield. Do you see it?"

"I do." My voice sounded far away. I concentrated on the image before me. In my mind, my shield glowed bright silver. It was beautiful to behold, a calming presence and a protective force at the same time. I heard Brigid's breath rapidly increase, but I didn't open my eyes until she let out a loud whoosh.

She looked pale and a little out of breath. I hadn't seen shock on her face before, but if I had to guess at the emotion, that would be it.

"I blocked you, didn't I?" I didn't mean to sound smug, but it came out that way.

Her expression soured, and then she relented. "You did. It was quite... good for your first time."

I knew it cost her to say the words. She was being almost nice to me. If she kept this up, she'd ruin her reputation.

"I will not!" she snapped. Anger darkened her eyes.

"You read my thoughts?" I didn't know why it surprised me, but it did. Shouldn't I be able to feel her presence if she was in my mind?

"I did." She shrugged like it was no big deal. "I told you that you simply reverse the process." I stared at her. I had no idea what she meant. She sighed as though I was slow. "You take your shield and you project it into another's brain."

I was bracing to try it when she dropped my right hand and held up two fingers. "Before you begin, you must know two things. First, when you project your shield out, you are vulnerable yourself, and second, you can only see the other's immediate thoughts. Nothing in the past, nothing in the future. If they're strong-willed and focus on— let's say—a rock. Well, then a rock is all you'll see. Understand?"

"Yes." As I spoke the word, I projected into her mind, hoping to catch her off guard. It worked.

I heard her thinking, *She's more skilled than I thought*, before she blocked me with an image of the sky. The cloud she pictured looked like a floating duck. A sharp pain pierced my forehead. She'd pushed me all the way out.

Panting, she said. "That's enough for today."

She turned and walked back to the fortress. Her back was rigid, her shoulders straight, but I noticed a little unevenness in her step. I had unnerved her. Instead of feeling pleased, I was scared. This was only my first lesson. What else was I going to learn?

I sat on the ground and let my feet dangle over the short cliff that overlooked the cove. The soft moss tickled my forearms when I leaned back. I stared into a bright blue sky and let the sun warm my face. My eyes closed, and the sound of waves grew louder. Gulls cried around me.

Footsteps told me someone approached. By the light sound of them, I guessed it was Ula. My guess was confirmed when her shadow blocked the sun as she leaned over me.

"Want to go for a swim?" Her grin was infectious.

"Can we?" I wanted to play in the water. My first time changing had been all business—just a means to get here. I'd yet to just enjoy my new form. I reached down to unclasp my bracelet and realized Brigid still had it. No matter, I could get it back from her later.

My anklet thrummed, sending tingles up my leg. "How do I Change? Do I have to dive in first?"

Ula shook her head. "Just like you turned back into your human form, you visualize it. See yourself as a seal and you'll be one."

I closed my eyes and did as she said. The world shrunk and

reshaped. When I opened my eyes, Ula towered above me. I barked impatiently, and she laughed.

"I'm coming!"

The image of Ula as a girl blurred and shifted until a small seal with red fur lay before me. I thought I'd never seen her in Selkie form before, but I was wrong. I spotted her several times when I lived in Peggy's Cove. I just didn't know it was her.

She turned and scampered across the rocks, sliding into the water with grace. I followed close behind, clunky and unsteady. Gracefulness must come with time. Or not. I sure didn't have it in my human form.

The light filtered through the water and highlighted the ocean floor. With my enhanced vision, I didn't need it. The underwater world shone crystal clear. All my senses excelled here. Schools of fish swam by, and I caught the subtle nuances in their coloring. A crab scuttled along the sand, and I heard the click of his claws. With air, scents came through smell. Under water, they were experienced through taste. My senses picked up fish, kelp, and other things I couldn't yet identify. Each scent was sharp and unique.

Ula rolled as she passed me, a shimmer of bubbles in her wake. I mimicked her moves. The awkwardness I experienced on land vanished here. I cut through the water with smooth, strong movements. The rightness of it settled in my heart. I flowed with the tides.

We played for a while, twirling and flipping with weightless delight until the cold hand of fear gripped me. What was wrong? I sought Ula. With relief, I spotted her just a few feet away. It took a moment to really notice her though. She was frozen in fear. It wasn't my emotions I felt— it was hers. Why was she afraid?

I had my answer a second later when a large shadow passed by me in a blur. It moved fast, but I caught the flash of white underbelly topped by dead, gray skin. A shark!

The shark ignored me and went for Ula, the smaller seal. If she didn't move, she would be shark bait in seconds. My heart skipped as her panic bled into me. She couldn't move; she was too scared.

I had to save her. I swam for the shark and butted its side with my head. Skimming around its tail, I sped away before its jaws could catch me. I made it angry. It pursued me, closing the distance. While the water was clear, I didn't know the landscape yet. Were there places to hide like underwater caves? I discarded the thought as quick as it came. Too late for that. The beast was almost upon me.

I tensed and prepared for the impact, but instead of the shark, I was pushed aside by another seal. Obviously male, it was at least twice my size and light gray. It wasn't my dad. I knew what he looked like. Who was it? My uncle Padraic?

The seal attacked the shark head-on. He slapped it hard with his tail and rammed into its underbelly. The shark moved to strike again, but before it could, the seal rammed it, rolling it over. The shark paused for a moment, and then swam away. Apparently, we were not a dinner worth fighting for.

The seal stood guard until the shark vanished into the distant darkness. Only then, did he turn and swim to me. I had the strangest feeling that I knew him. He motioned for me to follow, and we swam back to where I left Ula. She was no longer there. Had she gotten out of the water or had there been another shark? Praying she was safe, I swam toward the surface.

When my flippers touched dry land, I visualized my human form. My human form in jeans and a tank top. While grateful to the male Selkie for saving my life, I wasn't giving him a peep show as payment.

"Ula?"

I saw her small figure huddled up against a small boulder. Her wet hair hung down her back, and her head rested on her arms. Her body trembled. Was she okay?

I crouched by her side and touched her arm. "Are you hurt?"

She shook her head, but she didn't raise it.

"What's wrong?"

She lifted her head, and her eyes met mine. The misery in hers pierced my heart. What happened down there?

"I failed you," she said and looked away. "You could've been killed."

"I'm fine." I held my arms out to her. "See? No scratches."

I smiled. Her expression didn't change. Fresh tears rolled down her freckled cheeks. She looked behind me and paled. Before I could turn and see what startled her, she jumped up.

"I've got to go!"

She ran like the devil was after her. I called her name. She didn't turn back. As I watched her go, my blood turned to ice. What was behind me?

Chapter 6

I turned with a scream in my throat. When I saw what it was, I relaxed. The male Selkie, still in his seal form, lay on the pebbled beach. He lowered his head to the ground. His eyes held mine. This was why Ula ran? Who was it?

Uncertain, I called to him. "Uh... thank you?" If Ula was scared, maybe I should be, too. Then again, this Selkie just saved my life. I spoke again, trying for more sincerity. "Thank you for saving my life."

The Selkie's image shimmered and stretched vertically. As I watched, a familiar figure blossomed. With it, my temper grew.

"What are you doing here, Kieran?" I tried to sound mildly curious, but my trembling voice gave me away.

"Helping you, of course." He shot me a sexy grin. "Did you not just say you were grateful?"

I bit back a nasty reply. He was right. He did save me, but damn, did he have to look so good? Drops of water ran down his smooth, tanned skin. I was all too aware of his muscled physique. He hadn't felt the need to put on a shirt. At least he wore shorts. My eyes were drawn to the way they hung low on his hips. *Eyes up, Meara.*

Although his weathered baseball cap shaded his eyes, I could see the look on his face. He caught me checking him out. Great.

"How'd you get here?" I asked, eager to get my mind on something else. "I thought you lived in California."

"Near California, yes." He shrugged. "I like to travel."

I raised an eyebrow, but otherwise did not respond.

He stepped closer. "I wanted to make sure you were okay."

"I'm okay," I said quickly.

It was his turn to look skeptical. "Clearly not, since you came close to being a shark snack."

I snickered. "Is that like a Scooby snack?"

Now he looked confused. "I have no idea what you mean."

"Scooby Doo?" His face remained blank. I sighed. Pop culture was lost on Selkies. "Never mind."

His gaze fell to my top, and I realized too late that I picked white. White was not the best choice when wet. I cleared my throat, and his eyes jumped to my face. He grinned, and I realized the shark was not the only dangerous thing around here. I switched the shirt to black. No seeing through that.

"Does my dad know you're here?" I asked.

"Not yet." Kieran glanced in the direction of the fortress. I couldn't see it from where we stood in the cove, but clearly, he knew his way around the island. Then, I remembered what Ula told me about him. My eyes narrowed and pinned him down. "You were engaged to my aunt!"

He held his hands up in surrender. "Hey... we were betrothed. In the past."

"You broke up with her and had the nerve to come on to me." The anger built in my chest. It felt good. I'd take anger over the other confusing things he made me feel. I pointed my finger at him and scowled. "How dare you!"

He went from defensive to laughing. He laughed so hard that his eyes filled with tears. I tapped my foot and waited. Really, this was amusing to him? Why did everyone keep laughing at me?

"I broke it off over twenty years ago." He wiped his eyes, amusement gone as fast as it came. "You weren't even born yet."

"That's weird... I mean..." My thoughts scrambled. Why was Ula so upset about him? Did she still love him? "Why did you break up with her?"

"She is not powerful." His tone was matter-of-fact. "I need a partner who can help me rule, not one who needs protection."

"That's cruel," I said. "Doesn't love matter?"

He shrugged. "You think like a human."

"What's that supposed to mean? I am a human!" I seethed. He had a way of getting beneath my skin. What was the matter with me? Why was he affecting me so much?

My bracelet! Brigid had my bracelet.

Kieran saw me glance at my wrist. "I'm not doing anything to you right now. If that's what you're wondering."

"How'd you know I was thinking that?" I searched his eyes. Was he lying? Was he reading my thoughts? "How can I trust you?"

He lifted his shoulder with indifference, and his muscles rippled. I wished he wouldn't do that. "You can take my word or not, but I'm telling you the truth."

I resisted the urge to touch my lips when the memory of him kissing me breathless returned with a vengeance. It was the first and only time I betrayed Evan. He forgave me, and we moved past it. Our relationship was stronger than ever, but I had not expected to see Kieran again so soon. Or maybe ever.

"Did you do it then?" I asked, thinking about that night. That kiss. "Did you persuade me?"

His gaze grew hot, and his smile bitter. "It would make it easier for you if I said yes, wouldn't it?" Though flames engulfed my cheeks, I held my head high and waited. One second, two... then, "I didn't, Meara. Honest."

My breath caught. I turned to go, but he clasped my arm. His touch was gentle.

"Don't be angry," he said. "I won't try anything again. I promise."

Those were the words I wanted to hear, so why did I feel so disappointed? It wasn't going to be easy with Kieran around. "How long are you staying?"

"That depends."

"On—"

"How quickly you learn." He grinned at me. "I'm here to teach you."

"You... what?" He caught me off guard. I didn't know what I was expecting him to say, but this wasn't it. All I could think to ask was, "Does my dad know?"

"He's the one who requested me." Amusement rang in his voice and slid down my back like nails on a chalkboard. My dad asked him to teach me? What was he thinking? Ula told him about Kieran and the dance club. My dad and I were going to have a little talk later.

"Why you?" I blurted.

"I'm young. I'm strong." He leaned in and whispered, "And I'm much more personable than Brigid."

I couldn't argue with him on that, but I wasn't backing down. "Ula helps me."

His teasing expression softened. "Yes, she would. Unfortunately, she's not very strong or well versed in your gifts."

"How would you know?" I asked. "What gifts?" I didn't even know what I could do. Did he know more than I did?

"I can feel it. Your potential." Once again, he leaned in. He breathed deep, as if he could smell it on me. "You will be very powerful one day."

My heart raced with his words. I didn't know if it was fear or anticipation. What kind of powers would I have?

"If I'm so powerful, why am I still standing in wet clothes? For that matter, why are you?" I laughed to hide my nervousness.

It didn't work. He smiled at me indulgently. "You will be powerful; you just need to learn to use your powers. Which is why I'm here." He gestured to my clothes. "As to your wet clothes, just visualize yourself dry. It's that easy."

I did as he said and felt much more comfortable.

43

"As to why I'm still wet…" His hand swept past his chest and down his washboard stomach. I swallowed. When he laughed, my eyes flew to his. "Clearly, you enjoy it."

Face burning, I stomped away from him.

"Meara?"

I stopped and spun back. "Yes?" I bit out.

He tilted his head to the side. "Ronac is this way."

I seethed as I walked back to him. He held out his hand. "Shall we?"

I could refuse and walk back, or I could take his hand and transport like I did with my dad on my first day here. I couldn't do it on my own yet. I didn't know how. My muscles ached now that the adrenaline wore off. With a sigh, I placed my hand in his.

"Fraternizing with the enemy?"

Brigid stood at the entrance to the fortress with her arms crossed. She'd changed out of the velvet dress to fitted, leather pants and a blood-red blouse that billowed like silk. Something seemed different. I realized it was the first time I'd seen her in pants. She looked beautiful. And dangerous.

I dropped Kieran's hand and stepped back.

"Hardly an enemy." Kieran's voice was calm. "David invited me."

"Did he?" She slinked forward and wrapped her arm around his. Her lips curled up, but it was more sneer than smile. "Let's just see about that."

She flipped her hair and peered back over her shoulder at me. "I trust you can find your way from here, niece?"

As I watched them walk away, I couldn't decide if I wanted to laugh or weep, smile or scream. The day wasn't even half done yet. I thought about finding Ula. She was pretty upset. Would she want to see me? She looked so hurt before she left.

In the end, I decided to retreat. My room sounded like the perfect place to be.

Chapter 7

There was a knock at my door, followed by a polite, "May I come in?"

The voice was deep, masculine. I didn't recognize it. I rubbed my eyes and glanced around the dimly lit room. Had I fallen asleep? The sun was about to set. I must have napped for a few hours at least.

The knock was slightly louder. "Meara?"

Clearing my throat, I called out, "Come in."

A man with wavy, dark blond hair shouldered the door opened. I realized his hands were full, holding a tray of covered dishes. I bounced up and held the door back.

"Sorry," I said. "Had I known your hands were full, I would have opened the door for you."

"No worries." He set the tray on the chest at the end of the bed and turned to me with a smile. Something about his face looked familiar...

"I'm your uncle, Padraic." He offered me his hand. "You can call me Paddy, if you like."

"Nice to meet you." I studied him as I shook his hand. His coloring was completely different from my dad's, just as Ula's was different from Brigid. It made me wonder what my other uncles looked like. Uncle Ren was visiting, so I'd probably meet him, but I wasn't likely to meet the remaining two any time soon. Ula told me that they'd married into other clans and moved away.

He gestured to the tray. "I thought you'd be hungry. You missed lunch and dinner."

I smiled sheepishly. "I guess I was a little tired."

He didn't seem like he was in a hurry to leave, so I asked, "Would you like to have a seat?"

"Don't mind if I do." He positioned the pillows against the headboard and flopped down on my bed, stretching out his long legs. For some reason, he made me want to laugh. Once again, he gestured to the tray. "Go ahead and eat before it gets cold."

I perched on the end of the bed. Crossing my legs underneath me, I reached for the tray and rested it in my lap. The smell had my mouth watering. Before I lifted the lid, I knew.

"Scallops!" I cried happily. They were Dad's favorite dish and quickly becoming one of mine, too. When I popped a scallop in my mouth, it melted like butter. I closed my eyes and hummed in pleasure.

"You're a fantastic cook," I said when I reopened my eyes.

Paddy blushed and ducked his head. "I'm glad you enjoy it."

"Could you teach me?" I asked and immediately regretted it. I was probably unteachable. Who burned jarred spaghetti sauce? Taking another bite, though, I decided that if anyone could teach me, Paddy could.

"I'd love to," he answered.

I made a face at him. "You haven't seen me cook yet."

He looked amused. "How bad could you be?"

I stabbed another scallop and waved my fork at him. "Like a fish out of water."

He laughed, but promised to teach me anyway. While I ate, he told me about his kitchen, the staff, and his favorite dishes. We agreed that I would help with the meal preparations when I wasn't training.

When I finished eating, he stood and took the tray. I offered to help clean up, but he waved me off and said I was still a guest. He was just about to close the door when I remembered that I wanted to talk to my dad.

"Have you seen my dad?"

Paddy nodded. "He had dinner in the family commons with Brigid and Kieran."

"Are they still there?"

Paddy's brow wrinkled while he considered. "I don't think so. That was over an hour ago. I believe I saw Kieran go to his room."

His room? Was he here in the castle? I wanted to ask my uncle where Kieran's room was, but I didn't want him to get the wrong impression. I hoped it wasn't next to mine.

"And my dad?" I asked instead.

"He's probably in his chambers," Paddy said. "You're welcome there, of course."

"Thank you."

Balancing the tray on one arm, he reached out and touched my cheek. His hand was comforting. "No need to thank me. We're happy you're here, Meara."

After Paddy left, I shuffled over to my mirror. The reflection made me sigh. If I found a bird in my hair, it wouldn't surprise me. What a mess! I wish Brigid taught me how to conjure instead of shield. I could use a brush right about now. I tried to visualize straight, Pantene-worthy hair, but when I opened my eyes, the rat's nest stared back. With a growl, I resorted to dragging my fingers through the snarls. What good was magic if you couldn't even use it to make yourself presentable?

Several tearful jerks later, my hair managed to fall almost smoothly to my shoulders. Not quite as good as a hairbrush, but not bad. I visualized a long, patterned skirt and wrap top and felt the clothing adjust on my body. Admiring the outfit in my mirror, I wondered if I'd ever grow tired of this power. It was like shopping with a limitless credit card while never leaving your house.

Satisfied that I made myself presentable, I left my room and took the staircase closest to it, heading up to my dad's quarters. I knew when I reached the next floor that I was closest to the study. My dad's door was at the other end of the hall.

48

For a moment I paused outside Angus' room. Was he in there? He didn't really say much to me at dinner last night, but then again, he sat at the other end of the table. For some reason, he intrigued me. I wanted to talk to him and see what it was that captured my interest. With a shake of my head, I moved on. Tonight was not the night to bother him. I had more pressing concerns.

My dad opened his door before I could knock. He looked surprised to see me. The surprise melted into a warm smile. He stood back to let me in.

The first room felt like a living room. It reminded me of our apartment in Halifax. "Is this the same furniture?" I asked as I ran my hand along the arm of the couch.

He nodded.

"I thought you put it in storage." The furniture, along with some of my mom's things and some of my own, was supposed to be in a storage locker in Halifax. I was with him when we put it there.

He looked a little embarrassed. "I took it out. It reminded me of your mother, so I brought it here."

"You brought it here…" I left my statement hanging.

His face grew redder. "I brought it all here." He turned and walked through the living room into the bedroom. Stacked along the wall, floor to ceiling, were our boxes.

"My stuff!" I squealed. He said I wouldn't miss it, and I know I really didn't need it, but he was wrong. I did miss it, and I was ridiculously happy to have it back.

He laughed at my excitement. "I'll help you carry it to your room. And if there's anything of your mom's you want…"

His voice trailed off, and his eyes grew sad. I threw my arms around him and squeezed. "I love you, Dad."

In a voice choked with emotion, he said, "I love you, too."

Chapter 8

"Will we meet this elusive professor?" Evan's mom asked. He shrugged. His mouth was full of potato salad, so he couldn't give her a decent answer.

The Mitchell family sat at the patio table in their backyard. It was one of those warm June nights, and Evan's dad decided to barbecue.

Evan swallowed. "I can ask him."

"Do. See if he's free for dinner next Thursday. After all, you leave for Scotland the following week." Mom turned her attention to Katie. "Are your bags packed?"

"All set." Katie picked at her corn on the cob. She hadn't eaten much tonight, or for the last several weeks. Then again, she was going to Cancun with her best friends, Jen and Val. Two weeks on the beach and she insisted she needed to prepare. Katie's idea of preparation was losing ten pounds she didn't need to lose. Evan knew better than to tease her about it. The last and only time he did, she snapped. "Bikini, Evan. I will not look like a beached whale."

He tried to explain that even if she didn't lose weight, she wouldn't look like a beached whale, but she stomped out of the room. After that, he kept his mouth shut.

"Val's dad is planning to take you girls to the airport tomorrow, right?" Mom asked.

"Yep." Katie slid a potato chip under the table to Ebb, and then another to Flow.

"Don't feed my dogs," Evan muttered. "You'll make them sick."

"Really, Evan?" Katie's slim, blond eyebrow rose. "I don't think one potato chip will hurt them."

"Maybe not, but you gave them half of your hamburger, too."

Katie glared at him, but she didn't say anything. Their dad, who was reading the paper, snapped it shut and gave her a stern look. "Katie, eat your food. One dinner is not going to make you fat."

Katie's lip quivered. She stood up with her plate. "I'm not hungry. I guess I'm too excited. I'm going to call Val to finalize details."

Evan knew she was pissed, but it wasn't his problem. He didn't get most girls. He was glad that Meara was normal. If she were here, she'd eat a burger. Heck, she'd probably eat two if she were hungry enough. And she looked great. She didn't worry about gaining weight.

He took a long swallow of Coke and listened to his parents talk. The inn would be full of guests next week. The last week of June was always busy—the official start of the summer tourism season. His dad was staying in town all week to help his mom with the inn. Since he rarely did that, Evan knew it was going to be crazy. Would that really be a good time to invite Professor Nolan to dinner? Would he even come?

"Evan? Are you okay?" His mom frowned at him. She caught him staring off into space, he assumed.

"I'm all right. Just tired." He stood and cleared his plate. The dogs rose, too, tails wagging. "I'm going to take Ebb and Flow down to the shore for a bit."

"That's fine. Have fun." His parents smiled at him before resuming their conversation. Evan carried his dishes into the kitchen and placed them in the sink. The house was quiet. The one couple staying at the inn this week had gone into Halifax for the day. Katie must be up in her room with the door closed.

Evan found a couple of tennis balls in the front closet. He pulled on his windbreaker and a blue baseball hat. The sun would be start setting in about an hour, and June evenings were cool in Peggy's Cove. He didn't bother with the leashes. Ebb and Flow wouldn't leave his side unless he released them. They were well trained.

He thought about taking his car, but he chose to walk instead. The light breeze and warm sun caressed his skin. He already spent too much time cooped inside the lab. Summer break was a month in, and what did he have to show for it? Pale skin and no social life. It didn't matter; it was worth it if he was going to see Meara in two weeks.

Meara. He couldn't stop thinking about her. Did she miss him as much as he missed her? She promised to come and find him when he arrived. She knew he was staying in Aberdeen and that he was arriving on July 7. He knew nothing about where she was except that she was near Scotland. He wished he could call her, but she didn't have her phone. David told her not to bring it. She had to be somewhere remote if there was no cell phone service.

He crossed the street to the path that lead down to a popular stretch of shoreline. It was a small park, made up of a long strip of grass and two picnic tables. Not much, but the dogs liked it. He threw the tennis balls and commanded them to fetch. They took off.

The salty air misted his skin and calmed him. He felt closer to Meara. He couldn't explain it, but if he closed his eyes, he could picture her clearer here—her brown, wavy hair blowing in the wind, the light splatter of freckles across her nose, and her stormy, blue eyes.

He thought about the first time he saw her. It was late June last year. Since their mothers were best friends, Meara came with her mom to the house for a visit. While the older women went inside, Meara wandered into the backyard and introduced herself.

He wasn't looking for a relationship—his last girlfriend had been a piece of work—but when Meara smiled, he couldn't help it. He wanted to make her smile more. She hooked him that very first day.

The dogs made impatient noises at his feet. He picked up the balls, now damp with their drool, and threw them again. They repeated this pattern while the sun sank, large and glowing, over the churning gray sea.

Just two more weeks, he thought.

Chapter 9

A month passed and life at Ronac fell into a pattern of sorts, training followed by recovery. The physical nature of it surprised me. By the end of the day, I crawled into bed and crashed. I tried to read, but my eyes shut before I finished the page.

Most mornings, my dad attempted to eat breakfast with me. After that, he got caught up in the day-to-day running of Ronac. A few days after Kieran's arrival, I confronted my dad about him. My dad didn't budge.

"He's the most powerful, after Brigid and me," Dad explained. *Brag much?* I thought, but I wisely kept my mouth closed. "And I need to see what you are capable of."

"Why?" I was genuinely curious. Why did it matter if I was powerful or not?

I caught him with a mouth full of toast. He held up a finger, and I waited. He swallowed and then said, "We have enemies, Meara."

"Humans, I know." Brigid hammered that into my head every chance she got. At least I only had lessons with her twice a week. The rest were with Kieran.

Dad shook his head. "Humans are not our worst enemy."

"Then, who? Sharks?" I thought of the shark I encountered with Ula. We didn't tell my dad, and I knew Kieran kept it secret, too. If Dad knew, he'd probably never let me swim again.

He laughed. "No, not sharks. Sharks can kill us, but they are not our enemies. That's just nature, and we can avoid them."

53

I pushed pieces of omelet around my plate, as I grew annoyed. "You're not answering my question," I pointed out. My dad was good at avoiding answers. It took me months to get him to tell me about what we were—Selkies, and even then, Ula told me first.

Dad sipped his coffee. When he set his mug down, he sighed. "To start, there's the Blue Men," he said as though that explained it all.

The first image that popped into my head was that percussion group that painted themselves blue, and I almost laughed until I saw the look on my dad's face. He was serious. "Blue men? Seriously?"

He nodded. "The Blue Men of Minch."

When he said their full name, I vaguely remembered reading about them in one of the books I gave Evan last Christmas. I couldn't remember too much. I knew that they lived in some strait and sunk ships. "Why are they an enemy?" I asked.

My dad covered my hand with his. "They hate, and they destroy." His eyes grew sad, and he squeezed my hand. "They killed my parents."

I gasped. I couldn't help it. "When? How?"

"Many years ago." Dad's expression was far away. "It feels like yesterday though. They held them for ransom. When we wouldn't give in to their demands, they murdered them. Their bodies were found near Dublin, mutilated and almost unrecognizable."

"I'm sorry," I said. "I wish there was something I could do."

"There is," my dad said, surprising me. "You can train hard and be careful."

When he stood and kissed my cheek, I promised I would.

"You're not trying hard enough!" Kieran snapped.

"I'm trying as hard as I can!" I yelled, biting back the insult lurking on the tip of my tongue. I was exhausted. Last week, he drilled me on transporting. By the end of the week, I managed to move myself from the bottom of the cove to the top of the cliff. I was impressed; Kieran was not.

This week, he was teaching me weather control. A fluffy, white cloud floated above us. He told me to make it rain. As if I could make that silly thing do anything. I asked Kieran how to do it, and he told me to picture it like a sponge filling with water, then wring the sponge cloud in my mind and watch it rain. Ha! Like anything was ever that easy.

He blew out a breath and stalked over. His face was inches from my own. I could feel the heat radiating off his body. I wanted more than anything to take a step back, but I held my ground. I wouldn't let him see that he affected me.

"Clear your mind." He drew out each word between clenched teeth.

"I am. I did." My tone mimicked his.

He rubbed his temples and closed his eyes. I watched him with some level of fascination. Did I really have the ability to make him this frustrated or was this just his normal personality? Temperamental and irritating.

He smiled at me. Too bad it didn't reach his eyes. They still looked pissed. "Let's try again, shall we?" he murmured. "Close your eyes, Meara."

I did as he said. With my eyes closed, I could feel his breath on my cheek. Couldn't he back up a pace or two?

"Picture the cloud."

I saw the small cloud in my head. Not much bigger than a cotton ball, wispy and soft like one, too.

"Can you see it filling?"

I did. I saw the wisps growing heavy with dew, the white turning dark with moisture. The air cooled around me, and a breeze raised my hair off my shoulders.

"Good," Kieran whispered. "Good."

The edges of the cloud grew black in my mind, saturated to the point of bursting.

"Now, release it." Kieran's voice was a sharp command. I started and saw the cloud puncture like a water balloon. My eyes flew open when the rain drenched my skin.

Kieran beamed at me. "You did it!" His arms circled my waist, and he spun me around. I raised my face to the sky in awe.

I made it rain. *I. Made. It. Rain.*

Kieran set me down, but he pulled me into a tight hug. "You're amazing."

Without thinking, I slid my arms around his waist. My body fit against his easily. I missed this closeness with another person. My fingers brushed against his T-shirt. He rested his cheek on my hair.

My euphoria began to fade, and I stiffened and jumped back. What was I doing? This was Kieran, not Evan.

Kieran dropped his arms to his sides. I crossed mine over my chest. We stared at each other in silence until he cleared his throat. "That was good," he said. "You caught on faster than I expected."

"You were yelling at me before," I grumbled.

He shrugged and picked up his cap where it was laying on a boulder nearby. I tried not to notice how good he looked, even in basketball shorts and a faded T-shirt. "I'm not the most patient of teachers."

"You can say that again," I mumbled under my breath.

He turned back and grinned at me. "But I won't."

He was so infuriating! I tried to think of a smart reply. Nothing came to mind. I watched as he placed his cap on his head, adjusting it slightly.

"Oh, and Meara?"

"Yes?"

"Part two of your lesson today..." He paused until I motioned for him to go on. "Transport yourself back to Ronac." He winked and disappeared.

I stared in disbelief. Really? This was the best teacher my dad could come up with?

Chapter 10

"Evan, your ride's here," his mom called.

"Coming!" He looked around his room. It was so clean—didn't even feel like his. Everything he needed for the trip was packed between his suitcase and his carry-on. With any luck, he'd see Meara before the end of the week. At least, he hoped she find him right away. He didn't know how to find her.

He picked up his bags and went downstairs. His mom was at the door, looking out at the professor's car. When she turned, her face was shiny with tears.

"Mom, I'll be back in a few weeks."

"Over a month," she corrected with a smile. She reached up to frame his face with her hands. It was something she'd done since he was a little boy, only now, he was quite a bit taller than she was. He leaned down and kissed her on the cheek before hugging her.

"I love you, Mom."

"I love you, too," she said. "You'll call?"

"Regularly," he said. "And, of course, I'll call you when we land."

She nodded and dropped her hands, focusing again on the professor's car. "He won't come in and say hello?"

She'd been irritated ever since Professor Nolan declined the invitation to dinner. Evan tried several times to get him to come over, but he refused.

"He's socially awkward," Evan said after a moment. It was an excuse, but as good as any. It didn't really seem like the professor had friends. He barely talked to his colleagues and mainly barked orders or facts at students.

"Something about his profile seems familiar." She continued to squint at the car. "What did you say his name is?"

"Theodore Nolan. Uh, Ted."

"Ted Nolan… hmm… I don't recognize it." She frowned in thought. "Maybe he just has one of those familiar faces."

Evan shrugged. Professor Nolan looked like the stereotypical nerdy college professor—dowdy suit, tie, glasses, and untidy hair. He didn't really stand out.

He picked up his suitcases and waited. His mom wasn't moving from the entryway. "I need to leave, Mom."

"Of course." She stepped to the side and held open the door. "Have a good trip. Say hi to Meara for us."

His parents knew that Meara was one of the reasons he took the internship. It was probably the main reason they agreed to let him go. They knew how hard it was for him when she moved away with her dad. They also genuinely liked her. Meara was easy to like.

He paused to kiss his mom's cheek one more time. He would miss her, but she would probably miss him more. The house had been noticeably empty in Katie's absence, even when filled with guests. At least Katie was returning in a few days. She'd keep their mom occupied. And, Dad was coming home tonight and not traveling the rest of the week.

Evan hurried down the steps and put his bags in the trunk before sliding into the passenger seat. "Sorry for making you wait. I was saying goodbye to my mom."

"No problem." Professor Nolan didn't even look at the house. He simply took off. "Where is the rest of your family?"

"My dad's on a business trip. My sister's in Cancun."

"Your mom is alone?"

There was something in the professor's tone, but Evan couldn't pinpoint it. Whatever it was, he felt uneasy, but the feeling came and went just as quickly. "Not really alone," he said. "The inn is full right now. We're pretty much booked all summer."

"That's right." Ted nodded. "A bed and breakfast, correct?"

"Yes." Evan was surprised he remembered since he seemed to forget any detail that wasn't marine related.

The professor grew quiet, which Evan didn't mind. Classical music played at a whisper. It was pleasant and, after a while, Evan closed his eyes. He knew he wouldn't sleep on the long flight—flying made him nervous—so he might as well try to catch a bit now.

She touched his face, sliding her finger along his lower lip before moving her hand behind his head and drawing him closer.

"I missed you." She kissed him. "So much."

His hands tightened on her waist. He angled his head and deepened the kiss. She hummed in reply. It felt so good to have her in his arms again. He pulled her closer. He loved how she smelled, the summer scent of her. He sniffed her hair, but what he smelled was so rank that it made him gag. He pulled back and looked at her.

Her seductive smile stayed in place even as her face began to crack. A thick, black liquid oozed out, and the stench increased. He scrambled back and lost his footing. Reaching out to catch himself, he sliced his palm on a sharp stone. The warm blood trickled down his hand, but he couldn't look away from her face. Her beautiful face coated in smelly, black goo. Only her eyes remained untouched.

"Meara? What's happening?"

She opened her mouth to answer, and the blackness flowed inside. She coughed, doubled over, and retched. He reached for her just as she dissolved into a liquid puddle.

"Evan! Evan!"

He woke to the professor shaking his arm. Sitting up, he glanced around to get his bearings. Just a dream. They were still in the car. The airport was a few miles away.

"Are you okay?" Ted glanced at him uneasily. "You were crying out in your sleep."

"Yeah." Evan ran his fingers through his hair and reminded himself again that it was just a dream. His heart seemed to have a hard time believing him, the way it jumped in his chest. "I had the weirdest dream."

Ted raised his eyebrow. "Want to talk about it?"

"No."

"Okay." Ted turned his attention back to the road, and Evan tried to slow his breathing and pulse to match the tranquility of the music. It was just a dream. Meara was fine. He'd see her soon, hold her in his arms, and everything would be okay.

When they landed in Aberdeen, the professor rented a compact European car. Evan pushed the seat back as far as it would go. He still needed to bend his legs to fit in the car. It was mildly uncomfortable, but Ted claimed the car got excellent gas mileage. Hopefully, that didn't mean they would be taking any long road trips through the Scottish countryside.

As they left the airport, Ted explained that the airport was northwest of the city. It would take about a half hour to reach their destination. The house they were staying at belonged to another professor. They were going to work together, and he offered them free rooms if they chipped in toward the food. It sounded like a good deal to Evan.

Aberdeen itself was a beautiful city—old buildings mixed with new. It was early in the morning, and people bustled about. A few sat outdoors sipping coffee and enjoying the summer weather. Like Nova Scotia, Scotland was cold and damp most of the year. The natives needed to soak up the warmth while it lasted.

Outside of the city, the roads became curvy and narrow. The view became less metropolitan and wilder as buildings gave way to cliffs and manicured gardens to moss-covered boulders. A slender lighthouse in pristine white appeared on the horizon. It reminded Evan of home.

Ted cleared his throat. "We're almost there. Kenneth's house is just past the lighthouse."

With the term 'house,' Evan was expecting a cabin or small, weathered building like the homes in Peggy's Cove. He could not have anticipated the looming stone-and-wood structure that stretched before them. It looked like an English manor house, with two graceful turrets in the front and a steep, tall roof.

"That's your friend's house?" Evan's voice was filled with awe.

Ted chuckled. "It's something, isn't it? He inherited it from his great grandfather."

As they drew closer, Evan noticed that the house was gated. Stopping the car, Ted got out. He entered a code into a panel, and the doors swung open.

"It's well protected," Ted said as he slid back into the car.

From what? Evan thought. They were in the middle of nowhere. Why would this Kenneth need protection? The gate was probably leftover from his great grandfather's time. Things were rougher back then, highlanders and all that.

Ted parked the car at the end of the drive and got out. Evan followed. He stretched and tried to work the soreness out of his cramped muscles. The drive from the airport might not have been long, but it felt that way in the tiny car.

"Ted, you made it!" A tall, muscular man came down the front steps to greet them. His thick hair was white and silver and his eyes were blue-gray, so bright they almost glowed. Evan usually didn't pay much attention to what other guys looked like, but this man could give James Bond a run for his money. He exuded finesse and charm. The burr of his Scottish accent only added to his image.

The professor held out his hand, which Kenneth used to pull him into a hug. "None of that! We're family." He laughed when he saw the unsettled look on Ted's face. Evan almost laughed, too. Clearly, the professor was not used to hugs.

Ted straightened his glasses and looked at Evan. "Evan, this is my colleague, Kenneth Guthrie."

"It's Ken." His handshake was firm. "Let's not be formal. Welcome, Evan."

Evan turned to get his bags out of the trunk, but Ken's voice stopped him. "Leave your bags, the staff will bring them in." He started to walk away and motioned for Evan and Ted to follow him. "Come, I'll show you around."

He took them through the house, which was bigger inside than it looked from the outside. There were eight bedrooms and six baths, a den, a library, a large formal room, and an enormous dining room. The kitchen was huge, too, but mainly reserved for the staff.

"Unless you need a snack or drink," Ken said. "Then help yourself at any time. My home is your home."

Friendly guy, Evan thought. He wasn't sure he would act the same if someone came to his house, but it was nice to have such a generous host.

When they reached the room at the end of the upstairs hall and Ken told him, "This one is yours." Evan almost wept with relief. He was exhausted after the ten-hour flight and not being able to sleep on the plane. The seats were uncomfortable, and the cabin was noisy. *This room is perfect*, he thought, noting the bed was covered in plush blankets and fluffy pillows. Looking at it made him sleepy, he couldn't wait to change and crawl under the covers. His bags already sat in the corner of the room.

"I'm sure you're exhausted from the flight and time change," Ken said. "Please, rest. When you wake, press that button there." He pointed to a small box on the nightstand. "And someone will bring you a meal."

"Thanks," Evan said.

"No need to thank me." Ken resumed his conversation with the professor, closing the door on his way out.

Evan crossed the room and drew the curtain back from the window. It faced the ocean, which looked vast and endless.

Come find me, Meara, he thought. *Soon*.

Chapter 11

I woke to the sound of my name, but no one was there. The voice sounded like Evan. The glow of moonlight bathed my room in silver. It was early. Too early for the sun; too early for me to be awake.

How many days had passed since I left Peggy's Cove? In the beginning, I tried to keep a mental calendar, but I lost track. With all of my training, the days blended. I was getting stronger, better, and yet, I still had no idea of the extent of my power. Kieran was pleased with my progress; Brigid was irritated. I supposed that was as close to praise as she got. She harrumphed and sighed, but she continued to teach me, and I broke through her mental barrier on several occasions. I learned that was a quick way to end a training session with her. I used that knowledge to my advantage.

Ula recovered from the shark incident, but she was quieter than usual. I missed her bubbly cheerfulness, but I was glad to have her back nonetheless. She added warmth that Ronac lacked, and I really needed a friend.

I crawled out of bed and shivered when my feet touched the ice-cold stone floor. My room could use more rugs. Crossing to the window, I stared down at the ocean. Was Evan here? What day was it? I knew the day he would arrive was coming soon. Someone in this place must have a blasted calendar or know the date. In some ways, it was positively medieval here, but in other ways, it was modern. I'd yet to figure it out, and the oddity left me feeling slightly uneasy.

I turned, and the picture of my mom flashed in the moonlight. I couldn't resist picking it up and running my finger across the glass. "Where are you, Mom?" I whispered as I traced the outline of her face. "I hope wherever you are, you're happy." She suffered so much at the end. I wanted to believe that she was in heaven, healthy and young once more.

Putting the picture back, I opened the dresser drawer. I could visualize clothes, but all of my old ones were here, thanks to my dad, so I pulled out jeans and a T-shirt, dressed quickly, and slipped on my flip-flops. Paddy might know what day it is, and he was bound to be awake. He started baking well before the sun rose.

The sweet smell of yeast and sugar greeted me upon entering the kitchen. Paddy stood alone, slicing fruit at the counter. I sat on a barstool opposite him and snagged a strawberry.

"You're up early," he said. "Trouble sleeping?"

"Not really. Just woke up." I popped the strawberry in my mouth. The sweet tartness burst on my tongue. Everything tasted so much better here. Was it magic? When I finished, I leaned forward and broke off a small cluster of grapes.

"Hungry, are you?" Paddy laughed and handed me a small plate with berries and pineapple.

"Always," I answered. "Thanks."

I ate some more fruit, and he continued to fill a large, silver platter. I probably should help him, but unlike my magic lessons, my cooking lessons had been disasters. If it weren't for the fact that Paddy was my uncle and loved me, he'd ban me from his kitchen. I was sure of it.

"Do you know what day it is?" I asked.

"Not really. I don't track that closely. I try to pay attention when we're near a holiday, but the rest of the year, not so much." He stopped slicing and looked at me. "Why?"

My cheeks warmed as I considered what to tell him. I hadn't even told my dad that I was planning see Evan this summer. Evan told me about his internship on the last day I was in Peggy's Cove. After I said goodbye to him, Dad and I Changed and headed to Scotland. Not much time for explanations.

"My boyfriend has an internship in Aberdeen this summer. I promised to visit him."

Paddy looked surprised. "Does David know?"

I squirmed a bit in my chair. "No. I kind of forgot to tell him."

"Kinda, huh?" Paddy imitated me and smirked before growing serious. "You should, though, Meara. Tell him, I mean."

"Will he let me go?"

Now Paddy looked confused. "Why wouldn't he?"

Apparently, Paddy did not know the David I first met last summer, control freak extraordinaire and keeper of secrets. Then again, I could see how much more human he appeared here, where he was comfortable in his own skin.

"Why wouldn't he?" I repeated, more to myself than Paddy. I took a muffin from the cooling rack, broke off a piece and chewed thoughtfully. Blueberry. Yum.

"Are you having breakfast with him this morning or do you plan on eating your way through my preparations in the kitchen?" Paddy teased.

I rolled my eyes and hopped off the barstool. "How much longer until breakfast?"

Paddy glanced out the window. The sky was now a vivid pink edged in lavender. "I'd say he'll be up within fifteen minutes. I could serve you in his suite if you prefer. Your patience seems a bit limited this morning."

"You'd do that?" I was touched at how much my uncle, and the others, did to make me feel at home here.

"Of course. It's no trouble."

"Okay. I'll go wake him."

Paddy laughed. As I walked down the hall, I heard him say, "Good luck with that."

I knocked several times before I heard a muffled, grumpy, "Who is it?"

"It's me, Dad," I said. "Open up."

He opened the door and squinted at me. His hair stood up in small tufts, and a five o'clock shadow made him appear scruffy. He was wearing the same flannel pajamas that I remembered from the short time he, Mom, and I were a family. I missed that—being a family.

"What are you doing here?" Dad asked with a yawn. "Is something wrong?"

"No, but may I come in? Paddy's sending breakfast up."

"Here? Why?"

"I need to talk to you." I slipped past him and into the room when he moved to the side. I beelined for the couch and got comfortable. When I looked up at him, he was watching me with fear in his eyes. "Relax, Dad. I told you I'm okay."

He ran his hand through his hair and sunk in the recliner. "I haven't had my coffee yet this morning. I'm not awake."

A knock at the door had him rising again. It was a young Selkie girl. She appeared to be about ten, but I knew looks were deceiving. She was probably older than I was—in human years at least. Humans aged about seven times faster than Selkies.

"Your breakfast," she announced quietly. She set the tray on the table, curtsied, and left.

My dad wasted no time pouring himself a cup of coffee. After several sips, he sighed and sat back down. "Much better. Now tell me, Meara, why you are here this morning? Not that I don't enjoy a private breakfast with my daughter."

"Do you know what day it is?" I blurted. It probably wasn't the best opener, but I really wanted to know.

He frowned at me for a second before answering. "It's July 7, I believe. Why?"

July 7. My heart leapt. He was here. Evan was here. My euphoria didn't last. The hard part lay ahead of me. I had to tell my dad.

"I didn't get a chance to tell you before we left Peggy's Cove..." My voice trailed off as nerves took over. I still wasn't as comfortable talking to him as I had been with Mom. Then again, we had seventeen years to practice. I'd only known my dad for little over a year.

"Yes?" He calmly watched me over his coffee mug, although his expression darkened slightly at my nervousness.

I took a deep breath, and the words flowed out. "Evan's in Scotland for the next month. He's here on an internship. He told me right before we left, and I promised to see him. I meant to tell you, but I forgot when we got here and—"

"Meara—"

"—and I don't want you to be mad, but I really want to see him. I miss him so much, and he's only here for a month, and—"

"Meara—"

"—he's right in Aberdeen, which I don't think is far from here, I can swim there, and—"

"Meara! Stop and listen to me!" My dad sat forward in his chair. His brows knit together, but his eyes were full of humor. "And breathe, damn it, before you pass out."

I took another deep breath, feeling a bit winded. He walked over to the table and picked up a can of Diet Coke from the tray. They stocked it just for me. Popping the tab, he handed it to me.

"Thanks." The carbonated goodness made me feel instantly better.

He laughed and shook his head. Sitting next to me on the couch, he wrapped his arm around my shoulder and drew me close. "Do you really think I'd say no to you seeing the boy that you love?" When I looked at him in surprise, he kissed the top of my head. "I guess you did. I should do a better job communicating with you."

Did he just say I could go? Warmth spread through my chest. I was going to see Evan! "When can I go?"

"Today if you like," he said. "As long as Kieran doesn't mind cancelling your lesson and accompanying you on your trip."

"What?" My warm bubble burst. "Kieran?"

I could see it going down. *I'm introducing Kieran to Evan. Evan stares at me in disbelief. Kieran makes a wiseass remark. Boy fight ensues.* How would that ever work?

"Of course," Dad said. "You don't think I'd let you go alone, do you?"

"Does it have to be Kieran?" I couldn't hide the whine in my voice.

My dad was clearly confused. Did he forget about the Kieran club incident a few months ago? I know I told him. "What's wrong with Kieran?" he asked. "If you want to go today, he's your escort. He's available since he was already scheduled to work with you. If you prefer to wait, well, Brigid could accompany you tomorrow."

"Can't you take me?"

Dad's face softened. "You know I'd like to, honey, but I was gone for over a year. Our people need me. In a month or two, I'll be able to get away. Today, I can't. Your escort options are Kieran or Brigid."

Kieran or Brigid, who was the lesser of two evils? What it really came down to was that Evan was here today, and I wanted to see him as soon as possible. Kieran would have to do. I'd get Evan alone and explain. He'd have to understand.

"I'll talk to Kieran after breakfast," I said, although I'd already lost my appetite.

Chapter 12

I can't believe you're still interested in that human boy, Kieran's voice sneered in my head. I was beginning to regret my choice of escorts. Maybe I should've waited for Brigid. She might be witchy, but at least she didn't question my taste in men.

I love him, and it's none of your business, I bit back. He swam ahead of me, strong and sure. Even with my temper raised, I admired how swiftly he cut through the water. It took all my strength to keep up with him.

Thankfully, he lapsed into silence after his last comment. It was a relief from the mental berating the rest of the trip. I tried to put as much anger and irritation as possible into my response. I suppose it could've worked, but I doubted it. With Kieran, who knew what was on his mind. If I didn't know better, I'd say he was jealous.

Ha! Jealous of a human? He was back in my head again. *That's rich. You're joking, right?*

You know, I'm human, too.

You are not.

I am—

No, he snapped. *You are Selkie. Human is just a form you take.*

I sighed, and I hoped he heard that, too. Arguing in my head was exhausting. It didn't faze Kieran. He seemed to enjoy it.

How much further? I asked. He chuckled, and the sound rippled through me. I shivered involuntarily. I couldn't wait to take my human form again and get him out of my head.

We've arrived. Can you not see the slope of the shoreline?

As he spoke the words in my mind, I saw it—the upward slant of the ocean floor and the lighter, bluer water ahead. We approached quickly.

I'll go first and see that it's safe to Change. He turned back and looked at me. *Stay here until I tell you.*

I bristled at his commanding tone. With all the training, I should be used to his orders and demands, but they irritated me as much today as they ever had. *Yes sir,* I whispered. Instead of irritating him like I intended, he laughed.

A minute later, he gave me the all clear. I slid out of the water and onto the smooth rocks that made up the shore. Changing, I visualized a floral skirt and bright pink tank top. I learned my lesson about lighter-colored shirts. I ran my hands through my hair, drying and detangling it at the same time. It was one of my newest tricks and pretty darn useful, too.

Kieran paid little attention to me. He wore his baseball cap, cargo pants, and black T-shirt. Where I chose sandals, he wore practical tennis shoes. They were Nike, and for some reason, I found it funny that he chose a particular brand. He turned and caught me smiling.

"What?" he asked, and I almost sighed with relief that he spoke aloud.

I shook my head. "Nothing."

I looked around at the deserted shore. Like our island, this area was a cove, mostly hidden from the looming cliff above. "We need to go up there?" I asked, looking at the cliff.

"I imagine so. There's nothing down here," he said.

I closed my eyes to transport myself to the top when I felt Kieran's hand on my arm.

"Don't," he said. "Someone up there might see you. We have to go the human route." He pointed to the right, to a path flanked by tall grasses. I missed it on my initial inspection of the area, but it looked

72

functional. I followed Kieran to it. Stepping to the side, he motioned me ahead.

My heart thudded in my chest. I was mere steps from Evan now. I didn't exactly know where he was, but he was close. It was like a sixth sense that I had now. I could feel him, and if I tried hard enough, I might even be able to tune into his thoughts. I wouldn't do it, though, not without his knowledge. It wouldn't be right.

I stopped at the top and stared at the house, or rather, mansion, in front of me. From the heat at my back, I knew Kieran stood right behind me.

"So, these are the swanky digs of your human boyfriend," he said. "Nice spread."

I turned and looked at him. His eyes were on the house. Now was my chance.

"Kieran," I said. "Can you wait for me here?"

"No way." He crossed his arms and stared down at me. "David appointed me as your escort. You're not leaving my sight."

"What could possibly happen?" I asked. "They're just humans. You said so yourself."

A vein pulsed in his neck. His stance did not change. I held his gaze and waited. Finally, he sighed and shook his head.

"I have no desire to see you making out with your human boy toy." He looked at the house again and then at me. "I'm coming with you. I'll meet him and make sure it's safe. Then I'll leave you alone."

"Thank you!" In my excitement, I threw my arms around him and hugged him. His body stiffened, and he kept his arms at his side.

"Easy," he murmured. "You don't want your boyfriend to get the wrong idea."

"I'm not... I wasn't..."

While he laughed, I stomped away, knowing that he would follow. The anger wore off by the time I got close to the house. Fear replaced it. The place was huge and imposing. Evan was living here? Who owned it?

With a shaking hand, I rang the bell and waited. Kieran whistled "Funeral March" behind me. "Cut it out!" I whispered. He ignored me, but stopped when we heard footsteps approaching. The door was opened by a man dressed in a formal suit.

"May I help you?" he inquired politely.

"Hello," I said. My face burned, and I wanted the ground to open and swallow me. I felt so stupid. What if this wasn't the house? My gut told me it was, but could my gut be wrong? One way to find out. "Is Evan Mitchell here?"

The man's eyebrows rose in surprise. "He is indeed. Arrived a few hours ago with Master Nolan." His eyes narrowed as he studied me and then moved beyond me to Kieran. "Whom may I say is calling?"

"Meara Quinn," I said. "And Kieran—"

"Voda," Kieran added. I was grateful since it wasn't until that moment I realized I had no idea what his last name was. I said his full name to myself while I watched him shake hands with the man before us.

Peter. Kieran's teasing voice floated through my head. Damn. He could still speak to me telepathically in human form. So much for getting him out of my head.

Peter what? I had no idea what he was talking about. Was that the name of the man who answered the door?

Kieran Peter Voda, he said. *My full name.*

"I'll sleep better now. Thanks," I replied sarcastically. I didn't realize I spoke out loud until the man in front of me responded.

"Pardon me?" he asked.

"Nothing," I said, adding, "May we come in?" I didn't want to be rude, but really, how long was he going to make us stand on the porch?

"Of course." He stepped back smoothly and gestured for us to enter. The floors were marble tile. A deep mahogany table stood in the center, with a large arrangement of flowers on top. My nose told me they were fresh. They smelled as gorgeous as they looked.

"Please have a seat in the parlor. I will let Master Mitchell know that you are here." The man motioned to the room on the right. A large room full of formal furniture—antiques, if I had to guess. He started to walk away.

"Excuse me," I said, "but what is your name?"

The man stopped and turned back to us. "Stonewall." Almost reluctantly, he added, "Please call if you need anything."

"Thank you." Kieran and I spoke at the same time. Stonewall shook his head slightly before continuing on his way.

Kieran crossed the parlor and stood before the imposing stone fireplace. A large oil painting in rich, swirling color hung above the hearth. It reminded me of gilded-framed paintings I'd seen in museums.

It's original. Kieran turned back and met my eyes. *A Rembrandt.*

Could you get out of my head? I admonished. Evan might not notice, but I didn't want him thinking I was carrying on a sidebar conversation with another guy.

Sorry, he apologized. He sounded sincere. *It's hard for me to make the adjustment. I'm so used to communicating this way.*

Nodding once to show him that I heard, I sat on the edge of one of the chairs. From this angle, I had a good view of the hallway. Footsteps echoing in the hall made me jump to my feet. A moment later, I saw him. Last summer, he had a deep tan from working at the docks. Today, he looked pale with dark smudges under his eyes. He needed a haircut, too. It didn't matter. I'd never been happier to see anyone in my life. I launched myself into his arms. He pulled me into a kiss. My blood heated as the kiss deepened.

Meara, shield! Kieran's voice sliced through my stupor. I forgot he was in the room. Startled, I blocked him and everything else out. Evan broke away from me, gasping for breath. He hadn't been breathing!

"Omigod, are you okay?" I gripped his shoulder. Evan bent at the waist, his hands resting on his knees. He breathed deep, greedy gulps.

"Ye-yeah. What happened?" He straightened and stared at me.

Color was returning to his cheeks, but his stunned expression must have mirrored my own.

"I happened." I gestured down the length of my body. "Selkie seduction." I stole a quick glance at Kieran. He watched us with interest. "I'm so sorry, Evan."

"That's some power you pack in a kiss, Quinn." Evan grinned and rubbed my back.

"Don't remind me," I muttered.

"You seduced me when you were human, too," he teased.

"I don't recall making you forget to breathe."

"No," he agreed. "That's a new one. How'd you know I wasn't breathing?"

"I..." I couldn't tell him that Kieran was in my head, warning me. He wouldn't understand. I hated lying to Evan, but this was such a small one. "I could feel it."

Kieran cleared his throat. Evan's eyes immediately locked on him, and his brows drew together in confusion. I put my hand on his chest and braced for the worst. "Evan," I said, "this is Kieran Voda." I whispered the rest, although I knew Kieran could hear me. "My dad insisted that he escort me here."

Evan looked from Kieran to me. Neither of them moved to shake hands. I felt the tension like a hand at my throat. I tried to joke and lighten the tone. "Boys, play nice." Evan glanced at me with hurt in his eyes. He remembered. How could he forget the name of the guy I kissed?

"The only way I could come today was if Kieran escorted me." I pleaded for him to understand. It took a moment, but I felt him relax. He extended his hand to Kieran, who shook it. I let out the breath I didn't realize I was holding.

Kieran took off his hat and scratched his head. He looked around the room and then back at us. "You have two hours," he told me. "Then we need to go."

"Where should I meet you?" I asked.

"In the cove." He put his hat back on his head and brushed past us. I heard the door open and then close with a click.

"Where's he going?" Evan asked.

"I don't know," I said. "But he promised he'd keep his distance if he thought it was safe."

Evan's face darkened. "What do you mean? Why wouldn't you be safe here?"

"My dad..." I started to answer when a strange feeling crept up my spine. Someone was listening to our conversation. I knew it with certainty. I didn't get a sense of maliciousness, but I didn't trust my powers yet either. "Do you want to get some fresh air? Maybe take a walk?"

"Sure. Yeah. I mean, I don't know the area yet, but—"

"I can find our way around," I interrupted. Tapping my temple, I whispered, "Selkie sense."

"Is that like Spidey sense?" Evan whispered back and grinned. He loved comic books.

I laughed. "Something like that."

We went out the front door. I assumed Kieran went for a swim, so I wasn't worried about running into him. Not knowing where else to go, I headed back down the path to the cove. At least we could talk there without others overhearing. Evan followed me. I stopped when I reached the shore and turned to him.

"You okay?" he asked, searching my eyes.

I nodded. "Someone was listening to us. What I'm about to tell you... I didn't want anyone overhearing."

"How did you...?" He shook his head. "Never mind."

"My dad told me that my grandparents were murdered," I said. "He didn't give me details, but I know that he's worried. He won't let me leave the island without an escort."

"When were they killed? Does he think someone will try to hurt you?" Evan stepped forward and wrapped his arms around my waist. "Are you in danger?"

"I think they were killed a while ago, but I don't know for sure." I rested my head against his chest and listened to the steady rhythm of his heart. "I can't figure out why he's worried about me getting hurt. I haven't felt anything dangerous."

Evan's arms tightened around my waist. "I'll protect you."

It was a sweet thing for him to say, although I knew he stood no chance. If I made him stop breathing just by loving him, what would a Selkie with bad intentions do? I tilted my face up. His lips met mine.

He pulled away first, keeping his arms around me. "Can I ask you something?"

"Anything," I said.

"Why Kieran?" he asked, and my heart dropped. "I mean, there has to be other Selkies who could escort you, right?"

"There are…" I bit my lip. How much could I tell him? I could trust him, though. This was Evan. He loved me. I disentangled myself from his arms and took his hand. There was a flat boulder near the water, and I wanted to soak my feet. The ocean soothed me. "Let's sit."

I sat down and tugged his hand until he sat next to me. "There are others," I said, "but only a few are powerful enough, according to my dad."

"Kieran?" Evan asked again.

"Yes. And my aunt Brigid," I quickly added, "But she wasn't available until tomorrow, and I wanted to see you today."

He searched my eyes. "Do I need to be worried?"

"What? No! Of course not," I said. "Kieran's only here because my dad asked him to train me."

"Why doesn't David train you himself?" It was a fair question. One I asked myself.

"He's in charge of all of us," I said. "He doesn't have the time."

"For his only daughter?" While I understood the disbelief in Evan's voice, it still hurt to hear him say it aloud. I kicked the surf and didn't say anything. "I'm sorry, Meara. It's not your fault. I'm just jealous."

I placed my hand on his leg. "Don't be."

I leaned my head on his shoulder and closed my eyes. The breaking waves sang like the sweetest lullaby. Everything was right in the world. Evan was here with me.

"Do you have other powers now?" he asked. "You know, besides super seduction?"

I punched his arm playfully. "Not funny!" I figured he would ask about my powers. The problem was that I barely understood them myself. I could try to explain. He deserved an explanation. "I can read thoughts."

His eyes widened. "Can you read mine?"

"Not without pushing," I said. "And I won't do that."

He looked relieved. "What else?"

"I have an unlimited wardrobe." I stood and noticed how his eyes followed me. His face was open and intrigued. I visualized my sundress— the one I wore on my last day in Peggy's Cove and my first day in Ronac. I didn't need to look down to know that my jeans and T-shirt were gone, replaced by the sparkly, white dress I adored.

Evan whistled appreciatively. "That's a talent all girls would love. Katie will be green with envy." He stood and took my hand. Lifting it above my head, he twirled me in a slow circle before leaning down and whispering in my ear, "I remember the last time you wore this dress." His breath tickled, and his words had my pulse racing. The passion flamed down quickly when I thought about my powers. They were still in check. Until I learned to control them, they were going to be better than a cold shower for my impulses.

He kissed my lips softly and took a step back. He still held my hand. "Can I see you Change?" he asked. He almost sounded shy.

"You've already seen me Change," I said. "In Peggy's Cove."

"That didn't count," he said. "You were underwater."

"All right." I tugged gently, and he released my hand. Keeping my eyes on his, I took several steps back. I visualized my seal form and saw the air shimmer around me, saw my perspective shift as my form realigned and reshaped. When the change was complete, I sat upright and waited, never taking my eyes off his face.

He was enraptured. His eyes lit with delight as he moved toward me. "That was amazing," he breathed. He leaned forward, and his hand hovered above my head. "May I?"

I nodded and waited again. He tentatively touched my fur. His touch grew stronger, and he stroked his hand down my neck. Dropping to his knees, he wrapped his arms around my neck. "You are magnificent."

If a seal could blush, I would've—instead, my heart swelled. He knew what I was and accepted me for it. He loved me unconditionally. I could feel it rolling off him. It made me feel safe and treasured.

I shifted back while his arms were around me. He gasped. Then I was human again, and our bodies fit together as I remembered. I didn't want to think that we only had the summer. I let him go once. Was I going to be able to let him go again?

Chapter 13

"How's Evan?" Ula asked. She sat on my bed with several pillows propped at her back. There was a wicked gleam in her eye. I sipped my milkshake and made her wait. She'd brought my favorite—chocolate—to soften me up.

"We had a nice time," I answered vaguely. She grabbed one of the pillows and hit me, just missing the glass in my hand. "Hey! Milkshake here."

She giggled and wiggled back against the headboard again. "Come on, Meara. Give me some details."

I couldn't play along any longer. I grinned like a fool. "He's great. We're still totally in love. He really accepts me, Ula. All of me. What I am."

"He'd be a fool not to," she said. "When are you going to see him again?"

My smile wavered. "I'm not sure. He's here to work and, according to Dad, my escort choices are Kieran or Brigid." Ula frowned, and I immediately regretted my words. She continued to feel bad about the shark incident, although I didn't hold it against her. After all, in that moment, I was freaked out, too. "I'm sorry. It's nothing against you."

She held up her hand. "No. That's okay. I accept that I'm not powerful enough." She sat up straighter and looked in my eye. "It doesn't define who I am."

"That's true," I agreed. "What you are is the nicest person I've ever known."

"Aww." She leaned in and gave me a tight hug.

81

"Milkshake! Milkshake!" I warned as it almost slipped from my hand once again. I drank the rest quickly before she did actually spill it.

She giggled and wiped a few tears off her cheek. "You're a great friend, too, you know." She hopped off the bed and took my empty glass. While I watched, both glasses disappeared.

"Where'd you send them?" I asked.

She gave me a strange look. "To the kitchen, of course. Where else do dirty dishes go? We could've taken them, but that takes too long."

"What's the rush?" I asked. She seemed almost giddy.

"There's a dance tonight. I think we should go!"

"Where?" I didn't think there were any clubs nearby. As far as I knew, the only thing on the island was the fortress.

"In the caves. The clan puts on the best dances. Music, food, singing. It's so much fun. You'll love it."

"Like the celebration for me?"

"Not really." She shrugged. "That was more of a feast. This is a party or, what do you call it, a festive?"

"Festival?"

"Yes." She laughed. "That's it."

"What do we wear to this soiree?" I asked.

Ula pinched her chin between her fingers and studied me. She walked a slow circle around me while making humming noises.

"Wow. That big of a deal, huh? Is it like prom or something?"

Her green eyes met mine. "Prom?"

"You know, formal high school dance—flowers, limousines, fancy dresses?"

"It sounds lovely." She sighed. "I didn't go to high school, remember? Did you go to this prom?"

"No," I said. "No one asked me."

"Not even Evan?"

I shook my head, blinking the tears back. "After Mom died..."

Ula sucked in a breath and slapped her forehead. "Stupid. I'm

82

sorry, Meara. How could I forget?"

I gave her a watery smile. "It's okay."

"No, it's not." Her curls bounced from her agitation. "But we'll make it better. Tonight will be like prom." She frowned. "Only you don't have a date... oh! I know. I'll be your date. Don't girls go together sometimes?"

"Sure," I said. "It's called stag."

Her brows wrinkled in confusion. "Why do they call it that?"

This time, I laughed in earnest. "I have no idea. We're back to my original question, you know. What are we wearing?"

Her face broke into a grin. "Leave that to me. Close your eyes."

I did as she asked and wondered what I'd end up wearing. Ula favored the Flower Child era, so I imagined myself in a crocheted sundress or a tie-dyed number with bell sleeves. Fabric tightened at my waist and drew snugly to my chest and hips. The material slid and slipped against my skin—satin or maybe silk. I yelped in surprise when my tennis shoes were replaced by heels or platforms. I wasn't sure which without looking, but I grew three inches.

"Can I open my eyes?" I asked.

"Not yet." She sounded breathless. I wondered how much effort it took to dress someone else. So far, I'd only dressed myself.

My hair twirled up. I couldn't guess the style, but I felt the weight of it on top of my head. A necklace, earrings, and bracelet appeared next. It was a strange sensation, being dressed with my eyes closed. I wasn't sure I liked it, and I was growing impatient. Feeling the changes was one thing; I wanted to see what she did.

"Now?"

She didn't answer right away. From behind me, she maneuvered me forward, toward my mirror if my sense of direction was worth anything. "Now," she said.

I opened my eyes and gasped. The gown was gorgeous—prettier than anything I'd seen on the red carpet, certainly better than any ordinary prom dress. It was a flow of chocolate silk that hugged in all the right places, swirling at my ankles. A long slit started mid-right thigh. A panel of ice-blue lace made it discreet, hinting at the skin beneath.

Ula met my eyes in the mirror. "Look at the back."

The same blue lace covered my back in a deep V, ending at my tailbone. "I love it!" I squealed, and then laughed. "You know my dad's going to hate it."

Ula shrugged. "Only because every male eye is going to be on you."

My hair was piled in complicated coils on top of my head. The ends waterfalled down the back. Ice-blue crystals hung at my ears. The necklace and bracelet brought chocolate brown in with the ice blue. The effect was stunning. I didn't think I could look so sophisticated.

"Thank you." I kissed her cheek. "I'm speechless."

Ula grinned with delight. "You're welcome. Now, my turn."

She twirled in a circle. As she did, her cutoffs and tank top gave way to a bell-sleeved dress in deep emerald silk. The color was a good choice—it brightened the green in her eyes and her red hair popped against it. The dress' flouncy skirt ended just above her knees. The style of her shoes, I noticed, matched mine. Only mine were chocolate brown, and hers were the emerald of her dress.

"Can't have you be the only one who's taller," she said with a wink. "How should I style my hair?"

"Leave it down. It's gorgeous." I loved Ula's hair—all those coppery curls. It did have a tendency to look unruly though. "On second thought..."

I visualized an emerald clip and put it in her hair myself, pulling back the curls from the front. It smoothed her hair in all the right places and added the perfect amount of sparkle. She stood next to me, and we stared at our reflections in the mirror. We looked amazing, ready to conquer the world or, at least, a Selkie festival.

"So this is what going to prom looks like?" Ula asked, tilting her head toward mine.

"No," I said, wrapping my arm around her waist. "This is better."

I tried to calm the butterflies in my stomach. It looked like everyone turned out for the festivities. A young mother chased her toddler around the cavern, swooped him up in to her arms, and spun him in a circle. He grinned with delight. His laughter bubbled across the room.

"I thought the twins were the youngest?" I nodded to the mother and child. "He's clearly much younger."

Ula's eyes brightened. "That's my nephew, Nico, and sister-in-law, Atiya. My brother Ren must be around here somewhere. They're visiting right now."

"Where do they live?"

"Near Alaska." Ula started walking toward them, so I followed her. The closer we got, the more striking Atiya was—dark, almond-shaped eyes, long, black hair, and latte-colored skin. Nico looked very much like his mother, only his eyes were a vivid green like Ula's.

"Atiya, you're lovely, as always!" Ula hugged her sister-in-law tightly. As they embraced, Atiya watched me with friendly curiosity.

"Is this our niece?" she asked.

"I'm Meara," I said. "Nice to meet you." I shook her hand and laughed as Nico tugged on my dress.

"Pretty choc-late," he said before sticking his thumb in his mouth and grinning at me around it.

"He's adorable." I crouched down and held out my hand. "Nice to meet you, Nico. Looks like we're cousins."

He stared at my hand for a moment before he popped his thumb out of his mouth and placed his wet hand in my own.

"Nico!" Atiya scolded.

"It's okay," I said. "Would you like to dance, Nico?" He nodded solemnly. I glanced at Atiya. I should've asked her first. "Is it okay?"

"Of course," she said. "Have fun."

Ula and Atiya resumed their conversation. I picked up Nico and carried him to the dance floor. He was surprisingly solid for a toddler, but he wrapped his legs around my waist and his arms around my neck. It helped distribute his weight and made him easier to hold. The musicians played a bouncy tune with bagpipes, fiddles, and drums. I spun Nico in circles and dipped him back. He giggled and cried out, "More, more!"

I was enjoying myself, but dancing with him was exercise. My arms grew tired. I was about to ask him if we could take a break when I felt a tap at my shoulder.

"May I cut in?"

I turned. A tall, muscular man with glossy, dark brown hair and bright green eyes smiled at me. Atiya stood next to him. She reached for Nico, and he went to her willingly. Touching his brow with her own, she kissed his cheek. "Did you have fun, Nico?"

"Uh huh. Fun." He started to lean back toward me. "I want to dance again."

"You can dance with me, sweetie." Atiya looked at the man next to her. "Daddy's going to dance with Meara now."

She twirled him away. My uncle held out his hand to me. "May I have this dance?"

I took the hand he offered. He placed his other one on my waist, so mine went on his shoulder. The music switched to a waltz. I didn't know how to waltz, but Uncle Ren did. He led me around the dance floor with ease.

"It's nice to finally meet you, Meara," he said. "I wish it could've been sooner, but we had a few things to take care of before we could make this visit."

"It's fine," I said. "I'm glad you're here now. How long are you staying?"

"We'll leave on the Dispute Moon."

"What is that?"

He pulled back to look down at me. His eyes narrowed. "You are not familiar with the moons?"

"I have no idea what you're talking about." Why did it seem like every time I learned something new about being a Selkie, I realized how much more I had to learn?

"It's the full moon in the eighth month," he explained.

Okay, now I understood him. "So you're leaving in August."

"Yes, August."

"You could've just said that," I muttered. He chuckled and twirled us around. As we danced, he told me about Atiya's clan. Her parents ruled now. Someday, they would take over. He seemed curious about my human life, and he seemed especially interested when I summarized the last year with my mom and dad, their marriage, and Mom's ultimate death. It was easy to talk to him.

When the song ended, he pulled me into a bear hug.

"I do like you, niece."

"Thanks," I said as I fought to breathe. "I like you, too."

Uncle Ren excused himself to join my aunt and little Nico on the dance floor. I looked for Ula, but I didn't see her. I did spot refreshments on a long table against the far wall of the cavern. Brightly colored liquid filled large, crystal bowls. Fancy glasses sat nearby. No red Solo cups for the Selkies. I assumed the bowls contained punch, and I was thirsty. I filled a glass with lime-green liquid.

"I wouldn't drink that if I were you," spoke a voice near my right shoulder. "Horrible stuff."

"What is it?" I asked automatically. I turned and met the gray eyes of a male Selkie. This one, however, was much younger than my uncle was. He looked my age, which meant that he was still older than I was in Selkie years.

"Seaweed Swill?" he guessed. "I haven't the slightest idea really, but it's gross. Go ahead and try it if you don't believe me."

"It's not that I don't—" I took a small sip and made a face. "That's nasty!"

He laughed. "I told you. I don't know why Paddy insists on serving it. I think he's trying to make us eat healthy or something. Sneak in more vegetables." He pointed to another bowl. "Try the pink. It's sweet."

I held up my glass. "What should I do with this?"

"Set it on that tray. Someone will clean it up."

I sipped the pink punch. It tasted like vanilla and strawberries. "Mmmm. This is good."

"It's the best one," he said, holding out his hand. "I'm Arren, by the way."

"Meara." I shook his hand.

"Oh, I know who you are," he said. "We all do. My friends want to meet you. Unlike me, they're too shy to come over."

"Where are they?" I looked around. A group of teenagers sat at a corner table. Arren waved in their direction, confirming they were his friends. "Well, let's go over so I can meet them."

"Really?" He seemed surprised that I offered to meet them.

"Why not?" I didn't have anything else to do at the moment. It wouldn't hurt to make friends my own age, well, at least, friends that appeared to be my age.

"Follow me." He turned and strode away.

Mouths dropped open as we approached the table. Arren ran through their names. They recovered quickly, nodding or raising a hand as he introduced them.

"Nice to meet you," I said. "Mind if I sit?"

"Please." The girl closest to me with the short, blond hair scooted over to make room. She was the first blonde I met at Ronac. Most of the Selkies had dark or red hair. I sat and removed my heels. They were beautiful, but they were killing my feet. As I rubbed my sore toes, I skimmed from one face to the next. No one said anything. It was so awkward. I was about to excuse myself when Arren elbowed the boy next to him. I thought his name was Lyle.

"What was it like?" Lyle asked. They looked at me expectantly.

"What was what like?" I had no idea what he was asking me.

"Being human," Lyle clarified. "What was it like?"

"Did you go to the mole?" The blonde asked. I must have looked bewildered because she added, "You know, to buy things."

"You mean the mall. The shopping mall. Yes, I went there."

"What kind of music did you listen to?" Arren asked. He leaned on his elbows toward me. They all watched me intently.

"Rock music, I guess."

"Rocks make music?" The pretty brunette wrinkled her brows in confusion.

"Um, no." Were they serious? "Don't you ever leave the island? Haven't you been around humans?"

The blonde's eyebrows rose in surprise. "Leave the island? You're joking, right?"

The brunette shivered. "It's so dangerous out there. Humans have weapons that can kill us. Then there's the merpeople, kelpies, sirens—"

"They're real?" I couldn't believe the world could hold so many creatures. Ones I never knew existed.

"Of course, they're real. As real as you and me," she huffed. I didn't mean to offend her, but apparently, I had. We lapsed back into silence again.

"Well, this is a lively party."

I didn't have to turn around to know it was Kieran. I hated that my pulse raced at the sound of his voice. I wasn't the only one affected. The girls primped and preened next to me. Arren scowled at Kieran before glancing back at the blonde girl. They didn't seem to be together, but Arren obviously had feelings.

Kieran's eyes drifted over me. His mouth rose in approval. "Nice dress." He extended his hand. "Would you like to dance?"

I hesitated. The last time we danced, it went further than it should have. Sure, it was just a kiss, but I wouldn't like it if Evan kissed another girl. One time, forgivable. Two times, not so much.

"It's just a dance." Kieran noticed my hesitation. "I promise I won't try anything. You clearly love your human boy toy."

"You have a human boyfriend?" the girls squealed at the same time. Their reaction made me wince, although I tried to hide it.

"I'm human too, you know."

"But you aren't," Arren sputtered. "You're one of us."

I caught Kieran's smirk. He enjoyed this exchange a bit too much. "Told you," he said.

I stuck out my tongue. Childish, but I felt better afterwards. I'd hung out with the teenagers long enough. They were melodramatic and immature. Sheltered, like Ronac itself. I felt bad for them. Would they ever get a taste of freedom?

"Sure," I told Kieran. "I'll dance with you."

For a moment he appeared genuinely surprised that I agreed, but he quickly recovered. I left my shoes by the table. Kieran led us to the middle of the room. The band slowed the tempo. Around us, couples drew closer and swayed. He placed his hands on my waist and pulled me close.

"Kieran—"

"Relax, Meara."

My hands were on his arms, but I moved them up to his shoulders. If I looked straight ahead, I was staring at his white dress shirt and striped tie. I turned my head to the side and watched the couples around us. They seemed closer to my father's age than to mine.

"Kieran?" I looked up at him. He was already staring at me.

"Hmm?"

"How old does a Selkie have to be before you're considered an adult?"

"Why do you ask?"

"Arren and his friends." I nodded toward them. "They seemed to be my age, but they acted so much younger. They're really older than me, though, right?"

Kieran sighed. "Yes and no. They are if you measure in human years. They're younger if you measure by Selkie."

"I don't understand."

"You wouldn't," Kieran said, not unkindly. He lifted my chin and forced me to look in his eyes. "Because you're trying to reason things as a human. We're not human, Meara."

I jerked my head back, and he dropped his hand. "I don't know how to think like a Selkie," I persisted, "Why do you know so much about humans, and those kids know so little?"

"I'm older—"

"That's all?"

"You didn't let me finish," he scolded. "I'm also more powerful. As are you." When I rolled my eyes, he added, "You *are*, whether you believe it or not. We can defend ourselves against enemies. They cannot. They rely on us. Do you understand?"

His dark eyes bore into mine, and I did understand. Suddenly, I understood with great clarity. "They can't do magic, can they?"

"Not like us," he admitted. "They can change forms, of course. Some can do minor things, like visualize, but most have no powers beyond Changing."

The burden of responsibility weighed on my shoulders. Just as it was my father's role, it was my job to protect these people. Why hadn't my dad told me? Why hadn't Ula? Why was Kieran the one looking at me with sympathy and understanding?

"It's the same for me, Meara," he said. "When I return to our clan, I will take my father's place. He is old and ready to step down. I am the oldest, so the responsibility falls to me."

A new song began. This one slower than the last, if that was possible. Kieran tightened his hold and pulled me closer. I gave in and wrapped my arms around his waist. It was more comfortable than trying to put them on his incredibly high shoulders. He was so tall. I rested my head against his chest and soaked up his warmth. We could be friends. Our birthright made us uniquely positioned to understand each other. I had so much to learn, but he was teaching me more than anyone else was right now. That mattered. It mattered a lot.

"I think I'm done for the evening," I said when the song ended.

"May I walk you back?" Kieran asked rather formerly. "As friends, of course."

"I came with Ula…" I scanned the room once again for her coppery curls. Where had she gone?

"I saw her leave about an hour ago," Kieran said with a frown. "About the time I came, I suppose."

"She still cares for you." The words slipped out before I thought about them. Ula would be mad if she knew I told him, but he had a right to know.

"It's been years," he said.

"Love doesn't just go away," I replied. "Look at my parents."

His eyes grew distant and thoughtful. Finally, he nodded. "Perhaps you're right. Are you ready to leave?"

"I need to get my shoes first." I walked back to the table in the corner. The teens were gone, but my shoes were where I left them. I put them on and winced. At least it wasn't a long walk. Taking the arm Kieran offered, I tried not to notice everyone staring as we left the cavern and headed into the fortress. The halls were empty and quiet.

"I'm surprised my dad didn't make an appearance," I said.

"I'm not." Kieran glanced down at me. "Did you notice Brigid and Angus were missing as well?"

"I suppose," I said. "Why?"

"I'm not sure, but I think it might have to do with your side trip to Scotland."

Was he teasing me? He looked serious enough. "But why?"

"We have enemies, Meara. David's told you as much."

"He did," I said. "But I don't understand why they're worried about me. What kind of problems could my actions cause? I only saw Evan."

Suddenly, Kieran seemed angry. "Did nothing sink in? Do you not understand the magnitude of your position? You will someday rule this clan. You are their future protector, and therefore, you must be protected. Any time you leave the island, your father will risk almost anything to keep you safe, to protect his lineage."

"My aunts and uncles can rule instead —"

"No," Kieran interrupted. "It is not their responsibility. It's *yours*."

His words rocked me on my feet. Surely, I couldn't be that important? We walked the rest of the way in silence. I considered everything I learned this evening. I had a lot to consider. What was Kieran thinking? His emotions hid behind a blank mask. He stopped abruptly. We were at my door.

Kieran broke the silence. "I care for you, Meara." His voice sounded husky. "I meant it when I said I'd very much like to be your friend."

He was serious, even a little sad. I kissed his cheek and smiled. "I'd like that, too," I said. "Goodnight, Kieran."

For a moment, he looked like he was fighting something, but then he stepped away from me. "Goodnight, Meara."

He didn't return my smile.

Chapter 14

Bits of blue flashed in the corridor as she ran. The rest of her dress blended into the shadows. *She's fast,* Evan thought and struggled to keep up with her.

"Meara, wait!"

She turned a corner. When he lost sight of her, the walls began to close in and pain pierced his brain. He clasped his head and ran. *She was here. He would find her.*

Rounding the corner, he caught the flash of blue ahead and sped to catch up. She was quicker than he remembered, running with a strength and grace he never noticed. Still, he was faster, stronger. She glanced back over her shoulder as the distance closed between them. He reached out with a hand to grab her arm. His fingers grew into talons and cut angry, red strips into her flesh.

"Get away from me," she screamed. She sunk to the floor and wrapped her arms protectively around herself. Thin, red trails coursed down her arm. With the realization that it was his fault, his veins frosted over. *He did that. Hurt her. Hadn't meant to.*

Hands.

What happened to his hands?

He held them out. They shook, but they were only hands, not talons. *Had he imagined the whole thing? No, or her arm would be fine.*

"I'm sorry," he said. "I didn't mean to hurt you."

"Just go away," she cried. She hung her head, her hair falling in a riot of curls. It couldn't hide the tears on her cheeks or the fear in her eyes.

"Meara, it's me." He moved to crouch before her. She shot up and pressed herself against the wall, turning her face away from him.

"I said get away from me!" she screamed.

"Meara—"

Her scream cut through him, doubling the piercing pain in his head. What the hell was the matter with her? Why was she afraid of him?

"Evan! Wake up!"

A sharp knock sounded at his door. He slapped his hand on the alarm clock, and the screaming stopped. The headache remained, drilling through his teeth. Would his skull split? It sure felt like it.

"Evan." He recognized the voice on the other side of the door now—Professor Nolan. "Hurry down for breakfast. We're leaving in twenty."

Evan fell back against the pillow and closed his eyes. The dreams were getting old. He didn't mind dreaming about Meara, but he preferred her flirty and fun. He hoped to never see that look in her eyes. Pure fear. Fear of him. If dreams were supposed to tell him something, he needed help interpreting this one and the previous ones. What did they mean? Why was he having them anyway? Was it the change of scenery? Seeing Meara as something other than human? He didn't think so. She seemed human to him, even now.

He scrubbed his hands over his face and staggered out of bed. At least he packed Advil at his mom's insistence. He popped two pills without water and dressed quickly. A baseball cap would substitute for washing his hair. Given the choice, he'd choose breakfast over cleanliness, especially when he considered that they were most likely spending the day outside. Professor Nolan was vague about the whole internship program. At the time, it didn't matter. He took the job to be close to Meara. Now that he was here, though, he wanted to know what he'd be doing. Nolan told him so little. Today was his first day on the job. That was all he knew.

Breakfast consisted of sausage, toast, and stewed tomatoes. Evan ate it all and washed it down with two cups of black coffee. The sharp pain subsided to a dull ache at the base of his head. It was not ideal, but it was tolerable.

"Anything else, sir?"

Stonewall stood by the doorway, watching Evan with an amused expression. The man was odd; there was no doubt about that.

"I'm good, Stonewall. Thanks." He stood to carry his plate and cup to the sink.

Stonewall intercepted, taking them from him. "Very well, Master Mitchell. Master Nolan and Master Guthrie are waiting for you outside."

Outside could be anywhere, but they were probably in the front yard. Evan guessed right. The men stood next to the impossibly small rental car.

"We're taking that?" Evan asked the question before he could stop himself. The ride was uncomfortable enough in the front seat. He couldn't imagine folding himself up to fit in the back. The two men laughed, as if they shared a private joke.

"No, Evan," Professor Nolan said. "I was just getting some papers from the glove compartment. We're going to the pier. Our boat is docked down there."

They climbed down the steps that Meara and Kieran must have taken yesterday. Kieran—just thinking his name made a ball of jealousy grow in Evan's stomach. Did the guy have to look so perfect? Was he a model or movie star or something? Evan could hold his own. He had his share of girlfriends over the years. The problem was, next to Kieran, Evan looked plain. He looked plain, and he didn't like it. The fact that Meara kissed Kieran only made the green-eyed monster worse. She was attracted to Kieran, which made him a dangerous opponent. Evan refused to lose her.

"You okay, son?" Ken asked. "You're awfully quiet."

"I'm all right. It's a headache, but I took something for it already." Evan shook off the poisonous thoughts and started paying attention to where they were walking. Halfway down the hillside, the stairway split. One set continued down to the shoreline and beach, the other angled to a long pier. Docked on it was one very large boat. Unfortunately, the thought of being at sea didn't excite Evan this morning. Whether it was the dream, the headache, or the competition, his heart was not in it. He nodded toward the pier. "Nice boat."

"That's no boat." Ken laughed. "That's a fifty-foot trawler."

"Ken's pride and joy," Professor Nolan chimed in.

"It's great." Evan tried to drum up some enthusiasm. It sounded flat to his ears.

"Let's get onboard. Check her out," Ken said. "Ted, check the gauges, will you?"

"Sure thing."

For the first time, Evan had the impression that Ted worked for Ken Guthrie and not the other way around. What was their relationship? Did Ken finance this research? Whatever it was they were researching. The ignorance was killing him.

"What's on the agenda for today, Mr. Guthrie?" Evan asked.

"Ken. Call me Ken, son," he replied absently as he checked the rigs and various equipment on deck. Evan wasn't sure how he felt about being called 'son,' but he let it slide. Ken seemed to have a few quirks. If it got too annoying, he'd ask him to stop.

"You had some visitors yesterday, didn't you, Evan?"

It took Evan a moment to realize Ken asked him a question. He was still trolling the deck and his back was to him.

"Uh, yeah," Evan said. "My girlfriend, Meara, and her friend. I hope that's okay."

"Of course, of course. What's that saying, 'my house is your house'?" He paused and considered, then waved it off. "Ah, never mind.

The point is that you're welcome to have visits from your friends."

"Thank you."

"Where's your girlfriend staying anyway?" Ken looked at him now. His gaze was sharp and packed a punch for an old man.

Evan shrugged. "An island near here, I think. She's living with her dad."

"Ah. Divorce?"

"No…" Evan paused. He really didn't want to tell Ken about Meara's life, but he had to say something. "Her mom died a few months ago."

"Sorry to hear that." Ken looked sorry, too. "Pretty girl. You should invite her to dinner."

"Thank you," Evan said.

"How about this weekend?" Ken persisted.

"I would…" How could he explain that he didn't have a way of reaching her? He didn't like it himself, but she promised she'd come back as soon as she could. Ken watched him expectantly.

"Yes?" Ken prompted.

"Well, I don't have any way of getting ahold of her."

"What?" Ken's bushy, white eyebrows rose comically. "A teenage girl who doesn't have a phone? I didn't think they left the house without one."

"She did, but it broke and…" Evan felt increasingly uncomfortable. He really didn't want to explain Meara's lack of a phone to Ken or anyone else for that matter. Ken seemed to sense his discomfort.

"I'm just teasing you," Ken said. "Next time you talk to her, you invite her over. Tell Stonewall and he'll plan for another mouth to feed."

"I will. Thanks again."

"No thanks necessary." Ken looked up and yelled to Professor Nolan in the cabin. "Ted, you ready to get that engine purring?"

The motor roared to life and, within minutes, they were headed out to sea. Evan asked if there was anything he could do, but Ken waved him off.

"Take a seat," he said, motioning to the benches along the middle of the boat. "There'll be plenty of time to teach you. Just enjoy yourself today."

Ken went inside the cabin by Professor Nolan. Evan stayed on the bench, leaning back against the wall. The wind blew his hair, and the cool sea spray helped soothe the tension in his muscles. He closed his eyes and relaxed. Only when the boat slowed did he open them again. With relief, he realized that the ache in his head was finally gone.

He moved to the front of the boat and looked around. No land in sight. Too late, he wished he'd paid attention to which direction they headed.

"Ready to get to work?" Professor Nolan clapped him on the shoulder and smiled. Ken must have taken control of the boat at some point. They were still moving forward at a snail crawl.

"Where are we?" Evan asked.

"Northwest of Scotland. About fifteen miles out."

"What are we doing here?" Evan asked. He expected Nolan to give him a non-answer like he had every time before.

"This is top-secret research," Professor Nolan began. "We've discovered something big. The start, we think, of a mantle plume."

"Volcanic activity?" Evan was surprised. In this area, that would be unheard of. Although his focus was on marine animals, he took a couple of oceanography courses and studied plate tectonics. There were no plates in this area, at least that the scientific community knew of.

"Yes. We've seen the telltale emissions." As he talked, Ted began to lay out the scuba gear. The engine shut off, and Ken came out of the captain's cabin to join them.

"You told the boy about our find?" Ken asked, and Ted nodded. "Good, good. Mind you, this is top secret, Evan. No blogging on this one."

"Of course not, sir, I mean, Ken," Evan corrected when Ken raised one white eyebrow at 'sir.'

"You do know how to dive, son?" Ken asked.

"I've been certified, yes," Evan said.

"Then what are you waiting for? Suit up."

"I get to go down?" Evan's pulse raced. He didn't think he would actually get to go out on this first excursion. He figured he'd be assigned to man the ship.

"You and Ted," Ken said. "I'm conducting a few experiments on deck with my samplings from last week. We all take turns going down. I'll go next time." Evan stood, unmoving, and Ken added, "Go on. You'll find equipment in your size. Ted sent me the details ahead of time. I had everything ordered for you."

Evan changed and went to stand by Professor Nolan on the metal platform. He moved experimentally in his wetsuit, which was on the tight side. Maybe Ted should've asked him for his size instead of guessing. Evan added his diver's mask and air tank. Right then, he envied Meara. A flicker of thought and she could glide through the water—lightweight and carefree. His equipment weighed him down, and if it failed, it would cost him his life. He shook the thought off. He was lucky he had this summer job. He was going to see things few men ever saw.

"Ready?" Ken asked. They gave him a thumbs-up, and Ken lowered the platform into the water.

"Grab the scuba scooter in front of you. It'll get us there faster." Professor Nolan's voice floated around him, and Evan realized the scuba mask was outfitted with some kind of communication system. Until Nolan told him, Evan hadn't noticed the compact scooter in front of him, or the one the professor held. He unhooked it from the platform and tried to figure out how to operate it. A quick lesson on the deck of the boat might have been nice.

"Here. Take mine. I'll start yours. Watch what I do." He observed as Ted flipped a switch on the side and pressed a button on the top. "Hold in the levers to propel ahead."

Evan squeezed in the levers near the handle. He surged forward. He let up on the levers and slowed down. He could hear the professor laughing.

"You'll get used to it," he said. "By the way, if you want to talk, just do it. I can hear you."

"How far down are we going?" Evan asked.

"About three hundred feet." The professor sped ahead of him. "Just follow me."

They descended, and the water grew darker and darker. The headlight on the front of the scuba scooter lit the area ahead, but only about five feet. It was isolating and a bit disorienting. Evan focused on Ted's flippers and followed as the professor instructed.

The water cooled progressively as they moved down, but then it began to warm again. Evan attributed it to the mantle plume and wondered how active it really was. The professor wouldn't bring them here if it weren't safe, right?

"Almost there." Professor Nolan's voice startled him. He'd gotten used to the silence on their descent. "There it is."

He came up alongside Ted, their scooters illuminating the ocean floor. Evan gasped as he took in the view. The mantle plume was the cracked mouth of death from his nightmares. It spewed black and decay along its length.

"So much destruction," Evan murmured, not realizing that he said it aloud until the professor responded.

"The destruction is temporary, but the energy potential is tremendous." Evan heard the excitement in his voice. "Do you know what this could mean to the scientific community? It's believed that a mantle plume once raised an island and then sunk it within a hundred-year span. That kind of tectonic energy hasn't existed in this region for a millennia at least."

"What are we going to do with it?" Evan's throat tightened in discomfort. This was what his internship was about? Studying volcanic activity? He assumed they would be tracking native oceanic species.

"We'll gather samples, of course, and measurements. Try to determine how active it is and predict its growth."

"What is our assignment for today, sir?" Evan asked.

"I'll take some samples. You have the camera. Try to get some clear shots along the length, as well as some close-ups near the fissure."

Evan did as he was told. Digital was cheap, so he just kept clicking. The entire time he pondered the parallel to his dream. What did it mean? Was there any significance or was it just an eerie coincidence?

Chapter 15

"Are you awake?"

Ula stood in my doorway. All I could see was her silhouette against the pale glow coming from the hall. The room was pitch black. It was either the middle of the night or very early in the morning. I had no idea how much time had passed while I tossed and turned, thinking about what Kieran told me. I would rule this place someday, with responsibility for all of these lives. It scared the hell out of me.

"I can't sleep," I admitted.

"Are you alone?"

"Of course I'm alone. Who else would be here?" The words came out with a bit more edge than I intended, but really? What was she thinking? She knew I loved Evan. Did she think I would just throw myself at Kieran?

"Sorry," she murmured. "It's just..." Her voice trailed off. I waited for her to say something else. "Can I come in?"

"Of course," I said. She sounded so forlorn, I couldn't be angry with her. I scooted over to make room for her on the bed.

"Do you mind lighting some candles?" Ula asked. "It's awfully dark in here."

I waved my hand, and the candles on my bookshelf flamed to life. Ula's brows rose as she looked at them. "You're learning fast."

"Brigid taught me that last week." I shrugged. "It's useful, so I've been practicing."

I sat up and propped my pillows against the headboard. Sleep was not going to come tonight. I might as well get comfortable. Ula was a welcome distraction, even if I was irritated that she ditched me at the dance. It seemed to be a pattern, at least when Kieran was involved. I understood to a point, but when would she get over him? Hadn't it been decades?

She pulled her knees to her chest and rested her chin on them. Her eyes were still on the candles. "About tonight," she began. "I'm sorry I left. I was coming over by you and the children when I saw Kieran heading your way. It's hard for me to be around him. I panicked and fled."

"Being around him bothers you that much?" Her admission surprised me. Although I was starting to consider Kieran a friend, it didn't stop me from thinking he was egotistical and oftentimes annoying. Sure, he was hot, but a face and body only went so far. Eventually, good looks faded. It may take hundreds of years for a Selkie, but ultimately, everything aged.

My thoughts turned to Evan. He would age much faster than I would now. In twenty years, I'd look just a couple of years older. Kieran might look like he was in his twenties. Evan would have wrinkles and gray in his hair. Would I feel different then?

No, I decided. I'd love Evan the same as I did now.

"I still love him," Ula whispered. She looked miserable.

I leaned over and hugged her. "I'm sorry," I said. "I can imagine how hard it is for you to be around him."

"I see how he looks at you," she continued, as if I hadn't said anything. "He never looked at me that way."

"I don't know what you're talking about." If my heart sped up, I ignored it. Did he really watch me when I wasn't looking? "We're just friends."

She met my eyes, and I squirmed under her gaze. "You're lying to yourself if you believe that. I know you love Evan, but you feel something for Kieran, too." She drew in a deep breath before continuing, "And Kieran, he watches you all the time. He looks at you like you are precious and rare." She started to cry. "And you are. He's right."

"You are, too!" I said.

"He never loved me." Her voice held dejection. "He always thought I was beneath him. He must see you as an equal, and I know why. You're more powerful in a few weeks that I am after a century of practice."

How could I respond to that? Although I felt bad that I had more power than her, there was nothing I could do about it.

"When are you going to see Evan again?" She wiped her eyes and sniffed lightly.

"I don't know." I flopped back against the headboard again. "I have no way to reach him."

"Can't you go see him?"

I shook my head. "Kieran said I won't get many opportunities to leave. My dad's orders."

"He told you that?"

I nodded. "And he told me that eventually, it will be my job to protect this island."

Ula scowled. "He shouldn't have said anything. That was up to David to tell you."

"You knew?" I was hurt. Ula was my friend. Why hadn't she told me that I was next in line to rule or whatever they called it?

"Of course, but I promised David I wouldn't tell you. He wanted to give you time to adjust, and then he was going to explain it all to you."

"When?" I asked. "I barely see my dad. He's so busy."

My vision blurred, and my eyes filled with tears. Ula patted my hand. "He feels bad about that, too," she said. "Things should settle down by the end of summer. It'll get better."

Summer. Evan was only here for part of the summer. I had no idea when I'd see him after he went back to Peggy's Cove. I needed to make the most of his time here and see him as much as I could, but how?

"How can I see Evan if I can't leave the island?" I wondered aloud.

"I might be able to help with that," Ula said. "But don't tell your dad. Ever."

"My lips are sealed."

"What?" She gave me a confused look, and I remembered that she didn't know all the expressions I used. She knew more than the teenagers I met, but not all.

"It means I won't tell. I promise," I said.

"Good." She swung her legs to the side of the bed and stood up. "Follow me."

I thought we were going back to her room, but we passed her door and continued down the hall. We bypassed the stairwell and went down another hall. I thought these rooms were empty and said as much.

"They are," Ula confirmed. "We tend to use them for storage unless other Selkies are staying with us. Kieran's room is at the end of the hall."

"Oh." Were we going there? No, there was no way that Ula would purposefully contact him. We passed his room and turned to yet another corridor. She opened the third door on the left.

"This suite belonged to my mother."

My grandmother. Would this room tell me anything about her?

"Didn't she live with your father?" I asked.

"Sure." Ula shrugged. "But everyone needs an escape. She used it as a lady's chamber. She would gather in here with the other women. They'd tell stories, sing, knit, and sew." She looked around thoughtfully. "I think some of the women even painted."

Ula lit a candle near the door and entered the room. I followed and asked, "Couldn't they just use magic to create what they needed?"

"My mother could; she was very powerful. I asked her that once myself. You know what she told me? 'Where is the sense of accomplishment in that? Or creativity?'" She paused, her face lighting up as she remembered. Then, she shrugged. "Besides, most of the other women could not use magic. She preferred to create alongside them."

I looked around the room and wished I had met my grandmother. She sounded like a fair and caring woman, and she had elegant taste, too. The furnishings were beautiful. Tapestries on the wall portrayed sea life around the world, from tropical islands to the icy artic. Woven rugs covered the stone floor. Plush chairs invited one to sit and relax. They were set in a semi-circle before a large, stone hearth. It felt warm and inviting.

"Does anyone use this room anymore?" I asked.

"No." Ula moved toward a bookcase along the back wall. "It's been vacant for years. I don't like to come here. I miss her too much."

"How long ago did she die?" I wasn't sure if I should ask or not, but curiosity got the best of me.

"My parents were murdered sixteen years ago." Ula's voice was quiet. "It feels like it happened yesterday. I miss them so much."

She continued to search the bookcase, moving a few books on the shelf and talking to herself as she did. I stood back and watched. What was she was doing? After a few attempts, she hooted in triumph and spun to face me. She held a small, jeweled box.

"Let's go back to my room," she said. "And I'll explain what I have here."

The hall was less dim than before. Though dark outside, it was no longer black. Morning couldn't be too far off now. Ula opened her door and moved to the bookcase, lighting the candles. She sat in her favorite beanbag chair and pulled one close for me.

"My mother came from the clan near Nova Scotia." As she talked, she trailed her fingers over the top of the ornate box. "My father courted her for many years before her parents would allow her to marry him. During that time, he gave her a gift."

Ula opened the box and delicately fingered through its contents.

She pulled out a gold necklace with a pearl charm and handed it to me. I held it up. The charm was actually a tail—the tail of a whale or maybe a Selkie—wrapped around a pearl. Beautifully crafted, it was graceful and elegant.

"I love it," I said.

"It's yours." Ula smiled at me.

"No, I could never keep this." I tried to give it back, but she pushed my hands away.

"My mother would've wanted you to have it," she said. "Besides, you'll need it, along with this piece, for what I'm about to tell you." She lifted out another necklace. This one was a thicker gold chain, obviously meant for a man to wear. It was unadorned, but striking all the same.

"My father wore this," she explained. "And gave my mother the one that you're holding. When they were both wearing their necklaces, they could communicate with each other."

"How?" I could scarcely believe it. Had Ula discovered a way for me to talk to Evan?

"He charmed them. The wearers can communicate telepathically with each other. They wore the necklaces their entire lives, so they could always stay in touch, whether they were close or far. I'm not sure if it will work with a human, but I imagine it will." She smiled at me. "It can't hurt to try, right?"

I threw my arms around her and pulled her into a tight hug. "Thank you so much. You have no idea what this means to me."

"Can't breathe," she joked, and then laughed. "I think I do know what it means. I hope it helps you, Meara. I only want the best for you."

My excitement cooled when I realized I first had to get the other necklace to him. "How am I going to get over to Scotland to give him this? Kieran didn't think Dad would let me go back."

"You have lessons with Brigid today?" Ula asked. When I nodded, she said, "Let me talk to her. I think I can convince her to take you there. It will have to be quick, but you only need a few minutes to get him the necklace."

"You can convince Brigid to help me?"

"Sure, why not? I'll use my baby sister charm."

I laughed. "Maybe I should be taking lessons from you. Thanks for helping."

"Think nothing of it," she said. "We're family. Now go to your room and try to get at least a couple hours of sleep. I know my sister's lessons are brutal."

I clasped the pearl necklace around my neck, and Ula handed me the thicker chain. It felt heavy in my hands. If this worked, I could talk to Evan like he was in the room with me. It was almost as good as seeing him. I hoped it would allow us to meet up, too. I planned to make the most of our time together, in whatever way I could.

A sharp knock at my door woke me.

"I'm not waiting for you all day, niece. If you want to go, we're going now."

I flew out of bed and opened my door. Brigid was already heading down the hall. I visualized my pajamas becoming shorts and a T-shirt as I ran after her. Patience was not a word in her vocabulary.

"Ula talked to you?" I asked after I caught up. I hated that I was struggling to catch my breath, and she was cool as ever.

She raised one dark eyebrow and captured me with her cold eyes. "She did, although how she convinced me to help you on this little endeavor is beyond me. Don't push your luck. This will be a quick meeting. No long lovers' rendezvous, understood?"

"Of course."

Outside the fortress walls, she took my hand and transported us to the shore before I could take a breath. She didn't wait and dove in. I followed on her heels, too excited about seeing Evan and giving him the necklace to worry about my aunt's mood. Which, when I thought about it, wasn't really too different from her everyday mood.

She swam stealthily all the way to Aberdeen. How she knew where to stop, I had no idea. She must have talked to Kieran, because when we came on land, we were on the shore below the house.

"I'll wait here," she said. "Be back in fifteen minutes. Don't make me regret this."

I didn't waste time responding. I'd already visualized myself in shorts and a swimsuit. I sprinted up the hill and stopped at the top, out of breath. It was quiet, and the house was dark. Although a car was in the driveway, it looked like no one was home.

A motor roared in the distance. A large boat moved swiftly toward the shore. It slowed as it approached the pier. Of course! Evan was working today. How would I explain how I got here? I had no car. I'd tell his professor that someone dropped me off.

I didn't notice Brigid down in the cove. She'd either gone back in the ocean or found a place to hide and wait. They wouldn't see her.

Two figures stood on deck. When they debarked and tied it off, I recognized Evan and Professor Nolan. A third man with white hair stepped out of the cabin. I didn't know him. Indecision paralyzed me. Wait here or go to the pier? *Better wait here*, I decided. It might seem more coincidental that I had just arrived and been waiting for only a few minutes.

I paced nervously when a few minutes grew to at least ten. Brigid told me I had fifteen. How was I going to give him the necklace and leave without explaining myself? My plan was falling apart. I visualized a pen and envelope, wrote Evan's name on the outside, and took off the necklace and placed it inside. On the inside flap, I wrote, "Evan, a gift for you. Wear this and think of me. Love, Meara." Not that I was paranoid, but if anyone else found it, they wouldn't think anything of my message. I sealed it and looked down at the men again. They were lingering, probably putting equipment away on the boat.

I ran around the house to the front and rang the bell. Maybe the butler was here. He was odd, but he seemed professional. I was pretty confident that if I gave him the necklace, he'd make sure Evan got it. I'd know for sure when I tried to communicate with him later.

"Good afternoon, Miss." Stonewall looked the same as the day before, down to the dark suit and serious expression on his face. "Master Mitchell is not here. They are working today."

"I know. I..." I thrust the envelope into his hand. "I just wanted to leave this for Evan. Can you give it to him?"

"Of course, Miss. Would you like to wait? I imagine they will be home shortly."

"No, thank you." What I wanted was to get out of there before Evan or one of the other men spotted me. "Please just give him the envelope and let him know I stopped by."

"Very well." He stepped back and began to close the door. "Good day."

"You too," I called. "Thank you."

I hurried down the steps and around the corner of the house. As soon as I got there, I transported myself to the cove.

"Brigid," I called in a whisper.

"I was about to leave."

I jumped. She was directly behind me. "Did you say hello to your lover boy?"

"No. Their boat just came back, and they're standing on the pier. I left a message with the butler."

"How quaint," she said in a bored voice. "Time to get back and start your lesson."

"I still have a lesson today?"

She laughed. "Of course, and now that I've done you a favor, well, it's going to be a long lesson."

Why did she sound so happy about that?

My hair, plastered to my face, obstructed my view. I could, however, hear my aunt's cold voice. "Again," she commanded.

I sighed and sat down. She drilled me for hours in the pouring rain. For some reason, the rain didn't faze her. Her black hair was pulled back in a high, tight ponytail. Her clothes seemed to repel the water. I was soaked and she barely looked wet. How did she do it?

"Can we please Change?" I asked again. I thought the rain would bother me less in seal form. She insisted we stay human.

"What if you are attacked on land? You must know how to defend yourself. You can't very well change into a seal in front of the enemy, can you? How helpful would that be?"

"It would if the ocean was nearby and I could swim away," I muttered.

"What did you say?" Her voice was as icy as the rain.

"Nothing."

Next, I tried to explain that I'd been human for a long time, my whole life to be exact. She sneered at me. "I want you in human form, not human," she corrected. "Besides, as a human, you had no power. Now you do. Defend!"

I shot to my feet when she threw a bolt of blue light at me. From experience, I knew it hurt. I drew my shield and blocked her bolt. Another followed in its wake.

I was tired, cranky, and so done with this. I focused on my shield and its pliability. In my mind, I formed it into a glove and caught the bolt. It sizzled and encircled me, but it didn't touch my skin. I added my power, and it changed from electric blue to blazing orange. The orange engulfed me like flames. The power raised the hairs on my body. I wasn't afraid. If anything, I was energized. I threw my arms skyward and flung the orange bolt into the clouds.

"Enough!" I cried.

A flash of brilliant light blocked my vision. When I could see again, the sky was clear blue, not a cloud in sight.

Brigid stared at me, her mouth ajar. Several moments passed before she asked, "What did you do?"

"Sorry," I mumbled. I shuffled my feet and looked down. "I didn't mean to."

"Let me rephrase that." She pronounced each word with care. If I didn't know better, I'd say she looked shocked. "*How* did you do that?"

Tired of the damp clumps of hair clinging to my neck, I ran my hands through the strands, will them to dry. "I just pictured my shield as a baseball glove—"

"Excuse me?" Brigid's brow rose.

"Baseball. You know, American sport? A ball, bat, and glove?"

My aunt rolled her eyes. "Go on."

"I caught your power in my shield and added mine to it."

Brigid looked thoughtful. "That's when it turned orange."

"Yes," I said, confused. "Haven't you done that before?"

"Never," she said. "Selkies don't often work magic together, and we rarely fight each other."

I blew my now-dry hair out of my face and planted my hands on my hips. "Then why are you teaching me combat?"

Her eyes widened, and the corners of her mouth twitched. I thought she might be having a convulsion until a peal of laughter burst from her lips. "I was teaching you defense," she said. "You, apparently, are teaching yourself combat."

I stared at her, dumbstruck. Her violet eyes held warmth I'd never seen before, and her smile made her look years younger.

"You amaze me, Meara," she said. "And so few do." She caught herself, and the smile disappeared. "Speak of this to no one. I need a chance to talk to your father. You are dismissed." When I continued to stare at her and not move, she waved me away. "The lesson is over."

She disappeared, and I contemplated the strange turn of events. I wasn't sure if what I had done was good or bad. It certainly left an impression on my aunt. I sat on the mossy ground and turned my face to the sky. It was late afternoon. I could tell by the position of the sun. Give me another month or two, and I'd probably understand those crazy moon phases that my uncle told me about.

A gentle breeze caressed my skin. I stared out at the ocean and thought of Evan. Had Stonewall given him the necklace yet? Would Evan put it on right away, as I requested?

Tonight. I'd try to contact him tonight, not now. He could be with the professor and the other man. Late at night, I could reach him alone and explain.

Ula said they worked through mind speak, so Evan would hear my voice in his head, a form of telepathy. Would he realize it was me speaking to him? Would he believe it? If not, I'd have to convince him.

I stood and transported to Ronac. It was easy now. The clearer I thought about what I wanted, the more accurately it occurred. I was growing stronger. Brigid noticed and Kieran did, too. Did my father know? When Brigid told him what happened, would he be impressed?

I hadn't seen my dad since I asked for permission to see Evan. He was missing at breakfast, already starting his busy day of leading the people. Then again, for all I knew, he wasn't even on the island right now. When I decided to move here with him, I thought we'd get to know each other better. He was as distant as ever.

"Good lesson?"

I jumped and placed my hand over my heart. I was so lost in my thoughts that I hadn't seen Kieran. He leaned against the outer wall, close to the entrance.

"Sorry for scaring you," he said. "Brigid just came flying in like a bat out of hell."

I tilted my head and studied him. "How is it that you know slang and expressions, but other Selkies look at me like I've grown another head?"

He shrugged. "I grew up in California. I live closer to humans than most Selkies do. I've learned things over the years."

I nodded. It made sense. "What are you doing out here?" I asked.

"Waiting for you," he said. "Want to go for a swim before dinner?"

It was a tempting offer. My muscles ached, and my skin prickled from the energy I'd expelled. "I'm in," I said. "If we can walk to the cove. I'm not up for another transport right now."

"Too much magic today?" His expression was sympathetic.

"You could say that," I said.

"What happened?" He fell into step beside me.

"I'd rather not talk about it," I said.

"Some storm we had earlier. Funny how it cleared up so quickly." I felt his eyes on me, but I kept looking ahead.

"Hmm..." I gave him the noncommittal answer. When I added nothing else, he spoke again.

"Of course, the bright orange firework display might have had something to do with it."

"Really? I wouldn't know." I kept my voice innocent. "Why don't you tell me about your day?"

He laughed. "Today, I had the distinct displeasure of tutoring the children."

"The triplets?" I asked. They were cute, but mischievous.

"No," he said. "Your friend Arren and his entourage."

"My *friend* Arren?" I quirked my eyebrow at him. "I just met him the other night. I'd hardly call us friends."

"Oh, but he couldn't stop talking about you," Kieran teased. "He had a million questions. I wouldn't be surprised if he asks you out."

"Do Selkies date?"

Kieran shrugged and smirked at me.

"You told him I have a boyfriend right?" I glared at him.

He threw his hand over his heart. "What? And crush his dreams?" He playfully tugged a chunk of my hair. "Oh no, my sweet, that's for you to do. You can squish his heart just like you did mine."

"Really?" The sarcasm dripped in my voice. His eyes danced in response. I shoved his arm playfully. "Yeah, you look heartbroken."

We were halfway to the cliff when Kieran shouted, "Race you there. Last one has to surrender dessert tonight."

I ran after him, tight on his heels. Just before the cliff, I overtook him and jumped. I Changed and dove into the ocean. Delirious, I twirled in the water. I heard his deep laughter in my mind. He swam up to me and slid along my side.

That was impressive. His voice, like his body, caressed me. I shivered involuntarily. He affected me even in my seal form.

Anything for extra dessert, I replied lightly and dove down. I shifted course and sped to the surface, flipping in the air before diving under again.

Dolphins could do it, why couldn't I? I laughed inside my head, delighted. It was fun.

Kieran dove and flipped as well. For a while, we competed to see who could get higher. He won. He was more muscular and had years of practice. After a while, we slowed to a leisure pace and swam around the island. The water relaxed every muscle in my body, and I was glad I came.

A deep rumble sounded, and I heard Kieran's laugh in my mind again.

Was that your stomach? he asked.

I missed lunch, I said. *Training with Brigid, remember?*

Come to think of it, I missed breakfast, too. She was in such a hurry to escort me to Scotland. I didn't tell Kieran this.

Let's head back, he said. *It's probably dinnertime anyway.*

On the shore, back into our previous outfits, I dried my hair while Kieran rung the water out of his cap. "Double or nothing?" he asked.

"What are you talking about?"

"The bet." He grinned at me mischievously. "Let's race back."

"I've already won your dessert. What's the double portion?"

He twirled his hat on his finger. He looked like he was thinking about it, but I figured he was just pretending. "I'll take your next dish duty," he offered.

"You're on!" I took off running. I heard him behind me, gaining fast. I refused to turn and look; it would cost me time. In the end, it didn't matter. He flew past me in a blur. When I got to Ronac, he was back in his original spot against the wall, a smug expression on his face.

"You played me!" I said.

He kept his expression nonchalant. "I have no idea what you're talking about," he said. "A day in the sun and a long swim must have gone to your head."

I walked passed him, shaking my head. "You were totally holding back earlier. I can't believe I fell for it."

"Ah, don't be too hard on yourself," he said next to my right ear. "I can be quite convincing."

"Apparently."

He bumped my shoulder with his arm. "You're still rather impressive."

"Thanks." I fought to look angry. I wanted to laugh.

"Even if you're slow," he added. I punched his arm. "Ow!"

Chapter 16

Dinner was uneventful. Once again, Dad wasn't there. Neither were Aunt Brigid or Angus. I ate with Ula and my Uncle Ren's family. Kieran sat across the room, keeping his distance from Ula.

After dinner, we went to the study and played cards. My heart wasn't in it. I was relieved when the sun was low in the sky, and I could excuse myself and go to my room. I read for several hours, well past sunset. It was time.

"*Evan?*" My mind called out while I fingered the necklace. Was it my imagination or did it feel warmer in my hand? "*Evan? Can you hear me?*"

I paused and waited. Silence. Maybe Stonewall didn't give him the necklace. Disappointment settled in my chest. I really hoped this would work.

Meara? Evan's voice was clear, if confused. *Where are you?*

You can hear me? I sat up in bed. Ula was right. The necklace used telepathy. I heard Evan clearly in my head, the way I heard Kieran when he talked to me in seal form. *I'm at Ronac, Evan. The necklace... it's what allows us to communicate.*

His rumbling laugh warmed my insides. I wanted to see him.

Are you in your room? I asked.

Yes. Finally. He sighed. *I didn't think they'd ever let me stop working today.*

Are you alone?

Yes. His voice was deeper. Sensual. My stomach fluttered. Could I go? Would anyone know? I'd been to the house twice. I could picture it clearly in my mind. Who would miss me here? If I was back before dawn, there was no chance of getting caught.

Can I see you? I asked.

Do you have to ask? He paused. *But how?*

Just don't freak out. I closed my eyes to transport, and then realized I didn't know which room was his. *What room are you in?*

Second floor, last on the right when you're looking at the back of the house.

He knew that we came in from the cove then. That was good. Maybe I wouldn't shock him too much.

Close your eyes, I told him. *Don't open them until I say so.*

Meara—

Do it!

He thought I was joking, I could tell by the way he said my name. I closed my eyes and pictured the room. HIS room. I saw it clearly in my mind before I commanded my body to go there. I felt a pull deep in my abdomen and had the sense of moving really fast. When the movement stopped, I opened my eyes and grinned. I was in his room. He was sitting on his bed with his legs stretched out and crossed at the ankles. His eyes were closed as I requested, a smirk on his face, as if he were waiting for me to tell him it didn't work. I walked quietly to the bed and stopped by his feet.

"Keep your eyes closed," I whispered aloud, no longer needing the necklace to communicate.

I startled him, but he did as I said. I moved to the head of the bed and sat at his side. Leaning over, I kissed one eyelid and then the other. I slid my fingers through his hair before leaning down and kissing his full mouth. He wrapped one arm around my waist and placed the other hand on the back of my head. He kissed me back greedily. When the kiss ended, I rested my head on his chest, content to listen to his heart.

We were together. Alone. We could see each other every day while he was in Scotland.

"Can I open my eyes now?" he asked in a teasing voice.

"Oops." I looked up and met his blue eyes. "Sorry!"

"No need to apologize." He lifted the chain around his neck. "I think this has to go into the category of best gift ever."

I bit my lip and smiled. "Pretty cool, isn't it?"

"A personal communicator that allows me to talk to you? To arrange to see you in person? Freaking awesome I'd say." He lifted the charm on my necklace with his finger and studied it. "Where did you get these?"

"Ula found them," I said. "They belonged to my grandparents. They used them when they were courting."

"I'm glad we can carry on the tradition." He ran his hand along my cheek, cupping my face in his palm. "God, I missed you."

My throat tightened. "I missed you, too."

He leaned over and turned off the light. The room lit with the glow of the silvery moon, casting his face in shadows. "We have lots of lost time to make up," he said in a husky voice. I didn't get a chance to respond because his mouth covered mine.

When I woke, moonlight streamed into the room. Evan thrashed and moaned next to me. The sheets tangled around his lower body. His chest was bare, beaded with sweat. The room was cool, bordering on chilly. Something was wrong.

"Evan." I shook him. "Evan, wake up!"

He groaned and rolled away from me. I touched his head and jerked my hand back. He was burning up. In a panic, I visualized a cool washcloth and placed it on his forehead. He quieted as I dabbed the cloth across his fevered skin. I wished he'd wake up.

"Evan?" I called quietly, so I wouldn't startle him. "Are you awake?"

"Meara," he croaked. "So thirsty."

"Drink this." I handed him the tall glass full of cold water I just conjured. He gulped it down greedily.

"More," he begged. He pointed a shaky finger to his dresser. "Advil, too, please."

I got out of bed and walked to the dresser. Opening the bottle, I took out two pills. The bottle was half empty. Wordlessly, I refilled the glass and handed it to him with the medicine. He drank the water almost as fast the second time.

Falling back against the pillows, he closed his eyes. He no longer looked flushed, but he was pale.

"Are you okay?" I asked.

"I will be," he said. "Thanks to you." He patted the bed next to him. "Come back to bed."

I slid in next to him under the sheet. His warm body comforted my cold skin. Selkies weren't supposed to be affected by the cold. Could've fooled me.

"Does that happen often?" I asked.

"Just recently," he mumbled, already falling back asleep. "Better in the morning."

His reply didn't comfort me. I laid awake and listened to him breathe. His breath grew steadier as he fell into deeper sleep. I couldn't push tonight, because he needed his rest. Tomorrow was another story. Tomorrow night, he was going to talk and tell me what the hell was going on with him.

Time passed, and the room lightened. I knew the sun would rise soon. I slipped out of bed. Evan didn't stir. I closed my eyes and pictured my room at Ronac. When I opened them, I was there. I crawled into my own bed and pulled the covers over my head. The last thought I had before I fell asleep was that it worked. I could have the best of both worlds. I could be with Evan *and* live as a Selkie.

Chapter 17

*E*van woke. Had it been a dream? He lifted the chain around his neck. It looked like any gold chain. The kind some men wore. Evan never considered wearing jewelry, maybe a wedding ring one day. He didn't mind the necklace. It felt light and substantial at the same time. Last night, he was pleasantly surprised to find it was so much more than just jewelry.

Meara? He thought her name rather than said it aloud.

Her voice, though sleepy, rang clear in his head. *Yes?*

His lips twitched. No dream. *Good morning.*

Morning. Her voice was silk in his mind, erasing the lingering twinges of his headache. *Feeling better?*

Yes, he answered. *Thanks to you.*

I'll see you tonight?

Was it his imagination or did she sound tentative, unsure?

Tonight, he confirmed.

It wasn't like having a phone conversation, but it came close. One minute, he sensed her presence, and the next, it was gone. He glanced over at the clock. There was only ten minutes left until Ted knocked on the door, if he kept the same schedule as yesterday. Time to get dressed.

He was tying his shoe when the knock came. Evan laughed at the professor's startled expression when he opened the door.

"Oh!" Ted said. "You're up."

"Time for work, right?" Evan fought to keep a straight face. He gave up and grinned.

"Yes," Ted said slowly. His eyebrows wrinkled in confusion. "You're chipper this morning."

"No headache," Evan replied. "I feel great."

He stepped past Ted and ran down the stairs. The dining room table was already set with steaming dishes. This internship was feeding him well.

"Good morning." Ken sipped his coffee and watched Evan take his seat. "Sleep well?"

"Yes. Thank you." Evan filled his plate with bacon, eggs, and toast. Ted sat down across from him and began to do the same.

"Do you get headaches often?" Ted asked.

Evan shrugged, his mouth full. He swallowed and answered, "I never used to, but the last couple of weeks, I've been getting them on a regular basis."

Ted's gaze flicked to Ken, who waved his hand in reply. "It's Scotland," Ken said. "This overcast weather bothers everyone."

Evan didn't bother to point out that the headaches started back home, or that there had been very little rain since he arrived here, just that one day when it poured and then stopped abruptly. The rest of that day, the sky was a cloudless blue. Strange weather in Scotland, sure, but headache inducing? He didn't buy it.

They ate in silence until Ken spoke again. "New necklace, Evan? I don't recall seeing it before."

Evan had a strange urge to tuck the necklace into his shirt. Instead, he forced himself to smile and say nonchalantly, "It was a gift. I just decided to wear it today."

Ken nodded, still eyeing the necklace. "It looks expensive. The giver obviously cares for you."

Nodding, Evan continued to eat, although he wanted to squirm under Ken's gaze. Ted watched their exchange with interest, his fork paused halfway to his mouth.

Evan swallowed his toast. "Thank you. I like it, too."

When their plates were almost clear, Ken asked, "Did you have a chance to ask your girlfriend to dinner?"

"Not yet." Evan had completely forgotten. "But I will."

"Good, good." Ken rose. "See if she's free on Saturday night. She's welcome to bring her friend with her."

"Friend?"

Ken's brows rose. "Of course. The one who came to the house with her. Keith? Carter? I don't recall the name."

Evan was confused. "Did you meet them?"

"Stonewall told me," Ken said. "It is, after all, my house." Was that a warning? Evan tried to read Ken's expression, but there was nothing there really. He looked pleasant. Pleasantly neutral.

"We leave in five minutes," Ken said before walking out of the room.

Ted was quiet this morning. They finished their coffee and juice in silence, and he rose from the table first. "Are you ready?"

Evan nodded and followed him out. Once they were climbing down the stairs to the docks, Evan asked, "Why is Ken so interested in Meara?"

Ted made a dismissive noise. "It's not just her. He likes to entertain."

"Why?" Evan asked.

Ted shrugged and picked up his pace. "Don't you like parties? They're fun. Ken enjoys meeting people and showing off his house. If you want to know more, ask him."

The hours flew by at work, much to Evan's surprise. Gathering samples, he went through the motions, doing whatever Ken and Ted asked him to do. His mind was elsewhere. He thought of Meara and the necklace. He wanted to contact her again, see how she was doing now that he could talk to her at any time. He missed the daily interaction with her, and this was better than a text message. He tried not to think about it. It would look strange to the other men, and he didn't want to draw any more attention to himself or the necklace.

They broke for lunch. Amidst cold chicken, pasta salad, and bottles of water, the headache returned. It began as a dull throb at the base of his neck. By the time they docked, the pain seared behind his eyes. The neck pain felt like a knife wound. Sweat dripped from his forehead. He hastily wiped it out of his eyes, but not quick enough.

"You okay, son?" Ken studied him with concern. "You don't look too good. Why don't you go inside and get some rest? Ted and I can finish up here."

"Thanks," Evan murmured with gratitude. Even speaking that single word sent a shrill of pain through his skull.

"I'll have Stonewall send up dinner later." Ken eyed him sympathetically. "Feel better."

The stairs took an eternity to climb, then the trudge to the house, and again more stairs to his room. He swallowed three pills this time, chasing them with the remaining water in the glass by his nightstand.

His head met the cool softness of the pillow, and his eyes closed in relief. Meara's scent engulfed him. For a brief moment, he wondered if she were here. He could almost feel her cool, slender fingers on his head. The pain was too great to open his eyes. He breathed deep once and met the darkness.

Chapter 18

From the window to the door, I paced in my room. Evan's voice waking me had been pleasant, yet once I felt him disappear, I was edgy. Something wasn't right. Tonight, I would ask for answers, but what if he couldn't give them?

My stomach growled, and I stalked to the door. I hoped Uncle Padraic made something yummy like French toast or pancakes. He made the best pancakes, better than Mom's.

Mom.

I'd give anything to have her back. I missed her. Her laugh. The way she really listened to me. Her advice. I could use some now. I was breaking a major rule, but I couldn't help myself. I had to see Evan. I loved him.

"You ready?"

I jumped, my heart beating wildly. Kieran just raised an eyebrow. "A little jumpy this morning, aren't you?"

It was apparently a no shirt morning. Kieran had those often. Arms crossed over his chest, wearing only swim trunks, he leaned against the wall.

"You scared the crap out of me!" I snapped, trying not to stare at his muscled torso. "Do you have a shortage of shirts?"

His lips rose at the corners. "Why? Does my naked flesh bother you?"

"Don't flatter yourself." I elbowed my way past him, satisfied at his "oomph" when my bony elbow met his flesh.

"Where are you going?" He recovered quickly. I felt him directly behind me. He radiated heat like a furnace.

"To get breakfast," I said. "I'm starving."

"Are you forgetting something?" Kieran jumped in front of me. All I saw was his stupid, incredibly sculpted chest. I closed my eyes and prayed for patience.

"What?" I asked between clenched teeth.

"Your lesson." Irritation sharpened his words. "We should've started hours ago."

"How do you know?" My finger poked his chest, and he backed up. "How would I know? It's not like there are any clocks in this damn place."

"Grouchy much?" he snapped. "Fine, we'll get you something to eat, but then, we go to work."

"Fine," I snapped back before adding grudgingly, "Thank you."

Kieran wasn't kidding that it was late. Breakfast was long over. We found Paddy in the midst of lunch preparations. When I sat at the counter, he passed me a plate of fruit.

"Thanks." I popped a strawberry into my mouth, and then pushed the plate toward Kieran. He took a few berries.

Uncle Padraic poured us each a glass of juice before turning back to chop vegetables and prepare fish for a large pot of stew.

"Do you ever leave this kitchen?" I asked.

"Sometimes." He shrugged and didn't pause in his chopping. "I like it here. It soothes me."

Would I ever find a calling like that? Something I could be passionate about? Computers interested me, but I grew bored with them sometimes, too. I craved variety. Change was good. I liked being a Selkie. It was still new, still a challenge.

My uncle pulled a pan of rolls from the oven. He slid four onto a plate along with a bowl of butter, setting the platter before us. When the rolls cooled enough to eat, we ate them quickly. The rich flavor and light-as-air texture made a delicious combination. My crabbiness melted away like the butter. I always did better on a full stomach.

"You ready?" Kieran asked once I finished my juice. I nodded and followed him outside.

"What are you teaching me today?" I asked once we stood in the cove.

He tilted his head and studied me. "I want you to teach me."

I stared back at him. What could I possibly teach him?

"Teach me how you transformed Brigid's energy," he said.

My cheeks grew warm. "You heard about that?"

"Yes. Your father told me." His eyes held mine, his face serious. I felt a wave of anger at my dad. I hadn't seen him in over three days, but he found time to talk to Kieran? I tucked the anger away. It wasn't Kieran's fault. I would find my dad later.

"I'm not sure I can..." I bit my lip. "What I did was instinctual. If I think about it, I can't remember the steps. It just was."

"Please." His voice was soft, coaxing. "Try."

I nodded and shifted to a comfortable stance. "First, let's try to recreate it. I'll try to be more conscious of the steps."

"Can I listen in?"

I knew he meant my thoughts. I shook my head. "I need my shield. I used it to catch her energy, so I could transform it by adding my own."

Wait! That was it!

"Are you familiar with baseball?" I asked.

"Baseball?" His lips twitched. "Like the L.A. Angels?"

"Right," I said.

"I've seen a few games." His expression grew curious.

"Then this might make sense to you," I said.

His eyes lit up. "You remember?"

"Sort of," I confessed. "I still want to try it. Here's the gist. My shield was around me when I saw Brigid form the ball. I flexed my shield to form a glove and caught Brigid's energy. Once I had it, I grew it with my own."

Kieran shook his head, a smirk on his face. "Wicked."

I rolled my eyes, anxious to try now that I remembered the steps. "Are you ready?" I brought my shield around me and tested its pliancy. Perfect.

Kieran's hands rose in front of him. The ball of energy he grew was green. It glowed and floated in front of him while he hesitated.

"Throw it," I called. "I'm ready."

"You sure?" He frowned at the ball. "These really hurt."

"I know," I said, my patience snapping. "Kieran!"

He threw the green ball. I caught it. His energy tingled, but not unpleasantly. I concentrated on adding my own. As before, the original color gave way to my blazing orange. The fire spread around me. Kieran lunged forward.

"Stay back!" I yelled. "It's not hurting me."

As the energy swirled, I contemplated what to do with it. My target last time was rain clouds. Today's cloudless sky did not help me. Maybe I could ground it.

"Throw it back," Kieran called. "I'm ready."

He crouched in a catcher's stance. If it weren't for my concentrating to keep the energy contained, I would have found it funny.

"Are you crazy?" I asked. His wild grin told me he was.

He tapped one hand into the other like a catcher's mitt. "C'mon, Meara," he said. "I can do this."

"If you say so," I said.

Kieran's green orb had been the size of a baseball. As I reformed the orange fire into a ball, it was now the size of a basketball. With two hands, I lobbed it to him. He caught it with grace. The orange flickered and died. The ball once again glowed green, then spread out to spike around Kieran's shield.

No wonder Brigid freaked out. Like a special effect in a movie,

Kieran glowed, a magical wizard. His face lit with delight as he raised his arms and concentrated the energy above his head. The orb again doubled in size. He breathed deep and launched it into the bay. The water exploded like a torpedo hit. A rainbow arced across the sky.

I admired the beauty and size of the rainbow. I was so caught up in its beauty that I didn't see Kieran fall. He was on his knees, his head bent to the ground.

"Kieran!"

I dropped by his side. His skin was cold and clammy. He murmured in response, but he didn't raise his head. Rolling him onto his back, I listened to his heart. It was strong.

His arms came around me and trapped my body against his. "What a rush!"

I raised my head and looked into his eyes, which were now full of humor. I pushed to sit back on my heels, and he released me.

"What happened?" I asked.

His cheeks tinged pink. It was the first time I'd seen him embarrassed. "I think I released too much of my energy."

"Oh," I said. "Can you do that?"

He raised a brow. "I just did."

"You're okay?"

With a wince, he pushed himself up to sitting. "A bit sore, but I'll survive."

The red glow of the setting sun bathed the hallway as I hurried to the cavern. Would my dad join us for dinner tonight? Nearly a week passed since his last meal with the family. Where was he? I thought I was getting to know him. The time between Mom's death and our arrival at Ronac changed things. For both of us, I think. We had reached an understanding, but now I wasn't sure. He was so... absent.

I missed my mom. We could talk all night and laugh about anything and nothing. She knew me, understood me, and loved me. No one else came close to all three. Evan loved me and knew me, but he didn't understand my Selkie nature. Kieran and Ula understood, but they didn't fully know me. Did they love me? I didn't know.

The noise flowed in the crowded cavern. I paid little attention to it. My focus was the head table, the family table, and my dad was there. Smiling to myself, I hurried down the steps, nervously touching the edge of my top to ensure the necklace was safely tucked away. At the same time, my heart lightened. Mom was gone, but he was here. I needed to make the most of it.

He stood when he saw me approach and wrapped me in his arms. He hadn't shaved and his whiskers tickled, but I hung on and hugged him.

"How are you?" he asked, pulling out my chair for me.

"I'm good." I wanted to ask where he'd been, but what came out was, "How about you?"

"Entertained." His eyes lit with mischief. "I hear you've been keeping your tutors busy."

I laughed. Aunt Brigid sat at the other end of the table with Angus. She shot us a purple-eyed glare. My dad ignored her and winked at me. "I'm proud of you," he whispered.

Ula sat next to Brigid. She cast glances my way as we ate dinner. I knew what she wanted. She was dying to ask me if the necklaces worked. I touched my neckline. She raised her eyebrow in question, and I turned. I wasn't talking about that here or even acknowledging it. She had to wait if she wanted to find out.

I ate everything on my plate and took second helpings. Using my power made me hungry, and today's practice drained me. Had Kieran recovered or was he still weak? He trained me for another hour after he collapsed, but the rest of the lesson was almost tame. He rarely took it easy on me. I searched the room for him. He wasn't here.

"Kieran's not feeling well," my dad said.

"How did you know—?"

"Who else would you search for?" he asked. When I didn't answer, he continued, "I'd like for you to join me after dinner, if you will."

"Sure, Dad." Maybe he missed me, too.

He glanced at my empty plate. "Are you ready?"

Now he was impatient, after all that time away? I bit my tongue and followed him back to his room. Might as well see what he wanted before I picked a fight. When he opened the door, the stale air tickled my nose. Whatever he was up to this week, he hadn't been staying in his room.

"Where were you?" I asked as I settled on the sofa.

"That's what I wanted to talk to you about." He sat across from me in his recliner chair. It was strange seeing the furniture from our apartment here. Although I was glad he saved it, it felt out of place, from another time, another life. "Did you see Evan?"

"I did. I'm sure Kieran told you." After all, Kieran saw my dad more than I did. It annoyed me that he was ignoring my question once again. Could he ever give me a straight answer?

"He did," he consented. "But I wanted to hear it from you."

"He's good. The house is huge." A thread hung from one of the throw pillows. I wound it around my finger. It was difficult to meet his eyes. Would he see that I was holding back? Did he know that I saw Evan more than once?

"That's all?" My dad leaned forward, resting his arms on his legs.

"What else do you want to know? We talked. I miss him." In my nervous fumbling, I dropped the throw pillow and bent to pick it up. His eyes trained on the top of my shirt, and his brows drew together.

"Are you wearing a new necklace?" he asked. Before I could answer, he reached over and lifted it in his hand. He stiffened and said in a cold voice, "This was my mother's."

Crap! How did it fall out of my shirt? I thought it was well hidden.

"Yes, um… I found it." I wasn't going to mention Ula's involvement and definitely not Brigid's. If I did, I knew it would be the last time she ever helped me.

"Where did you find it?" He stood stiffly before me.

"In a chamber," my voice squeaked. "With a fireplace."

"My mother's chamber." He paced across the room and back. "I take it that Evan has the other one?"

I watched him with wide eyes. Could I lie? Would he know? Was he going to demand that I give them back? I wouldn't. I couldn't. It was the only way that Evan and I could communicate. I wasn't going to lose it.

"Meara?" He took a deep breath and sat next to me. "Tell me the truth. Does Evan have the other one?"

"Y-yes," I stammered in a quiet voice. The thread broke away from the pillow, leaving a small hole in its wake.

He sighed and leaned back. "Very well. What's done is done."

"Do I have to give them back?" I asked. "It's the only way we can communicate, Dad. My cell phone doesn't work. I can't see him unless I have a chaperone—"

"You may keep them," he interrupted, and I breathed a sigh of relief. "My mother would've wanted you to have them anyway, but you must not see Evan anymore."

"What?" I turned and stared at him. "You're kidding, right?"

"I am not." He shook his head. "You are not to leave the island."

"Are you grounding me? Is this because I took the necklaces? I'm sorry; I didn't know."

Now it was his turn to face me. He took my hands in his. "You misunderstand. I am not familiar with this grounding, but from your other question, I assume you think you are in trouble. You are not."

"Then… why?" I looked down at our joined hands. My dad's fingers were long, but his hands were strong. There was a quiet strength within him, but right now, he looked worried. "What's wrong?"

He stood and paced to the far wall where the window faced the ocean. It was dark now, but the moon washed his face in soft light. Everything about him spoke of tension, and maybe even fear. "I don't know, and that's the problem. We lost two of our clan."

"Lost...?" Did he mean that they died?

"Two of my stronger guards. They were patrolling our borders and went missing several days ago."

"So they're missing, not dead?"

My dad shook his head. "Their bodies washed ashore. One yesterday, and the other today."

Two Selkies were dead. A chill traveled down my spine. What happened? "How'd they die?"

Leaning into the windowsill, he crossed his arms and rested his forehead on them. "Hard to tell. The bodies were almost unrecognizable."

"I'm sorry, Dad. Is there anything I can do?"

"Yes." He lifted his head and turned to me. His eyes burned into mine. "Stay here. Stay safe." He crossed the room and knelt before me. "Promise me this, Meara. I lost your mother. I don't want to lose you, too."

"You won't lose me." He was being a little overdramatic.

He took my hands and shook them. "Promise me, Meara."

"Okay. Okay. I promise," I said with my fingers crossed behind my back. So, it didn't really count, did it?

My dad calmed down after that, and we talked for a while. He asked about my training, and I filled in some of the details that Kieran and Brigid left out, or, in Brigid's case, corrected some of the details she provided. I asked him more about what he was doing, why he was gone so much, but he refused to tell me. "It's not your worry," he said.

"Maybe it should be," I argued, but he didn't budge. The old resentment rose inside me. When was he going to trust me? Would he ever see me as grown up? When I realized that he was not going to say another word on the subject, I excused myself, kissed his cheek, and left. How could I love someone who irritated the hell out of me at the same time?

"Meara? Is that you?"

Ula's door was ajar. She beckoned me in. "Close the door behind you."

I dropped into the closest beanbag. Her room really was comfy.

"What's up?" I asked, knowing perfectly well what she wanted to know.

"The necklaces," she hissed. "Did they work?" I grinned, and she bounced in her chair. "They did. Excellent! Are you going to see him again?"

I couldn't tell her that I saw him last night. She'd freak. Instead, I said, "Dad just told me that I can't leave the island. He's worried about my safety."

She frowned. "He told you about Malcolm and Henry then."

"Well, I didn't know their names..." The names weren't familiar at all. I must not have met them. "But yeah. He told me they're dead."

"Dead!" She scoffed. "They were murdered. He knows it, too."

I didn't argue with her, having got that impression when he told me. I twirled my necklace. "Why does he treat me like a child? Why won't he tell me anything?"

Ula leaned forward and patted my knee. "You are a child." Before I could object, she added, "More than that, you're *his* child, and he just got you back. Give him time, Meara."

"If he loves me so much, why do I hardly see him?"

"You know the answer to that," she admonished, but her tone was gentle.

I stood and walked to the window. In the early moonlight, the ground below appeared gray, the ocean silver. "He makes time for

Kieran and for Brigid. Even Angus. Why not me?"

She came behind me and rested her hand on my shoulder. When I looked back at her, her eyes were full of sympathy. "He conducts business with them. They are not meeting for pleasure. He wants to see you more. I know it."

"How do you know?" I asked bitterly. My throat constricted, although my eyes were dry.

"He told me." She wrapped her arms around me. "He loves you, Meara. Once he ensures our safety, he'll make time for you. I promise."

"Funny thing about promises," I said, thinking of the one I made to him earlier. "They're easily broken."

Ula wanted me to stay and talk to her. I made a flimsy excuse about being tired and left. I was eager to contact Evan. Luckily, I encountered no one else on my way to my room. I closed the door and breathed a sigh of relief.

Would my dad check on me during the night? So far, people only came by in the morning, not during the night. If I was back before sunrise, would I be able to safely escape? I crossed to my window and stared at the moon. I was getting better at reading its position. I deduced that dinner, my conversation with my dad, and my visit with Ula took about two hours. Evan would be home. Hopefully, he was alone.

You there? I asked.

Always, came his immediate reply. *And I'm alone. You can come.*

I closed my eyes and pictured Evan in his room. It was easier this time since I'd been there before. When I blinked them open, he sat before me on the edge of his bed, grinning.

"Amazing." He pulled me forward and into his lap. "I don't think I'll ever get tired of seeing you do that."

I returned his smile. "I'm glad you like it."

"Not as much as I like this." He wrapped his arms around my waist and kissed me. When we pulled apart, we were both breathless.

"Wow. Someone's feeling better."

Apprehension flitted across his face before his smile returned. "It was just a headache. No big deal."

I scrambled out of his lap and stood before him. "It wasn't just a headache, Evan," I said. "You were sweating and delirious. What's going on? Has this happened before?"

He shrugged. "A few times. I take some Advil. It goes away. I'm fine."

"How long have you been having them?"

"Jesus, Meara." He raked his fingers through his hair, leaving it disheveled. "Are you my mother now?"

"As your girlfriend, as someone who loves you, I can't be concerned?" I tried to keep my voice calm. He was clearly defensive, which made me think the headaches were worse than he was letting on. "Have you seen a doctor?"

"What? No! I'm fine."

"Evan, I just lost my mom to cancer." I took his hand and sat next to him. Could I help him the way my dad helped my mom ease her pain? I'd have to ask Ula and find out. When he looked at me, I said, "Will you at least see your doctor when you get home?"

He rested his forehead against mine and closed his eyes. "Yes," he relented.

I put my hand to his cheek and kissed him softly. "Thank you."

"You didn't come here to talk about my health, did you?"

He was teasing again, so that was a good sign. Unfortunately, I had to bring the mood back down. "I almost didn't come at all," I said.

"Why not? You were that upset about my headache?" His voice rose in confusion.

"No," I said. "My dad doesn't want me leaving the island. Two Selkies were found dead. He's worried."

"Were they murdered?"

"He doesn't know." Goose bumps broke out across my skin. Evan pulled me back into his lap and kissed my neck. "I've never seen him like this."

"Maybe you shouldn't come back." Evan's voice was quiet, but firm.

I drew back and stared at him. "How can you say that? We only have a few weeks as it is."

"This isn't about us." He looked resigned. "If your life is in danger, I won't risk it."

"It takes me seconds to get here. No one knows that I can transport myself this far. What danger am I in?"

"I don't know, Meara. I bet those other Selkies didn't think they were in danger either. Why would anyone want to kill them?" Evan held me tighter. "I know little about what you are now and less about your enemies."

"Do you think we really have enemies?" I shuddered. "Why would anyone want to harm us? We pretty much keep to ourselves."

"Should we see if we can find anything? I brought my books with me." Evan set me to the side and crouched to pull his suitcase out.

As he lifted the books onto the bed, I resisted the urge to laugh. "You brought books with you?"

"Why not? I reference them often." He paged through the thickest book. With his free hand, he pushed another tome toward me. "You look through this one."

I sighed and flipped the book open. This could take all night.

"I found something!" Evan slid his book toward me. I blinked rapidly to clear my vision. I may have dozed off. We'd been at this for hours, and I was exhausted.

"What'd you find?"

"Aumakuas," he said proudly.

"Amawhatis?" I had no idea what he was talking about. Was he delirious?

"Ow ma ku as," he pronounced slowly. "Shark people."

"Shark people?"

"What?" He laughed. "You're seal people. Why not shark people?"

"I guess." I thought about the shark I encountered in the cove when I was swimming with Ula. "Sharks are scary enough."

"You're right," he said. "It says a seal's natural enemies are also a Selkie's, so sharks and killer whales are two of the bigger ones."

I pulled the book closer and read the paragraph. "It makes sense, but if a shark or whale attacked those men, wouldn't their bodies be gone? I mean, not to be gross, but the sharks would've eaten them, right?"

Evan nodded. "Exactly. That's why the Aumakuas are more plausible. Perhaps they're planning an attack of your island."

"Why?" There wasn't much in the book on them, but I didn't see anything that would explain why they hated Selkies, only that they saw them as a food source. I didn't hate cows, but I'd been known to eat a hamburger.

"That's what we have to find out." Evan closed the book. "But enough for tonight." He set the books on the floor and lay on his side. He patted the space in front of him, and I stretched out to face him. His fingers raked slowly through my hair and down my side. "I was supposed to ask you to dinner."

What he said was so unexpected that I didn't even comprehend it. "What?"

"Ken, the man who owns this house," he explained. "He wants you to come to dinner. And, he wants you to bring Kieran, too."

I frowned at him, trying to make sense of it. Why did this man want to meet me?

"He recommended Saturday, if you're free." Evan said it lightly, as if he were joking. "I'll make up some excuse why you can't make it."

"Let me check with Kieran—"

"Are you crazy? No! Until we figure out who's after you, you shouldn't come back here. I only told you about it because I promised Ken that I would." He lifted my chin until our eyes met. "You're not coming. David's right. You need to be safe."

"I want to be with you," I said.

"For tonight," Evan whispered. "You can't come back until we know it's safe." I nodded, and he wiped the tears from my cheeks. "Don't cry. We'll figure it out. I love you. Nothing changes that."

I wrapped my arms around his neck and kissed him with desperation. When would I see him again? I didn't want to let him go.

The sky was inky black when I transported back to my room. The moon and stars hid behind thick, dark clouds. I moved through the familiar darkness and crawled into bed.

That was when I realized I wasn't alone.

A hand snaked around my head and covered my mouth, muffling my scream. The voice spoke near my left ear. "Did you have a nice time with your boy toy?"

I jabbed my elbow back hard and met a solid wall of muscle.

"Cripes, Meara! Are you trying to kill me?" The words came out in raspy bursts. My aim wasn't half bad.

"Maybe you shouldn't sneak into a girl's room in the middle of the night!" I snapped back. "What are you doing here, Kieran?"

With a flick of my wrist, the candles in my room flared to life. Kieran leaned against the headboard, rubbing his side where my elbow made contact. He scowled at me. "I came to ask you something about the transfer of energy, but you weren't here. David left again, and Ula's room was quiet. That left only one option. You went to see Evan, so I decided to wait for you."

"Are you stalking me?" I glared back at him. How dare he keep tabs on me! Who did he think he was? My babysitter?

"I'm not stalking you!" He ran his hand through his hair. It was so short that it didn't even muss it up. "And, you're avoiding my question. You're more like your father than I thought."

"Don't bring my dad into this." The last thing I wanted was to be compared to my dad. I was nothing like him. "And, you get plenty of answers from him. More than me."

"If you say so. Where were you tonight, Meara?" He leaned forward and waited.

I stomped across the room and sat in the chair near the bookcase. It was making me distinctly uncomfortable sitting next to him on the bed. "I was with Evan. There! Are you happy?"

His hand went to his hair again. "Are you crazy? Do you have a death wish?"

"No, I'm not crazy." First Evan, now him. "Why does everyone keep asking me that?"

Kieran raised his eyebrow, and his lips twitched. "Who else asked you if you were crazy?"

"Evan." I hated telling him, but I did anyway.

Kieran slid down and sat at the end of the bed facing me. He looked amused. "Why would Boy Toy ask you if you're crazy?"

"Please stop calling him that." I shifted in the chair. It wasn't comfortable. I debated telling him about the dinner and decided that maybe he'd have a different perspective. "Ken, the owner of the house, asked Evan to invite us to dinner."

"Us?"

"You and me." Before he could say anything, I added, "I guess Stonewall told him about you, too."

"And Boy T—, I mean, Evan, didn't want us to go?"

"No," I said. "When I told him about the dead Selkies, he told me not to come back."

"You shouldn't have told him." He pointed a long finger at me.

"That's Selkie business, not his. At least he finally said something smart. You shouldn't have gone there, and you can't go back."

"Stop telling me what to do." Why did everyone think they knew what was best for me? "I transport there in minutes. Who would catch me?"

Kieran laughed. It sounded sharp and brittle. "Who would catch you? Any number of magical creatures. You think we're the only ones out there?" He came over and crouched in front of my chair. He was so close that I could smell the mint from his toothpaste. "We're not alone, and not everyone is as friendly as we are."

I moved in so our noses were almost touching. How dare he get in my face and challenge me? "Then enlighten me, Kieran. Who else is out there?"

He'd sucked in his breath when I moved closer. He let it out in a minty whoosh and stood, pulling me up with him. "Fine, I will." He held my wrist and pulled me toward the door.

"Where are we going?" I asked, alarmed. It was ridiculously early. Hours until sunrise. What could he possibly show me now?

"Do you want answers?" His hand flexed on my wrist. It wasn't painful, but his grip was firm. I wasn't getting my wrist back unless he released it. When I nodded, he said, "Then extinguish the candles and let's go."

I waved them out with my free hand. He slid his hand down my wrist and locked his fingers with mine. My pulse thrummed in my throat. He'd never held my hand before. His was warm and strong. I never thought of mine as delicate, but it felt that way in his.

His fingers squeezed mine briefly before he loosened his grip. "Follow me and be quiet. We don't want to get caught."

He led me down the hall and up a flight of stairs. When we passed my dad's room and then Angus', I figured we were going to the library, but instead, he turned left. He chanted something under his breath, and the wall that I thought was solid stone wavered. An opening appeared to another hall. When I gasped, Kieran squeezed my hand again before pulling me in.

There were no windows in this corridor, only darkness. I was grateful for his guiding hand. I stumbled a few times over uneven stones, and he steadied me.

"Some light would help," I offered.

With a sigh, he created a small, glowing orb that cast the hall in green light. The hall was narrow enough that I couldn't see past Kieran's back. I was about to ask if we were almost there when he stopped.

"Stairs going down ahead," he said. "Just a few of them."

He started down the stairs, and I followed, counting as I went. Ten stairs ended on a landing. The heavy, wooden door creaked as he opened it.

"Let's have some real light."

As he said it, several torches lit in the room. In awe, I stepped around him and entered first. The room was cavernous, lined with bookcases, maps, and globes. A large table ran the length of the room and crossed most of the width.

"What is this?" I asked.

"The strategy room. Only the elders use it." He stepped behind me. I didn't turn, but I felt him to my right. "I took a big risk bringing you here. Don't tell anyone."

"How did you know about it?" I asked. When he didn't say anything, I turned around. He looked uncomfortable. "Kieran?"

"I know..." He paused. "Because I'm one of them."

"What?" My dad made Kieran an elder and not me? Was I important to him at all?

"Not of this clan," Kieran added quickly. "But of my own. My dad made me an elder several years ago. David honors that." His voice faded at the end. He stepped around me and walked toward a bookcase. "Try not to take it too hard, Meara. Your dad just found you. It's going to take time."

"Everyone keeps telling me that, too," I mumbled under my breath.

Kieran turned to me with a confused expression. "What did you say?"

"Nothing." I walked over to where he stood. "What's here that you were going to show me?"

He grinned. "Well, everything here is worth showing you. Your dad has an amazing collection of information." He trailed his hand along the shelves. It seemed that he shared a love of textbooks with Evan. "You specifically asked about our enemies, though, so..." He scanned the shelves in front of him, his slender fingers tapping on the volumes until he found the one he wanted. "We'll start here."

Carrying the book over to the table, he pulled a chair out for me and took the one next to it. I sat and tried not to think about how much I liked the way he smelled, like spring rain and clean air. I cleared my throat, "Do we start at chapter one?"

He laughed. "No. I've read this a few times before." He flipped through the pages, and then slid the book in front of me, pointing to an illustration. My heart stopped. The creature had the head of a shark and the body of a human. "Sharkna. Very common where I'm from, not so much here in Scotland. They like warmer water."

I swallowed my fear and stared at the killing machine. "Evan found something similar yesterday. The book called them 'Aumakuas'."

Kieran nodded. "Same creature. That's just the Hawaiian name for them. They view the Sharkna as sacred."

"Have you ever seen one?" I asked.

Kieran stared at the book and frowned, his brows drawing together. I wasn't sure if he was going to answer me.

"Yes," he said quietly. "He killed my mom before my dad killed him."

I placed my hand on his arm. "I'm sorry, Kieran."

He looked at my hand and then into my eyes. His shimmered

with unshed tears. He blinked them away as I watched. "Thanks," he said. "It was a long time ago."

The creature stared up at us with beady, black eyes and a mouthful of razor teeth. This image alone could give me nightmares.

"What's next?" I asked, eager to move away from the Sharkna.

"Leviathan," he said and pointed to another picture. "Typically live alone, which is good. Makes them easier to kill. A pack of Leviathan means certain death."

One glance at the image on the page, and I believed it. The Leviathan was a giant sea snake with two heads. In the image, the heads intertwined, but both heads were hideous with glowing, yellow eyes, forked tongues, and long, thin fangs dripping with blue venom.

Kieran tapped the book. "You have to watch out for the mouths, too. The venom is deadly."

"And this is easy to kill?" I gave him a skeptical look. "Have you killed one?"

"Once. I came across its cave. Lucky for me, he had just woken up and was slower than normal." He shook his head at the picture. "He had nasty breath, too."

"You know you're not filling me with confidence here," I said.

"I'm not trying to." He leaned in and looked into my eyes. "I'm trying to instill some fear into that pretty little head before you find yourself without it."

I tried not to notice how my heart jumped when he called me pretty. "Point taken. What's next?"

Kieran took the book back and flipped through a few more chapters, muttering as he went. He paused and said, "You can look at all of those later. They're not really threats to us, more of a nuisance, like bugs are to humans. But these..." He stopped, and his finger drilled into the page in front of him. "These you must take note of."

He slid the book back over to me. The image was a collage of beings. Some looked human with different-colored skin, some looked half human, half fish like a mermaid, but uglier.

"What are these called?"

"Merfolk, Blue Men, Water Demons, and Kelpies." He identified each one as he said its name. "Like us, these creatures can appear as human. You might meet one and not even know it at first. It takes experience to recognize them."

His description reminded me of when we met last year at that dance club. I didn't know at the time that Kieran was a Selkie. I had no idea until I found out that my friends had no memory of the evening or of Kieran's Selkie friends. It scared me to think of how easily he tricked me, and how I could be fooled again.

"Can you recognize them?" I asked.

"Usually." He shrugged. "I'm still learning. I haven't encountered all species yet."

"The ones you've seen," I said. "What do you look for?"

He moved the book so it was halfway between us. "I'll tell you what I know from experience and what my father told me. When you get the chance, ask David his opinion."

"You told me not to say anything."

"Tell him you found the information in Evan's book," he said. "Lie."

"Okay." Kieran was telling me more than David ever had. If I had to lie, I would.

He pointed to the merman. "Merfolk. Sometimes friendly, sometimes not. Easily bribed, so they often work for our enemies or the highest bidder. In human form, they don't have a belly button."

"That's it?" I asked. When he nodded, I laughed. "What do you do? Go around lifting people's shirts?"

He rolled his eyes at me. "They're not fond of human clothes either, so their chest or midriff typically shows." I continued to snicker at an image of Kieran lifting people's shirts. He didn't share my amusement. "Shall I continue?" he asked drily.

"Yes." I took a deep breath and reminded myself that these

creatures could kill me. Had killed two of our own. The thought sobered me quick enough.

Kieran nodded and continued. "Blue Men of the Minch. From what your dad has told me, they are vicious, self-serving, and thrive on destruction and chaos. I've never seen one. They have blue eyes, skin, and hair. I don't know if they can disguise this or not. When your dad fought them, they were in their true form like you see here."

My dad fought them? I looked at the picture of the muscular man. From head to toe, he was a deep royal blue. He smiled with a mouthful of pointy, blue teeth, vicious and scary. My dad was not only powerful, but also brave.

"I know that they killed my grandparents," I said. "I didn't know Dad fought them."

"He tried." Kieran's voice was soft. "He lost. It was only David, Brigid, and Angus against all of them. Your family retreated while they had the chance."

I tried to picture my dad and aunt fighting throngs of these creatures. A shiver ran down my spine. Maybe I was a fool. The world was much more dangerous than I thought.

"What's that one?" I pointed to something that looked like a sea horse. "It doesn't look dangerous."

"Looks deceive," Kieran warned. "That's a Kelpie. They're dangerous all right, unless your wish is to drown to death. They lure you into the water and hold you captive for hours until you take your last breath."

"Sounds awful."

"I imagine it is. Thankfully, I've never encountered one. I understand they have hypnotic powers. Never look in their eyes. As humans, their eyes are all black, so you can easily spot them."

"I thought I'm not supposed to look at their eyes?" I asked.

"I didn't say this was easy." Kieran looked down at me. "Are you beginning to understand?"

"Yes." My voice sounded small. We had so many enemies. "The last one is a water demon?"

"Right. Water demon." Kieran's lip curled at the monster. It had deep red skin and green hair, gills, and fins. "Nasty creatures. Ruthless and tough. Their human disguise is strong, but they cannot purge their stench. If you encounter a human who smells of dead fish, you've met a water demon. If you're alone, run."

I sat back and stared at him. He put his arm around my shoulder and pulled me against him. "I know I scared you. I'm not going to apologize. David should've showed you this a long time ago. Now you understand why he wants you to stay here."

I slid out from under Kieran's arm and stood up, gesturing around the room. "Why didn't he take me here or at least tell me about our enemies? When I asked him what killed those Selkies, he told me not to worry about it. How could he say that? Now that I've seen them, I have a lot to worry about."

Kieran walked over and placed his hands on my shoulders. "I'm not arguing with you, Meara. I don't know what David's motives are, besides keeping you safe. Maybe he thinks he needs to shelter you to do that. He underestimates you. You're strong."

"Do you think so?" I searched his face to see if he was joking, but his eyes were serious.

"I know so. What you've already accomplished is amazing. You taught me something new, something powerful. You're a force, and you're only getting stronger."

A flush heated my face. I lowered my head and hoped that Kieran didn't see. "Thank you," I said. "For showing me this."

"No need to thank me," he said. "Keep yourself safe."

He placed the book back on its shelf and snuffed the torches. His eyes glowed a soft bronze in the darkness. I wondered if mine were luminous, too. "Your eyes are glowing," I said.

"Yours, too." His voice was quiet as he moved closer. "Selkie trait."

He stopped in front of me—close enough to touch but not touching. When he clasped my hands in his, my breath caught.

"We're the same, Meara," he whispered in my ear. "You and I."

His warm breath tickled my ear and made my pulse pound. Could he hear it? He was so close. It would be easy to turn my head and meet his lips.

I stepped back and broke the connection. "We better leave. It must be close to dawn now." I betrayed Evan once; I wouldn't do it again.

He walked around me and led the way to the door. "Follow close. I'll get you back to your room safely."

I heard the disappointment in his voice and allowed myself to imagine what it would've been like to kiss him. It didn't take much imagination since I'd done it before. I was moving into dangerous territory, and it wasn't just the monsters that scared me.

Chapter 19

"He's having a reaction. Bring us up now, damn it!"

Evan heard the professor talking, but he couldn't focus on the words. His head was splitting. A knife in his skull, the pain's sharp edge slicing his reason. He longed to pass out; the blackness would be a relief.

"Hold on, Evan. Ken's bringing us up." Professor Nolan clipped something around his waist, and then they were slowly rising toward the surface.

He blacked out.

"Evan! Evan, can you hear me, son?" Ken sounded far away.

Blinking his eyes, Evan croaked, "The light. Too bright."

"We're outside, Evan." Professor Nolan's voice now. "Ken, can we get him inside?"

"Grab his legs," Ken's voice commanded. "I'll lift his shoulders."

The sudden movement shot pain through his head. With a cry, he lost consciousness again.

The room was quiet, the air cool and damp. He tasted salt and smelled coffee. Slowly, Evan opened his eyes. The only light came from a small lamp. He was in the cabin below deck. Ken and Ted were not there. His temples thrummed with his pulse, each wave of pain making him want to clench his teeth. What was happening to him? Maybe Meara was right. Maybe if he waited to see a doctor, it would be too late.

"You're awake." Ken stood in the doorway with a glass of water. "I don't have much onboard, but I have some aspirin." He handed Evan the pills and glass.

"Thanks." Evan swallowed them and drained the water. After handing the cup back to Ken, he lay down and closed his eyes.

"Do you have episodes like this often?" Ken asked. "Are you epileptic or something? Is there anything we need to know?"

"I dunno," Evan muttered. It hurt to talk. "I never had them before this summer. Now I have them almost daily."

"I'm going to call for a doctor when we get back," Ken said. "Right now, rest up. We'll wake you when we get to the pier."

"Thanks," Evan mumbled. The click of the door was the last thing he heard.

Evan fluttered his eyelids and willed them to open. When they did, he wished he could close them again. A row of sharp, white teeth filled his vision before a bright light blinded him.

"You're awake?" the soft voice murmured. "Good, good."

The light brightened slightly and blocked everything out. When it receded, Evan blinked the black shadows away. A man with a round face peered down at him. Thick, heavily framed glasses magnified the man's pale blue eyes. He smiled kindly and, to Evan's relief, his teeth were perfectly straight and decidedly not pointy. Must have been the leftover remnants of a nightmare.

"I'm Dr. Martin Tenuis," the man said. "Ken mentioned that you're having headaches?"

Evan nodded, and then winced. Apparently, he still had one.

Dr. Tenuis frowned in concern. "When did these headaches first start?"

Evan remembered that when he was young, his head hurt during severe storms. His mom gave him a Tylenol and called it, "sinus headaches." He stopped having those around age twelve. He didn't think the doctor would care about that.

"Beginning of summer," Evan said. "Before that, I rarely got headaches."

"How frequently do you get them?" The doctor took notes on a small notepad he pulled from his pocket.

"In the beginning, about once a week. Once I arrived here, I started waking with headaches daily, but I take Advil." Evan's voice trailed off. "Uh, I took the last of my pills this morning..."

"Don't worry about that," the doctor said. "Once we figure out what's going on, we'll get you more medication." He looked down at his notes. "The ibuprofen works then?"

"No," Evan said. "The pills dull the pain, but the headache doesn't always go away."

"I see." Dr. Tenuis set his notepad aside and sifted through his medical bag on the bed near Evan's feet. "Do you mind if I conduct a physical examination?"

"Not at all." Evan winced as he sat up. "I want to know what's going on, Dr. Tenuis."

"Please, call me Marty." The doctor smiled at him, his blue eyes crinkling behind the thick lenses. "Sounds strange to hear myself addressed so formally in this house. Ken and I have known each other forever."

Marty checked his vitals and shined the bright light in his eyes again. He scribbled notes on his pad and muttered to himself. Whenever he caught Evan watching him, he gave him an encouraging smile.

"Your vitals are all excellent," Marty said. "You are in great shape.

My preliminary analysis has not turned up anything that could cause those headaches. Would you be willing to come to the lab for further study?"

"Lab?" The word struck him as strange. Doctors didn't usually refer to their offices at laboratories. It was a term used by scientists.

"Of course." Marty straightened. "I'm a medical doctor by trade, but I currently head the disease research department at MMB Industries in Aberdeen. We have all the equipment I need there. I'd like to start with a brain scan and x-rays."

Evan smiled. It was a relief knowing he could get help. "Whatever it takes, Doc."

The doctor laughed. "Not comfortable calling me Marty, are you?"

"No," Evan admitted.

"Doc is fine." He grinned. "In fact, I kind of like it."

Evan watched Dr. Tenuis meticulously repack his bag and asked, "When will we start?"

"As soon as possible," Dr. Tenuis said. "I'll ask Ken or Ted to bring you by around eight am. Don't eat beforehand; we'll need to put you under for some of the procedures."

Evan's heart sped up. He'd never been anesthetized. He split his lip during a hockey game senior year, and they just numbed the area when they stitched him. What kind of procedures was the doctor going to do?

Dr. Tenuis squeezed Evan's shoulder and gave him a reassuring pat on his arm. "Don't worry, Evan. The tests are painless. We just require you to be absolutely still, and anesthesia is the best way to ensure that. You'll wake feeling quite rested."

Evan relaxed and nodded. He was about to ask what procedures would be done when a sharp pain pierced his upper arm. His eyes narrowed on Dr. Tenuis and the needle in his hand.

"Painkiller," Dr. Tenuis explained. "And a little something extra to help you sleep."

The doctor continued to talk, but his words were now a low hum. The room started to spin, so Evan closed his eyes.

The bitter smell of antiseptic seared his sinuses, waking Evan up. His eyes adjusted to the darkened room. He wasn't in his bedroom at the house. This was in a hospital bed. Sensors were taped to the backs of his hands. He felt them on his chest and forehead, too. Not counting the machine beeping next to his bed, he was alone.

He heard footsteps in the hallway, some light and hurried, others heavy and slow. A thin band of light seeped under the door, flickering whenever somebody passed his room. A dull pain thrummed in the back of his head, and his muscles ached. He tried to swallow and grimaced at the metallic taste in his mouth. He noticed the table next to him and sighed in relief. At least someone had the foresight to leave water. He picked up the Styrofoam cup and sipped greedily. The water was ice cold. Whoever brought it must have come into his room recently. Maybe that was what woke him.

Heavy curtains blocked the one window in the room. Enough light seeped around the edges to show that the walls were light and bare, and the room sparsely furnished. Besides the bed, table, and machine next to him, there were two small, uncomfortable-looking chairs.

The door opened, and Evan blinked when the bright light from the hall hit his eyes.

"Ah, good. You're awake." Dr. Tenuis stepped into the room, flicking the light switch. He carried a tray of food, which he set on the table next to Evan. "I'm sure you're also hungry."

The doctor busied himself adjusting the bed so Evan could sit up. He handed him the tray. "Here you go. I'll update you while you eat."

Evan lifted the cover off the plate to find meatloaf, mashed potatoes, and green beans almandine. He lifted a forkful of the meat and tasted. It was good.

"Not your typical hospital food." Dr. Tenuis winked at him. "We're not your typical hospital."

"Do you have many patients here?" Evan asked before taking another forkful, this time of potatoes. When Dr. Tenuis entered, he left the door ajar. Although Evan could see people who looked like medical staff in the hallway, he hadn't seen anyone else in a hospital gown or even street clothes.

"Not on a daily basis, though we're obviously equipped to do so." The doctor pulled over one of the guest chairs and took a seat. "When we have patients, they're usually volunteering for research."

As Evan ate, the headache receded. He felt remarkably better. Better than he had in the last week, maybe longer. "When do we start my tests?"

Dr. Tenuis' eyebrows rose above his glasses. "Why, my boy, we're already done!" He chuckled and shook his head. "I thought you knew that. I told Ted you seemed groggy when he brought you in this morning."

"I'm done?" Evan didn't remember this morning. He didn't remember anything except the shot that the doctor gave him the night before. "I was talking to you when Professor Nolan brought me in?"

"Of course." The doctor's voice softened. "We needed standard medical information, insurance and all that. You don't remember?"

"Not at all." There were no clocks in the room. How much time had passed? "What time is it?"

Glancing at his watch, Dr. Tenuis said, "Four o'clock. We wanted to get some food in you, but then you're free to leave. I already called Ted. He's picking you up in an hour."

"I've been unconscious for eight hours?" Evan pushed the tray aside, the last few bites forgotten.

"No, no." Was it his imagination or did Dr. Tenuis look a bit nervous? He glanced at the doorway, and then back at Evan. "You were only out for about four hours. The rest of the time, you were awake. You really don't remember any of this?"

Evan shook his head. How did he forget four hours of the day when he was supposedly awake and responsive? The idea freaked him out, but he'd worry about it later. Right now, he wanted answers. "Did the tests show anything?"

"Nothing you need to worry about." Dr. Tenuis flipped through a few papers. "Your physical makeup is fine. Nothing's wrong with your brain." He looked up and smiled at Evan. It didn't reassure him. How could nothing be wrong with his brain, yet he didn't remember half the day?

"We did discover something in your blood work... " Dr. Tenuis hesitated.

"What?" Evan sat up straighter and turned to the doctor. His pulse quickened. What was wrong with him?

"A strain of bacteria," Dr. Tenuis said. "Easily treatable with an antibiotic." He held up a syringe filled with an aqua-blue liquid for Evan to see. "Are you ready?"

"That's it? One shot and my headaches will go away?" Evan eyed the needle dubiously. He wasn't a fan of needles, doctors, or hospitals, and in the last twenty-four hours, he'd experienced all three.

"One shot, and you'll be right as rain." The doctor turned his head and the light caught his eyes. For a moment, they were bright turquoise like the medicine. Before Evan could react, the needle sunk into his arm.

The impact was immediate. Evan felt the liquid burn through his veins. It didn't burn like fire. Icy cold, it was more like frostbite working its way through his body. Nauseated, he lowered his head to his hands as his senses overloaded. Children screamed, their tortured cries piercing his ears. Behind his closed lids, broken bodies writhed in a massive pile of pain, their blood pooling into a red lake. The smell of tar and smoke filled his nostrils, and his tongue thickened while he struggled to breath. He barely registered the other prick in his arm before he succumbed to darkness.

Chapter 20

After Kieran showed me the strategy room and the faces of our enemies, I couldn't fall asleep. As it was I got to bed ridiculously late, and I knew I've suffer the next day. Sure enough, I did. My lesson with Aunt Brigid was horrible. She didn't need to lecture me. I knew how badly I performed. Then, when I collapsed in my bed that night and tried to contact Evan, he didn't respond. All I heard was static. Was he wearing the necklace or was that what it sounded like when he took it off? If he removed it, why? Before I could think about it more, my mind shut down from sheer exhaustion.

I woke early and tried Evan again. Nothing. Images of monsters played through my head the entire time I trained with Kieran. What if one of them got Evan while he was diving? Kieran would tease me if I asked him, but my father would know if Evan was safe. I wanted answers, which is why I found myself standing outside of Dad's room after he didn't show at dinner. I slammed open the door to his suite and stomped inside, only to be disappointed. He wasn't there either. I stood for a moment and wondered what I should do now. I could wait for him, but when was he coming back?

A loud crack exploded down the hall. Someone dropped something heavy. The sound came from Angus' room. Would he give me answers that my dad wasn't willing to? It was worth a shot.

I knocked on his door and waited. Shuffling footsteps drew close before the door was yanked open. "Who's there? What do you want?"

I stared into my great uncle's stormy eyes. They softened slightly when he saw me. "Oh. It's you. Been wondering when you'd pay me a visit." He stepped back and waved me inside. "Ula told you then?"

"Told me what?" I asked.

"You'll see." He chuckled as I entered his room, and my mouth fell open in shock. It looked like a modern apartment. He had a flat-screen TV, Blu-ray player, and tower speakers faced by a curving, leather couch. A kitchenette to the left housed modern appliances, including a microwave.

"Where," I asked, "did you get all this stuff?"

"I have a small obsession with human luxuries." His cheeks tinged pink as he stroked his beard and looked around his room, not meeting my eyes.

"Does it all work?"

"I can make it work," he said. "Except I don't get any signals of course. The Blu-ray is strictly for movies. No scraping with your friends."

"I think you mean Skyping," I said. "Which reminds me, why can't we have phones or internet access?"

"If we're on the grid," he said, "we can be found. Do you understand?"

I did understand. After what Kieran told me, I knew there were definitely creatures that we didn't want to find us.

"You're interested in humans?" I asked. "Most Selkies don't seem to be."

"I'm not like most Selkies." He moved to the kitchenette and filled a teakettle. "I'm going to have some hot chocolate. Would you like some?"

"Yes, please."

He motioned for me to sit in one of the two kitchen chairs. I watched with humor as he took a box of Swiss Miss from the cabinet and emptied a packet into each mug. When the kettle whistled, he filled the cups and gave one to me before picking up his own and joining me at the table.

"I know you're wondering why I have all this stuff." He moved his arm to indicate the room at large.

"I am," I admitted. "It's a little unusual."

"Not when you consider that I'm half human." His eyes twinkled at my intake of breath, and he leaned back in his chair with satisfaction. "I knew I could trust that urchin, Ula, to keep my secrets."

"How—? Who?" I stumbled over my questions as my words clung to my throat. Angus chuckled and reached across to squeeze my hand.

"I'm quite old, Meara, even by Selkie standards. I have lived as Selkie for many centuries, but I was born and raised as a human the first fifteen years of my life."

His eyes grew distant. He absently blew on his hot chocolate to cool it, although he put the cup back down without taking a sip.

"I grew up in the Scottish highlands. My father was human, a farmer, and an occasional fisherman. It was on one of those fishing excursions that he met my mother, trapped her in his nets to be precise. Imagine his surprise when he goes to check his catch and sees it's a beautiful woman."

"He caught your mother like a fish?" I couldn't imagine it. The hot chocolate was cool enough to drink now, so I took a few tentative sips.

Angus laughed and wiped a few tears from his eyes. "That he did, Meara. That he did. Not only did he catch her in his net, he caught her heart as well. They married, and they had me."

"So quickly?"

His gaze locked on mine. "Things happened fast in those days. Humans lived much shorter lives. It wasn't uncommon for people to wed in their teens and have children shortly after."

"Did your mother stay?" My dad told me that after living with humans for a straight year, a Selkie's powers disappeared. Had Angus' mother chosen to become human?

"She tried. She stayed with him until after I was born. I wasn't even a month old, though, and she was gone." Angus stared into his mug, swirling the steaming liquid with a spoon. "My dad raised me."

His mom was like my dad. Were there others like us? Half-Selkies who didn't even know what they were? "Did you ever see her again?" I asked.

"I did," he said. "Which is how I ended up at Ronac. She came back for me when I was fifteen. She brought me here and taught me the Selkie ways."

"And your father was left alone?"

"Not alone, no." Angus nodded toward my mug. "Are you finished?"

I drank the last bit and handed the mug to him. "I am now."

He stood and took our cups to the sink. He hadn't touched his, but I didn't say anything. With his back turned, he continued his story. "Dad remarried while I was still a babe. I had two half brothers and three half sisters. When my mother came back for me, he encouraged me to go with her. He was a good man. Not a day goes by that I don't miss him."

His voice cracked, and I looked up in alarm. I couldn't see if he was crying.

"I'm sorry, Uncle Angus," I said. "He sounds like a great father."

"Aye, that he was." My uncle turned and gave me a shaky smile. "But you didn't come here to listen to the ramblings of an old man. What can I help you with, my dear?"

"I was actually looking for my dad—"

"He left with Brigid yesterday. They're meeting with the Icelandia clan in the north, hoping to find answers about the deaths." Angus shook his head and sat back down. "Such wasted lives. Do you know it has been decades since a Ronac Selkie died?"

I had no idea. Death was such a regular occurrence in human life. I never considered how infrequently Selkies lost one of their own. His question seemed rhetorical, so I cleared my throat and continued. "I wanted to ask him about our enemies. I know so little, and I don't want to put myself and others at risk from my ignorance."

"Your father has not tutored you about our enemies? What has he been doing?" Angus' roar filled the room. He thumped his hands on the table and pushed himself up, practically overturning it in the process.

While Angus glared, I swallowed nervously. I knew his anger wasn't directed at me, yet it was scary to behold. "He hasn't been teaching me," I said in a meek voice. "I haven't seen much of him. He ordered Aunt Brigid and Kieran to help me learn my powers and defense."

Angus lowered himself back into the chair and leaned on his arm, looking thoughtful. "Good choices for tutors. At least he's not completely hopeless." His gaze sharpened on me. "I trust you've been learning and practicing?"

"Yes," I said. "Every day."

He stroked his beard and seemed to consider me. I waited, growing impatient. Finally, he spoke. "I can teach you about our enemies. David's reasons be damned. You need to know."

He stood and crossed the room to open an old, black chest. It sat in a corner where I hadn't noticed it. He pulled out a bundle wrapped in faded velvet. The folded bits showed that the fabric used to be black. Now a mottled, dark gray, the velvet shined in places where the soft texture rubbed away. Angus placed the package on the table and unfolded it. He held up a polished, silver dagger, its handle heavily inlaid with coral and gemstones that were smoothed from years of use. For such worn wrapping, the weapon was meticulously cared for.

"It's beautiful," I said.

He held the handle out to me. "It was my mother's. Now, I want you to have it." When I made no move toward it, he said. "Go ahead and take it."

I wrapped my hand around the polished gems and felt warmth travel up my arm. The weight of the knife balanced in my grip. It was surprisingly light for a weapon that looked so substantial.

"I'll teach you to use it," he said. "That dagger tasted the blood of many an enemy. It's a powerful weapon. Keep it safe, and you'll be able to summon it when needed."

I twisted my wrist and watched the light reflect off the blade. I had no idea what to do with it, but I felt stronger with it in my hand.

"You have a firm grip," he said. "That's useful. Does it feel comfortable in your hand?"

"It does," I said. "Like a part of my arm."

"As I thought." He nodded with approval. "It was meant to be yours. Of course, a blade is only useful in human form. Call it to you, and it will appear in your hand in the heat of battle."

"Cool." My eyes locked on the blade, mesmerized by the intricate carvings and gem work. Angus gently pushed on my wrist until the knife lowered to the table. With his other hand, he raised my chin until my eyes met his.

"Did you father explain your vulnerabilities in human form?"

I frowned. "I don't think so."

"Idiot," Angus muttered and huffed out an irritated breath. "Your seal skin is an anklet, correct?"

"Yes." The leather band circled around my right ankle three times.

"That's a good form to choose. Inconspicuous and easily carried. I sometimes wonder what my niece was thinking when she chose hers."

"Ula?" I wondered. Brigid's choker wasn't too different from my anklet, but Ula's backpack was unique. "What's wrong with hers?"

"Something easily stolen or lost." He shook his head with disgust. "If your skin's destroyed, you will no longer be a Selkie. You live as a human and age as one, too."

I nodded. Now, I did remember. Last year at the museum, Evan and I saw the Selkie exhibit, the story about the fisherman who stole the Selkie's skin. He forced her to stay with him and become his wife. I shuddered and reached down to stroke the soft leather. Now that I had my skin, I couldn't imagine being without it.

"Your father has neglected your studies," Angus continued not without a level of disgust. "You must come here for lessons, starting tomorrow."

"I have lessons with Kieran or Aunt Brigid during the day."

"We'll train after dinner," Angus decided. He took the blade from me, wrapped it in the velvet, and handed it back. Pulling out my chair, he offered me his hand. "Come now, it's getting late, and you must have other things to do than hang out with the likes of me."

I let him help me stand. Without thinking about it, I threw my arms around him and hugged him tight. He returned the embrace, his arms surprisingly strong.

"Thank you," I said. "For everything."

"Of course." He seemed surprised by my emotional display. "You are Selkie and my niece. We take care of our own."

As I left his room, I couldn't help but wonder why my great uncle was more willing to provide for me than my own father was. I was losing faith in him fast.

Chapter 21

The ocean floor stretched before him. Evan watched a school of fish pass in a flash of silver, their underwater dance both graceful and quick. Again, he wondered what it would be like to swim amongst them, unrestrained by his heavy scuba gear, free to race with the currents. He caught himself humming a perky tune and abruptly stopped.

"Feeling better?" Professor Nolan's voice, full of humor, echoed in his ear. "Really, Evan, go on. I was enjoying the background music."

His face grew hot, but Evan laughed because he *was* feeling better. After Dr. Tenuis gave him the second shot, he woke an hour later rested and relaxed. If the drug was experimental, Dr. Tenuis should consider patenting the stuff. It worked miracles.

When he woke up at the hospital, Ted was waiting for him. They drove back to the house, and Evan spent the rest of the evening eating ice cream and playing video games.

The only thing he regretted was his conversation with Meara. She'd been so worried about him, and he snapped at her, "Am I supposed to be at your beck and call?" She grew quiet after that, and before long, they said goodnight. He didn't like leaving things that way, but he didn't know what to say to make it better.

"Okay, now you're really quiet," Ted said. "Everything okay?"

"Fine. Just working on gathering the last couple of samples Ken wanted."

This was Evan's fifth trip to the crevice, the first one where he was pain free. He looked at the fissure with new eyes. It wasn't the death and destruction trap he once deemed it to be. Life moved in and around the hot springs, small, gray crabs and slick, black eels. He was collecting samples of everything in the area—the mantle floor, ash, and cooled lava, as well as a crab and the limited flora. The subjects were the same from the previous week, but Ken studied them for signs of distress or change. So far, the area was relatively stable, but with a mantle plume, that could change overnight.

Ken never came down on the dives. He preferred to stay onboard. Evan asked the professor about it, but Ted just shrugged it off. "He just prefers land, I think. Maybe he's claustrophobic."

That could be a plausible answer, though Evan wasn't sure. In any case, it meant more diving trips for Evan, and he loved it. The hard part was staying focused on the mantle plume. There were so many amazing creatures. He longed to study them.

He closed the cover on his last sample, placed it in his pack, and gave Ted a thumbs-up. Using their scuba scooters, they began a slow ascent.

Ken was waiting when they broke the surface. He helped them into the boat and took their packs. "Did you find everything?"

"We got it all," Evan answered. "It sure is a lot easier when my head's not pounding."

"Glad to hear it." Ken patted Evan's shoulder. "Dr. Tenuis helped you then?"

"I feel much better," Evan said. "Thanks for calling him."

"Anytime, my boy." Ken smiled at him. "Just glad you're all right." He lifted the bags and nodded toward the cabin. "I'll store these samples, and we'll head back."

For a brief moment, Evan wanted to grab his pack from Ken, open the vials, and return everything to the sea. A shudder ran through him, and the feeling passed. He sunk onto a bench on the side of the stern and took off his scuba fins.

His headaches were gone, but was he losing his mind?

Chapter 22

"He said that to you?" Ula shook her curly head in disbelief. "That's crazy."

"He's never spoken to me like that before. I wasn't nagging either. I just asked where he's been. Is that so unreasonable?"

"Of course not, sweetie. Here, I think you need some more." Ula held out the container of ice cream we'd been sharing. In my first lesson with Angus, I asked him where he got the Swiss Miss. He admitted to raiding a grocery store on the mainland. He transported the items to his suite and left money at the service desk. I laughed, and then laughed even harder when his cheeks reddened. In the end, though, I asked him to show me how and he did. The result was the caramel-swirl ice cream we were currently enjoying.

"Besides boy trouble, what have you been up to?" Ula leaned back in her beanbag chair and studied me. "I feel like I haven't seen you in days."

I let the ice cream melt on my tongue a little before I swallowed it and spoke. "I guess lessons have been keeping me busy, especially now that I added the ones with Uncle Angus."

"How are those going?" Her eyes twinkled.

Holding up the ice cream, I grinned. "Pretty well." I set it down and poked her in the arm with my spoon. "But why didn't you tell me Angus is half human?"

"He asked me not to," she said. "It was his secret, not mine. Besides, you know now."

166

"I guess." I handed Ula the container. "I can't eat any more of this. I feel like I'm going to explode."

"I certainly hope not." She looked at me in mock horror. "What a mess that would make!"

She giggled at her own joke while scooping out the last few spoonfuls of ice cream. I curled into my beanbag chair and relaxed. It was easy to be around Ula. In some ways, she reminded me of my best friend Kim, and in others, she reminded me of Mom. In either case, I felt closer to her than anyone else here, even my father.

"Thanks, Ula," I said. "You always cheer me up."

"Anytime." She smiled. "That's what aunts are for."

"Did Brigid get that memo?"

"Memo?" Ula's eyebrows wrinkled in confusion. "What memo?"

"Nothing," I said. "It's just a human phrase. It means that she doesn't know about it."

"Oh, of course. Funny." Ula's expression clearly said she didn't get it, but I let it go. Mom would've laughed. It was a phrase we used often.

"I think I'm going to head back to my room." I stood. "See if I can reach Evan. Maybe he was just having a rough night with the medicine wearing off."

"You want me to come with you? I can use your necklace and verbally beat him if he hurts you."

"That's okay, Ula." I smiled at her. "I think I've got it. Thanks for sharing the ice cream with me."

"Anytime." She tossed the container in the air, and it disappeared. "For future reference, I also like strawberry."

I paced in my room. Part of me wanted Evan to make the first move. He was such a jerk last night. Shouldn't he apologize or at least reach out to me?

A cool breeze brought the sweet scent of brine. I longed to swim and clear my head, but I couldn't. My dad would kill me. If he didn't, Angus, Brigid, Ula, and Kieran would be waiting in line. If anything were left of me, Padraic and Ren would take a shot. It was nice to have a family that was caring and stifling at the same time. My dad forbade swimming for all Selkies until he solved the mystery surrounding the deaths. I was stuck on land.

Pulling back the covers on my bed, I crawled in. It was getting late. The moon spilled silver light across the stone floor, and Evan hadn't called to me. Was he angry? How could he be angry when I was just concerned?

Meara! Evan screamed my name.

I winced in surprise. *What is it?*

My voice met silence. What was going on?

Evan?

Evan!

I called his name several times. He didn't respond. What was wrong? He could be sick like the last time I stayed over.

I had to go. I didn't have a choice.

I'm coming, Evan. I spoke in my mind. *Hang on.*

I closed my eyes and focused on every detail in his room. I heard his moans before I opened my eyes. He thrashed in his bed, his hair matted to his head, his chest bare and beaded with sweat. His legs, tangled in the sheets, struggled to break free.

Not wanting him to kick or hit me by accident, I approached with caution. His cheeks were flushed crimson, but the rest of his face was markedly pale. I pressed my hand against his forehead. He was burning up. Could I help take away the pain the way my dad helped my mom?

I visualized cool air flowing from my hand to his body, and then I felt it. The coolness flowed from my fingertips into his skin. His thrashing slowed, and his breathing regulated. It was working!

A blue light sparked in the dark and shot up my arm. Crying out in surprise, I pulled my hand back, fingertips biting. The pain was cool and sharp like an electrical burn. I blew on each finger, and the pain receded. When I looked up, Evan's eyes were open and glowing in that same, strange blue. What was wrong with him?

He flipped on the bedside lamp. His eyes returned to their normal, deep blue. Had I imagined it?

"Meara?" His voice was groggy and confused.

"Turn the light out," I whispered. He did as I said and pitched us into darkness. His eyes no longer glowed. "Okay, you can turn it on again."

"What was that about?" he asked. When the light came back on, he was sitting up. The sheet pooled around his waist. "Why are you here? Didn't we decide it was best for you to stay away?"

"You screamed my name. Don't you remember?" I sat on the edge of the bed and reached for his hand. "I tried to reach you after that, and you didn't respond."

He ran his hand through his hair and studied our joined hands for a brief moment before tugging his free. "I was having a nightmare. I don't remember calling to you. You should leave."

"Evan, are you mad at me?" This was my first serious relationship, but I knew what to watch for when someone was losing interest. Evan had all the classic signs, the hot and cold treatment, not wanting to hold my hand, not looking me in the eye. Had he met someone else?

"What?" He looked up at me then. "I'm worried about you. Meara, you told me that your dad thinks it's unsafe for you to come here. You need to listen to him—"

Evan was interrupted by someone knocking at the door. "You okay, Evan?"

"Go," Evan mouthed silently, but it was too late. The door opened, and the professor stepped in, a shocked expression on his face when he saw me.

"Oh, you have company. Forgive me." He turned to leave, and

then turned back to give me a confused look. "How did you get in?"

"I let her in," Evan blurted before I had the chance to consider a response. "I'll see her out."

Professor Nolan's face relaxed. "Not a problem, Evan. Although I think Ken likes to be aware of visitors in his house."

"Of course," Evan said. "It won't happen again."

Once the professor left, Evan stood and threw on a T-shirt. He placed his hand on the small of my back and guided me forward.

"Where are we going?" I asked.

"Isn't it obvious?" he asked. "I'm seeing you out."

He led me down the hall and a flight of stairs until we stood in the entryway where I'd first met him in this house.

"Evan, who is your visitor?"

The voice came from the formal living room. A man sat in a chair near the fireplace, a book open in his lap and reading glasses on his nose. In his red velvet smoking jacket, he looked a bit like Santa Claus in that his hair was white and he had a beard, although his was more trimmed and elegant that Santa's was. He watched us over the top of his glasses, which also added to the jolly elf look.

"Ken," Evan said. Was that reluctance in his voice? "This is Meara."

"Meara!" Ken set the book on the table and crossed the room. "What a delight to finally meet you."

"Uh...nice to meet you, too." I shook his outstretched hand.

"I assume Evan extended the invitation to dinner this Saturday night? I do hope you'll join us."

Behind Ken, Evan shook his head furiously. "I-I don't think we can make it," I stammered. "We already have a commitment."

"Are you sure?" he asked. "You're welcome to bring your friend as well. I believe Evan said his name is Kieran?"

"That's right." My eyes flickered to Evan's, and I was surprised to see how furious he looked. Was I doing something wrong? Did he want me to decline or not?

"Truly, I insist. If not Saturday, what about Sunday evening? Surely you can't have plans two days in a row."

"Sunday…" I considered. What could I tell him? Before I could speak up, Evan spoke for me.

"She'd love to come. I'm sure Kieran will be here, too."

Ken's expression relaxed into a smile. "Wonderful. I look forward to getting to know you."

"Thanks," I managed before Evan grabbed my elbow and steered me toward the door. Once we were outside, I spun around to face him. "What the hell was that about? One minute you're telling me to decline, the next you're accepting the invitation for Kieran and me. What's gotten into you?"

"If you hadn't come back here, you wouldn't have been in this situation. You should've listened to me. You couldn't decline right to Ken's face. That would be incredibly rude. Ken's been nothing but a gracious host to me. He's offering to make you dinner, not serve you as dinner. What's the problem?" Evan's voice grew colder with each word, and his eyes began to glow. "As for Kieran, he's your personal bodyguard, isn't he? You two are a packaged deal, aren't you? That's the only way your daddy will let you come."

"Your eyes." I stepped back and tried to keep my voice from trembling. "What's happening to you, Evan?"

"What are you talking about?" he snapped. "I feel better than I have in weeks. You're the one who told me to see a doctor. I did, and now you're on my case about it? Go home, Meara."

"Evan—" I took a step toward him.

"I'll see you Sunday," he said and slammed the door in my face.

Chapter 23

What's wrong with me?

Evan paced in his bedroom. He sent the girl he loved out the door as if she were a vacuum salesman. He worried about her safety, but that was no reason to treat her so rudely.

Then there was the dinner on Sunday. He couldn't remember why he felt it was important that she come and bring Kieran with her. Kieran, of all people. Evan hated that guy for flirting with Meara. Yet, he heard himself asking Meara to bring him. It was like he was talking but someone else was pulling the strings. It creeped him out.

He wanted to reach out to her and tell her he was sorry, but he didn't think she'd believe him. What if he tried to apologize, only to say something horrible? He didn't trust himself. What did it mean when you couldn't predict your own behavior? It sounded like a sign of madness.

Someone knocked once, a loud rap, on his door.

"Come in."

Ken stepped in the room, looking concerned. "Everything okay, Evan? You seemed a little upset downstairs."

"I'm fine." Evan sat down on his bed. "We just had a fight. That's all."

Ken's face fell in sympathy. "Too bad I didn't know. I wouldn't have pushed her to come to dinner. Should we cancel?"

Yes, Evan wanted to say, but something told him not to. Meara would be safer if he went along with this. He didn't know why he knew that, but he did. "No need to cancel. It was nothing major."

172

"Good to hear." Ken clamped him on the shoulder with his strong grip. "I'm looking forward to it. I haven't entertained in ages."

"We're looking forward to it, too, sir."

"Ken, son. Call me Ken. Remember?" Ken slapped him on the back, and Evan tried not to wince. Walking out the door, Ken called over his shoulder. "We're like family here. No need for those formalities."

"Goodnight, Ken. Sorry for the interruption earlier."

"No need to apologize. It gave me a chance to meet your girl. She's a lovely thing." He grinned at Evan, who smiled weakly in return. "Why don't we take the day off tomorrow? Head into town, have lunch, and pick up some new clothes for the dinner."

"Um... okay." This was turning into a bigger event than Evan originally anticipated. He really wished that Meara had obeyed him and her father and stayed away. It was too late for that now.

"Great! See you in the morning." Ken closed the door, his footsteps echoing down the hall. Evan rubbed his sore shoulder and cursed. What had he gotten Meara into?

Chapter 24

Kieran charged and I stood my ground, judging the angle of his attack. At the last minute, I repositioned and threw him over my shoulder. His breath whooshed out when I dropped and pinned him in place.

"You're getting strong," he said. "And fast." I let up slightly, and he used the move to his advantage, flipping me onto my back. "You still show too much mercy."

"Would you rather I knock you out?" I pushed his arm off and sat up.

"I'd like to see you try." His grin was full of conceit.

"Don't tempt me," I muttered while scratching at my skin. It had been a week since I last Changed. I missed it. "Can we go for a swim?"

Kieran's expression sobered. "You know your dad forbade it."

"He's not here, is he?" I swept my arm to take in the island. It was beautiful, but it was starting to feel like a prison. "Besides, you can protect me."

"As if you need me to protect you." He stood and moved beside me to look out at the ocean. "You can protect yourself."

I wasn't above begging. "Kieran, please?"

I took his hands in mine and tried to ignore the wave of warmth that tingled up my arm. If I didn't Change soon, I'd go mad. My dad had to know how terrible of a sentence he gave us. I wanted to chew him out, but he wasn't around.

I felt the moment when Kieran's resolve broke. "Okay, we'll go for a quick swim. Any sign of trouble, we transport back here instantly. Agreed?"

"Of course."

With our hands still joined, Kieran transported us to the cove. He eyed me warily before the air shimmered and he took his seal form. Tossing his head, he gave an impatient bark. I laughed and Changed, gliding into the water with a sigh of relief. Only once I was swimming through the waves, lost in the current, did I realize what this meant. How could I give this up? How could I choose to live as a human when a mere week of being forbidden to swim was pure torture?

You okay? Kieran's voice filtered through my head. *You seem sad. I thought you wanted to swim.*

I'm fine. Just thinking.

Well, stop, Kieran ordered. *I don't know when we'll get to do this again, so let's take advantage. Race you!*

He took off, and I struggled to catch up. He was faster underwater, more powerful, more experienced. I kept him in my sight and raced after him. I lost track of how far we'd gone. I almost ran into his tail when he stopped short.

What's this?

His voice sounded worried. I peered over his shoulder and jerked back in shock. In front of us, death and decay stretched as far as I could see.

Was there an oil spill? I asked.

I've seen oil spills and their destruction. Kieran's voice was soft. *This is not the same.* He lowered himself to the ground and nosed at the sediment. *There's something else going on here. Something I've never seen before. We'll have to alert the elders.*

Is everything okay? I watched him move slowly along the perimeter, nudging at random plants and animals that were either dead or dying. *Kieran?*

I... I don't know. He sounded insecure, afraid even. *Let's head back.*

We didn't talk on the swim back. I paid closer attention and determined that we must have been about twenty miles away from the island when we ran into the rotting mess. There seemed to be more schools of fish as we neared home. I hoped that meant these were the survivors. The only things that died were the plants and animals that could not move or move fast enough. Would the destruction keep spreading? Which way was it moving, away from or toward Ronac? And if it was moving toward us, how long would we be safe?

Kieran changed back first. His jeans clung to his wet skin, and he didn't bother with a shirt. This time, I knew it was from distraction. He wasn't trying to seduce me. As I changed, I consciously dried off. Wet denim was so uncomfortable. I visualized jeans and a T-shirt, with tennis shoes on my feet.

Ready? Kieran grasped my hand and transported us back to the entrance. He was poised to run, and I wanted to keep up. Running on land was a close second to racing under the waves. I thrilled with the power and matched his stride. How did he know where to go? Was he heading to the strategy room?

Do you think Brigid and my dad are back? Although I could speak aloud, running up the stairs, it was easier to speak to him telepathically.

We'll find out. If not, we'll tell Angus.

Are you going to tell them we were swimming? I asked, already guessing the answer.

I have to, Meara. I could practically hear the eye roll in Kieran's voice. *How else would we know what's happening at the bottom of the ocean?*

I swallowed my fear. Dad was going to be pissed. I ran down the hall silently, trying to be brave.

Kieran sensed my worry. *Don't worry*, he said. *They'll be more concerned about our report than what we were doing at the time.*

Don't be too sure about that, I said.

My dad and aunt weren't back. We tried both of their doors with no success. We checked the strategy room, too, but it was dark. I was disappointed and relieved at the same time. I wanted to see my dad, but maybe it would be easier to break this news to my great uncle.

Kieran knocked at Angus' door while I shifted on my feet. I hoped he wouldn't be too disappointed in me. He understood how hard it was to stay out of the water.

Angus opened the door and was clearly surprised to see us. "Kieran! Meara! What brings you two to my door?"

His broad shoulders filled the entrance. He looked from Kieran to me, pulling on his beard in speculation.

"We'd like to talk to you, sir." Kieran's voice filled with deference. His head bowed slightly toward my uncle, although they were the same height.

"Of course." Angus stepped back to give us room. "Come in, come in."

Kieran's eyes widened as he took in the furnishings. Apparently, this was his first time in Angus' quarters. He raised an eyebrow at me in question. I just smiled and shrugged. Let Angus explain it.

"Let me just turn this down." My uncle muted the movie playing in the background. It was one of the blockbusters from last spring. He caught me watching. "Have you seen this one, Meara? It's quite good."

"I saw it with some girlfriends."

"In the theater, no doubt?" His gaze held mine with interest. "I do love movie theaters."

"Yes—"

"If you don't mind, sir." Kieran shot me an impatient look when he interrupted. "We have some rather unsettling news to share with you."

"Do you?" Angus looked at me for confirmation. I nodded. "Then please, sit. Let's at least talk in comfort."

177

Kieran and I each took one end of the leather couch. Angus sat across from us in his chair. Clearing his throat, Kieran started, "We encountered mass destruction, about eight leagues northwest of the island."

Angus thumped his hand on the chair and glared at us. "And what were you doing out in the ocean?"

"That's hardly the point, sir," Kieran corrected, managing to sound polite at the same time. "The decay stretched as far as we could see. I tried to determine a source, but could not."

Angus stroked his beard and didn't say anything. Kieran's expression remained polite and patient. With a sigh, Angus sat back, his anger replaced with concern. "Do you think it's spreading?"

"My guess would be that it is, but I don't know for sure." Kieran leaned forward. "The waters surrounding the island are crowded with fish. More than I've seen before. It's like they're being forced out."

"Any idea how widespread it is?" Angus asked. His beard was a mess of corkscrews from worrying fingers.

"No, sir. As I said, it was black as far as we could see, but we didn't venture into the space. We came back to tell you."

"A wise choice," Angus said before piercing me with his eyes. "Even if your initial decision was poor." Angus stood, and I knew he was dismissing us. "I'll contact David and Brigid. Thank you for bringing this to my attention."

"Is there anything I can do?" Kieran rose to meet my uncle eye to eye.

"Yes," Angus said. "Guard Meara. Keep her safe."

I jumped up and was about to tell my uncle that I could protect myself when Kieran's words took my thoughts away.

"Always," Kieran replied. "With my life."

Angus visibly relaxed and pulled me into a hug. "Our lessons are suspended for a few days," he whispered. "I'll contact you when we can resume. Be safe, niece."

"You, too, Uncle Angus." I kissed his cheek and stepped back. Kieran placed his hand on the small of my back and guided me toward the door. Unlike Evan, his touch was gentle and not pushy. Did he mean what he said? Would he give his life for me?

Dinner that evening was quiet. With my dad, Aunt Brigid, and now Uncle Angus gone, only Ula and I sat at the table with Uncle Ren, Aunt Atiya, and my little cousin, Nico, who insisted on sitting next to me. At the moment, his sticky fingers tugged on the ends of my hair.

"No, Nico. Let Meara eat her dinner," Atiya scolded while she untangled his hand. He took a few strands of my hair with him. I would be using extra shampoo tonight.

"Meara's pretty." He patted my arm. "Love you."

I looked down at him. His bright green eyes were so exotic against his dark skin and hair. He was a cute kid even when covered in tomato sauce. "I love you, too, Nico."

"Can Meara play with me?" he asked his mom.

"Not tonight, Nico," Atiya said. "It's bath night for you."

"Tomorrow?" His voice lifted in a whine as his bottom lip pouted.

"I'll play with you before dinner tomorrow, okay, kiddo?" I ruffled his hair, and then confirmed with my aunt and uncle. "Will that be okay?"

Atiya smiled. "He'd love that. Don't feel like you have to, though. I know you're busy training."

"My pleasure," I said. "I've never had a little cousin before."

"Come by our room. He wakes up from his nap around three."

While Atiya began the enormous task of cleaning Nico's dinner off his skin, my uncle leaned over and smiled at me. "I'm sure that's all we're going to hear about until you come by tomorrow. Nico talks about you almost nonstop as it is."

My cheeks warmed from the attention. Ula grinned from my

uncle's other side. She already teased me about Nico's crush. The one thing I learned was that toddlers share sticky, gooey affection. Several wet cloths later, Atiya decided Nico was clean enough. When she released him, Nico stood on his chair and wrapped his chubby arms around my neck. Pressing his lips to my cheek, he blew his cheeks out like a blowfish in an impression of a kiss.

He finished saying goodbye by patting my face with soft hands. I bit my cheek to keep from laughing and gently held his hands at bay.

"See you tomorrow, Meara." He climbed down and took his mom's hand.

"Goodnight, Nico."

I watched the three of them walk away, Nico in the middle, holding hands with his parents. They were such a close family. What would it be like to be raised by two loving parents? Would I get the chance someday to show that kind of love to a child of my own? I was in no hurry to have kids, but I missed the closeness I shared with Mom.

"They're so loving," Ula said once they were out of earshot. "Sometimes it's sickening."

"I think it's sweet."

"It is," she said. "I'm probably just jealous. Anyway, do you want to come back to my room? I had Angus pick up some of those magazines you like."

I was tempted, but I really needed to find Kieran. I hadn't asked him about dinner on Sunday night yet, and I knew it was going to take some serious convincing.

"I'd like to," I said. "But I can't. Tomorrow night?"

She looked disappointed, but cheered up a little when I rescheduled. "Okay. What are you doing?"

"I need to talk to someone." I didn't want to say his name, but she asked anyway.

"Kieran?"

"Yeah."

"You sure spend a lot of time with him." She sunk in her chair and sulked. I raised my eyebrow, and she waved her hand at me. "I know, I know, you're training and all that. Fine. I don't like it, but as your aunt and friend, I'll try to understand."

I stood and gave her a quick hug. "Thanks, Ula."

"What are friends for?" she murmured, returning my hug.

I straightened and noticed Kieran leaving the cave. If I hurried, I could catch him before he got back to his room. Ula followed my gaze and gave me a slight push.

"Go," she said. "I'll see you tomorrow."

I hurried up the steps and down the hall. He was nowhere in sight, but I caught up on the second-floor landing.

"Kieran, wait!" I called, slightly breathless.

He turned and smirked at me. "Are you chasing me? 'Cause all you have to do is ask, and I'm yours."

"Well, yes, but no, thank you," I stammered, suddenly nervous. He wasn't going to be happy when I asked him. He raised an eyebrow and waited. I took a deep breath. "I need to ask you a favor."

He studied my face. "Must be a big one," he commented.

"Can we talk somewhere?" I didn't want to have this conversation in the hallway where anyone might hear us.

"It is serious. You have my full attention now." With a flirtatious edge, he asked, "My room or yours?"

I wanted to say neither, although that would probably offend him. "Your room," I decided. What would his room look like?

Both eyebrows went up, and his lips curved into a slow, sexy smile. My insides turned to jelly when he looked at me like that. *You're doing this for Evan*, I reminded myself.

"Follow me." He headed down the hall. When we reached his room, he held open the door. "After you."

I stepped around him, careful not to brush against him. His room was slightly smaller than mine with fewer windows. His bed was unmade, the sheets navy blue. A lighter blue blanket spilled off the corner and pooled on the floor. A few posters of basketball players hung on his wall. I didn't know all the athletes, but I recognized some of the older, more famous ones like Michael Jordan and Magic Johnson. A basketball hoop hung on the wall opposite the bed. A jersey lay over the back of the only chair in the room. Kieran pulled it off and folded it with care, placing it next to him when he sat on the edge of the bed. He gestured for me to sit in the chair.

"It's not much, but it's home," he said.

"I didn't take you for a basketball fan," I said.

"Why not?" He looked around the room. "Selkie's need to have hobbies, too."

"Have you ever played?"

"With some of my cousins back home. Just for fun."

I glanced at the jersey next to him. "Whose jersey is that?"

"Michael Jordan's. I met him once, and he signed it." He shifted on the bed. "You're stalling, Meara. I know you didn't come here to talk b-ball."

"No." I studied the posters on the wall, unable to meet Kieran's eyes. Better to get this over with, I thought. "I need you to escort me back to Aberdeen on Sunday."

"What?"

My eyes flicked to Kieran's at the disbelief he conveyed in one word. "I promised Evan we'd join them for dinner. Ken, the owner of the house, invited us." My voice fell to a whisper. "I couldn't say no."

"I'll say it for you. No. Absolutely not." He crossed to the chair and crouched in front of me. "Your dad will have my head. It's bad enough he's going to find out that we were swimming against his wishes. Are you trying to get me killed?"

I raised my chin. "Then I'll go alone."

"You'll do no such thing." His voice lowered with the threat.

"I will." My voice grew stronger, although my lips trembled.

"Watch me."

He leaned in close, his breath hot on my face. For once, I could see why others found him dangerous. "Meara—"

Before I knew what was happening, he was kissing me. His lips crushed mine as he pulled me close. I would've protested, but my mind went blank, and all I could do was respond or drown. I shoved him away when my sense of reason returned. At first, he looked as shocked as I felt, but he quickly recovered with a smug expression.

"Consider that payment," he said. "If I'm risking my life for you, I deserve something in return."

I ignored the first part of his statement, and instead focused on what he left unsaid. "You'll go?" My heart hammered in my chest, and my blood was on fire. I tried to take a few deep breaths without Kieran noticing. I needed to show him I was cool, that his kiss didn't affect me.

"I'll go." He shook his head. "Against my better judgment." He stood and offered me a hand to pull me up. I reluctantly took it and swore at the power humming between us. His breath hitched and with a deep voice, he said, "I think you should leave now."

"Night," I mumbled as I fled.

Chapter 25

"What do you think?"

Evan ran his hand down the front of the suit and turned to get a better view in the mirror. His tuxedo for prom hadn't looked this good. He looked rich. Elegant. Then he glanced at the price tag — too bad he couldn't pay for it.

"It's great." Evan met Ken's eyes in the reflection. "But I can't afford this."

Ken laughed. "Who said you had to? My treat."

"I can't accept that kind of gift—"

"Sure you can," Ken interrupted. "Consider it a bonus for all of your hard work."

The saleswoman hummed appreciatively. "I'd take him up on it, hon. It looks amazing on you."

Evan glanced at the clerk and wondered why he hadn't noticed her before. Thin, but curvy in all the right places. Her straight, black hair hung to her waist. She watched him with wide, brown eyes, and he realized he was staring.

"Thanks," he said, not sure if he was thanking Ken or the girl. "I'll take it. I'm going to change now."

Ken chuckled as Evan walked away. The clerk was already checking the fit on Ken's suit. The last thing Evan saw before he turned away was a thin strip of skin at her waist when she stretched to adjust Ken's collar. Why did he feel the urge to run his finger along that stretch and feel her shiver in reply? Why was he thinking about her anyway?

He felt more like himself once he was back in his jeans and T-shirt. He went to the lobby to wait for Ken, handing the salesclerk his suit. She placed it in a garment bag, and then did the same with Ken's when he gave it to her a few minutes later. As promised, Ken paid for both and took the garment bags from the saleswoman.

"Hungry?" Ken asked.

Stomach rumbling in reply, Evan laughed and said, "I guess so."

He hadn't realized he was hungry until Ken said something, but now he was ravenous. Hunger was a sharp, desperate pain in his gut.

"I know just the place. Follow me."

Evan assumed they'd eat at one of the mall's many restaurants, but Ken led him outside. They walked to his sleek, silver sports car, and Ken placed the suit bags in the trunk. The rich scent of leather wafted out as Evan took his seat. He felt a twinge of guilt that he was glad Ted opted to stay back at the house. If he'd come along, they would've taken the cramped rental instead. This car was amazing.

The engine purred to life, and Ken took off. Once they left the city, the roads changed from straight and crowded to curvy and open. Ken lowered the top and grinned at Evan.

"Great day for a drive."

Evan agreed. The misty sea air was silk against his skin. He relaxed into the seat and enjoyed the ride. "Where are we going?"

"A little dive I know." Ken adjusted his visor before glancing at Evan. "They have great seafood."

They drove through miles of unbroken green and hills before civilization appeared again. The homes here were small and modest, more cabins than houses. Yet they were lovingly cared for, with colorful flowerbeds and thriving vegetable gardens. A few locals waved as they drove by. Evan waved back.

"Friendly people here."

"It's a nice town," Ken said. "I come here sometimes to get away. They make the most of little. It humbles me."

The streets changed. The well-tended homesteads gave way to ramshackle buildings that barely stood. A strong wind could wipe out the whole neighborhood. Unlike the previous blocks, this street was deserted. No one greeted them. It looked abandoned.

"The poorest of the poor," Ken said. "Destitute. And yet, our destination ends here." He pulled to a stop outside of a two-story shack, the wood blackened and cracked with age and smoke.

"The Shack," Evan read the sign aloud. "Not a very creative name."

"Doesn't have to be," Ken replied. "The food speaks for itself. C'mon."

As they approached the door, the smell of roasting meat grew stronger, smoky and spicy. Evan's stomach rumbled. He followed Ken in, staying close as the thick air and low lighting made it difficult to see. Music thrummed in a loud, steady rhythm.

When his eyes adjusted to the dark, Evan saw the stage. Three exotic dancers captivated the room. Their hair varied from neon blue to bright green. He wondered what kind of makeup trick made their eyes glow so brightly. The little clothing they wore shimmered under the lights like the scales on a fish.

"The entertainment's even better than the food." Ken winked at him. "Follow Deanna. I've got a table."

Their waitress, Deanna, was dressed like the dancers. She led them to a table in the corner. She smiled at Evan and ran her hand down his arm before walking away.

"I think she likes you," Ken observed, chuckling. Evan's face grew warm. What was this place? Now that he had a better view of the room, he could see the only women in here were either waitstaff or dancers. The men eyed them hungrily, but whenever a man reached for one of the girls, she twirled out of his reach with a tinkling of laughter.

"What are you having?" Ken asked, breaking Evan out of his reverie.

Evan stared at the one-sided menu. The options were limited. "I don't know. What do you recommend?"

Ken drummed his fingers on the table in rhythm to the music. "The shark. It's excellent."

"Sounds great," Evan agreed. He'd never tried shark, but he trusted Ken's judgment. After all, he said this was his favorite place to eat.

"Wonderful. I'll do the ordering." Ken's teeth glowed blue in the stage lights when he smiled. Everyone looked blue under this lighting. Evan was surprised to see how blue his own skin looked. Was it getting hot in here? He felt a little queasy.

"Where's the restroom?" Evan asked.

Not taking his eyes off the stage, Ken motioned toward the back corner. "Down the hall, last door on the right."

"Thanks." Evan stood and made his way to the back. His head spun as if he were drunk, but he hadn't even ordered a drink yet. The music drilled into his skull. His head pulsed with it. It wasn't a headache exactly, but it felt strange.

"You're new here." Deanna stood in the shadows. She pushed off the wall and crossed to him, running a finger up his arm, and then along his jaw. "I'd remember you."

This close, Evan noticed that her long, wavy hair was a pale green. Sections of it hung in braids decorated with smooth beads of blue and green or shiny, white pearls. Her large eyes were a shade of green only slightly darker than her hair. Her skin glistened like the pearls, luminescent and smooth. She licked her lips, drawing Evan's attention. They beckoned him to kiss her.

He shook his head to clear the fog. The restroom, he was looking for the restroom.

"Restroom?" he croaked.

She stepped back with a pout, revealing the hall behind her. "Last door on the right."

He made his way down the hall, berating himself. He almost kissed a girl he didn't even know. He wanted to kiss her, wanted to do more than that if he were honest with himself. What was he thinking?

The door swung shut behind him. The music was muffled and indistinguishable here, and no one else was in the bathroom. He splashed cold water on his face, feeling more like himself. A glance in the mirror revealed that his skin was its normal tone. It was just the lighting in the bar, nothing more. He dried his hands and hoped he could avoid the waitress on his way back to the table.

A glass of foamy, dark liquid waited for him at the table. "I hope you like Guinness," Ken said. Evan had never tried it, but he didn't want to admit that to Ken. He took a drink and decided it wasn't bad.

They lapsed into silence and watched the girls. Their voices floated around the room while they danced with precision and harmony. Evan found he couldn't take his eyes off them. They were exceptional. What were these girls doing in a seedy bar?

"Here are your dinners." Deanna set their plates in front of them. "Enjoy."

Evan nodded and stared at his plate. The meat was a deep red. It could be the lighting, but it didn't look cooked. "Is this—?"

"I ordered it how I eat mine. Rare. Try a bite." Ken motioned with his fork. "If you don't like it, you can send it back to whatever doneness you want. With shark, cooking takes away the tenderness of the meat."

Evan gave Ken a dubious look before cutting a small piece. He chewed it slowly, waiting to be disgusted, but Ken was right. It melted in his mouth like the most expensive cut of beef. The flavor was an intense blend of spice and something richer.

"Well?" Ken watched him carefully.

"It's amazing." Evan laughed and shook his head. "Best thing I've ever eaten."

"Told you," Ken said with a smug smile. He finished his drink and motioned to Deanna to bring them refills. She brought fresh drinks over, her eyes glued to Evan's face. It thrilled him that she was so obviously interested. In the past, he was the one doing the pursuing.

The girls on stage announced a ten-minute break and the room brightened by several degrees.

"I need to make a phone call," Ken said. "I'll be right back."

Ken pulled out his phone and headed toward the parking lot doors. Deanna took his vacancy as an opportunity to steal his seat. She reached across and took Evan's Guinness, taking a long, slow sip.

"Will you be staying for the next segment?" she asked.

"I don't know," Evan said. "Ken's in charge."

For whatever reason, that made Deanna giggle. "Clearly," she managed.

"What does that mean?" Evan asked, which made her giggle more. Her voice had a melodious quality to it. Evan couldn't be mad, although he had the distinct impression she was laughing at him.

"I'm up next," she leaned forward and whispered.

"You dance?"

"I sing," she corrected. "You won't want to miss it."

"Okay."

Deanna disappeared to get ready. Evan finished his meal and his beer. The lights dimmed again, and Ken hadn't returned. Whomever he called, it was taking a while.

When Deanna glided onto the stage, Evan swallowed with difficulty. She was beautiful, her hair twisted on top of her head in a complicated style. Her makeup was darker, which made her pale eyes more striking. She caught his gaze and began to sing.

She sang of love and loss, sailors and tides. He saw, rather than heard, her words. The room fell away, and there was only Deanna. The song ended, and her lips curled into a slow, welcoming smile. She gestured for him to follow her, and he did.

Deanna. He'd follow her anywhere.

"You're awake."

Ken sounded amused. Evan rubbed his temples. They were in the car, driving fast. It was getting dark outside, although he could see the house in the distance.

"What happened?" Evan's thoughts were foggy. He remembered Deanna, their waitress, singing. She had a beautiful, clear voice. That's the last thing he recalled.

"You passed out, son." Ken clucked his tongue. He was definitely amused. "I guess I gave you one too many drinks."

Evan didn't think he'd even finished the second one, but he wasn't thinking very clearly in that bar. "That's strange," he said. "I feel fine."

"That's good. Work starts early tomorrow." Ken pulled into the drive and cut the engine. "I gave you one day off, not a long weekend."

"Yes, sir." Evan felt admonished by Ken's sharp tone.

Ken lowered his sunglasses and glanced at Evan. "Relax, son. I'm teasing. We are working tomorrow, but it'll be a short day. We've got to get ready for our dinner guests this weekend, right?"

"Sure." Evan opened his door, anxious to get out. He didn't really understand Ken. Couldn't Stonewall and the other staff clean the house and prepare a meal? What was the fuss about anyway? Meara was coming to dinner, not the queen.

He started toward the house when Ken called him back. "Yes?" Evan asked, turning.

Ken held up a bag. "Your suit?"

"Oh yeah. Thanks again."

"You're welcome." Evan reached for the bag, but Ken didn't release it. "Evan, where I took you today… best we keep that our little secret, okay?"

"Sure." Who was he going to tell? Meara? Somehow, he didn't think she'd approve of him eating at a restaurant staffed by beautiful, scantily clad women.

190

"And we'll keep what happened there secret, too."

"What happened?" Evan asked.

Ken winked. "Exactly." He took his suit and headed into the house. With a growing sense of dread, Evan stood in the driveway and watched him walk away.

Chapter 26

I studied the magazine in front of me, wondering if I could imitate the complicated hairstyle. I took a deep breath and closed my eyes, picturing the twists and braids. With a few gentle tugs, my hair arranged itself. I opened my eyes and judged the results.

Not bad.

The updo, a little looser than the one on the actress, allowed a few curls to fall and frame my face. I mimicked my makeup after hers, too, although I swapped the brown shadow for a pale gold that matched my dress. I hung crystal and pearl strands in my ears and was just clasping my bracelet when I heard Kieran's knock.

"Come in."

He wore a trim, black suit. His eyes lit up when he saw me. "You look amazing."

I eyed his gold tie with dismay. "We match," I said. "Evan will think we planned it."

"Really?" He lifted his tie and observed it curiously. "What color should I wear?"

"Silver? Black? Blue? Anything but gold."

The gold faded to silver. He adjusted the tie and smiled. "Better?"

"Much," I said. "You look good."

He crossed the room to my dresser and lifted one of the framed photos. "Any idea what to expect at this soiree?" He was trying for indifference, but I heard the catch in his voice.

"Are you nervous?" I asked.

He shrugged. "I have a bad feeling, but I told you I'd go so..." He set the frame down and spun around to face me. "Here I am."

As I crossed the room, his smile faltered.

"Is there something you're not telling me?" I asked. I was nervous, too, but he looked almost green.

He tugged at his collar and grimaced. "If something goes wrong tonight, if something happens to you, it could cause a war between our clans."

He couldn't be serious. A war? Over me? I doubted it.

"It's dinner, Kieran, nothing more. Relax." I wrapped my shawl around my shoulders and linked my arm through his. "Shall we go?"

"In a minute," he muttered. He took my hand in his. We were mere inches apart. He held my gaze. "If I sense anything out of place, even something minor, we're leaving. If I tell you we're going, we go. No arguing. Do you understand?"

"Of course," I said. "Aren't you overreacting?"

"I'd rather be safe." He tucked my hand back into the crook of his arm. "Let's go."

We arrived in the cool darkness of the cove. The night sky was cloudy, which provided further coverage. Not that anyone else was out.

"Do you think they're going to wonder where our car is?" I asked as I climbed the steps in front of Kieran.

"We'll say your dad dropped us off," Kieran said smoothly. "He's overprotective and wanted to see the house."

I laughed. "Not too far from the truth."

"Exactly." Kieran's voice was soft in the night. "The strongest lies are based in truth."

I paused and looked back at him. "Sounds like you have

experience with that."

He shrugged and motioned for me to continue. "We don't want to be late."

The butterflies whirled in my stomach the closer I got to the house. Why was I so nervous? Something about this house didn't feel right to me. Still, Evan was here, and I loved him. I shouldn't worry. What could happen?

I hadn't realized that I stopped at the front step until I heard Kieran right behind me. "Having second thoughts? We could leave and go back."

I straightened my shoulders and stepped onto the porch. I heard him sigh. I rang the bell, and there was no going back. Stonewall opened the door almost immediately.

"Good evening."

Had he been waiting on the other side?

"Please come in," he said. "The others are waiting for you in the parlor."

Stonewall took my shawl and disappeared down the hall. Evan sat on the couch, a glass of wine in his hand. Ken and Ted each held their own glass and sat in the chairs opposite him. Ken stood when he saw us.

"Welcome, my friends. So glad you could make it. Please, have a seat." He motioned to the couch. Evan moved to the far end. He hadn't looked at me yet. He was watching Kieran with undisguised hatred on his face. I didn't expect them to get along, but hate seemed unwarranted.

His eyes flickered my way. "You look nice."

"Thanks." I took the seat next to him. Kieran sat stiffly on my other side.

"Can I offer you a drink?" Ken held out the bottle of wine for our inspection. It could be a grocery store label or a high-end winery for as much as I knew, but Kieran seemed impressed and nodded his consent. Ken turned his gaze to me.

"Sure," I said. "Thank you."

The wine sucked the moisture from my mouth. I smacked my lips and wished I had a glass of water. Ken noticed and laughed good-naturedly. "Not a fan of cabernet, are you?" He poured a pale pink liquid in a fresh glass. "Try this one."

I took a sip and smiled. The new wine was light and citrusy. "It's delicious. Thank you."

We settled back with our drinks, and Ken started the conversation. He told us about Evan's internship. They were studying a portion of the ocean floor off the coast of Scotland. Ted jumped in with funny stories about their diving excursions, like Evan's first time using a scuba scooter. It made me remember the scene Kieran and I encountered on our swim the other day. I was about to say something when he spoke in my mind.

Don't tell them anything.

I shot him a questioning look, but he didn't meet my eyes. He was nodding politely at Ted as if he hadn't spoken to me at all.

Meara, stop looking at me. They're going to think something is going on.

Oh. Sorry, I apologized. *Why don't you want me to say anything? I don't trust them.*

I slid my hand over by Evan. We were sitting close, but not touching. It wasn't like him. He usually made the first move and was quick to take my hand, touch my hair, or kiss me. Tonight, he seemed distant. I placed my hand over his and smiled at him. He smiled back, but it seemed forced. He patted my hand with his free one, and then took them both away.

Leaning forward, he rested his elbows on his knees with his hands clasped between them. To anyone else, it must have looked like he was engaged in the conversation. I knew it for the rejection it was. Evan never dropped my hand like that. Again I wondered if I had done something wrong. The absence of his touch was like a slap. I stared at the back of his expensive suit and wondered what he was thinking. Why did he invite me only to ignore me?

"You're living with your father, correct?"

Evan turned to look at me, and I realized Ken was talking to me.

"Um, yes," I said. "I moved in with him this summer."

"And where in Scotland is that?" Ken asked.

Be vague, Kieran warned.

"Not too far from here," I said. "About twenty minutes away." I didn't elaborate if it was twenty minutes by car, foot, or boat.

Ken smiled pleasantly. "And are you planning to stay in Scotland?"

Why was Ken so interested in me? I glanced quickly at Evan hoping for a clue, a smile of encouragement, something. He didn't look at me.

"I'm not sure," I said. "I haven't picked a college yet."

"No?" Professor Nolan spoke this time. "Most universities start in just a few weeks."

"I'm taking some time off," I said.

"Her mother passed away last year," Kieran said. His voice was firm, but polite. He shot Evan a dirty look. A wasted effort since Evan was staring straight ahead and didn't see it. "She needs a little time."

"Of course," Ted murmured. "My sympathies."

"Thank you," I said. What was Evan's problem? He hadn't said two words to me.

Are you okay? I asked him through our necklace link.

Fine. His voice was short. *I think we should only talk out loud, don't you? It's rude to talk this way in front of others.*

I heard the unasked question, "Can you communicate this way with Kieran?" I felt no need to tell him that Kieran and I could talk telepathically without jewelry, and thankfully, Evan couldn't hear us. That much I knew about the necklaces. Ula had explained that it only worked when words were directed at the other necklace wearer. This protected both parties from sharing unwanted thoughts or words. In any case, Evan's attitude was really starting to get to me. If he wanted to break up, I'd rather he just did it than string me along.

My apologies, I said, sending plenty of sarcasm with it. He got the message. His mouth twitched downward at the corners. Other than that, he didn't acknowledge me again.

Ken and Kieran began discussing art. They appeared to have common interests. Ken seemed pleased and offered to take us on a tour of the house to see his other paintings. We followed him out of the room. I was between the professor and Kieran. Evan seemed content to bring up the rear. He didn't try to walk next to me.

What's going on, Meara? Kieran asked. *Evan's being a jerk. Did you have a fight?*

Not that I know of. I blinked back tears at Kieran's concern. At least someone cared about me. *I don't know what's wrong with him.*

I'm getting a weird vibe, he said. *I can't put my finger on it. Remember, if I say we need to leave, we're leaving, okay?*

I'm ready to go now, I admitted. *I don't want to be here if Evan's going to ignore me.*

Hang in there. Kieran sounded sympathetic. *Just act like nothing's wrong. Don't let him know he's getting to you.*

Every room was impressive. Beautiful works of art by both unknown and famous artists. The famous ones Kieran announced to me, but even I recognized the Birth of Venus by Botticelli.

Is it the original? I asked Kieran.

Not possible, he said. *It's an amazing replica.*

I studied the painting. "She's beautiful, isn't she?" Ken's voice came from directly behind me. I hadn't heard him walk over. "Some think Venus was the first mermaid."

"The first?" I asked, turning to look into his eyes.

His eyebrows rose. "Of course. You of all people must know that mermaids exist."

I felt Kieran's presence in my mind, though he didn't say anything. I knew that he wondered, like me, where Ken was going with this conversation. Dread weighted my stomach, but it didn't stop me from asking, "What do you mean?"

Ken held my gaze as if challenging me. I raised my chin slightly, and I didn't break eye contact. What was he implying? What was he trying to get me to say?

He smiled pleasantly. "You've been dating Evan for over a year. Surely, he's told you many of the myths are real. I know he's a fan of ocean lore, sirens in particular."

Ken winked at Evan. Confused, I watched Evan's face turn slightly red. He laughed awkwardly before asking, "Isn't it time for dinner, Ken?"

"You're right, of course, my boy." Ken laughed and patted him on the back. "You're right. Let's all head down to the dining room."

That was strange, Kieran said.

You're telling me. Did you get the feeling that he wanted me to say something else?

Yeah, Kieran said. *I did. I don't like it.*

"Are you two coming?" Ted asked. Ken and Evan were already on their way downstairs, lost in a conversation.

"Right behind you," Kieran said. When Ted turned and started down the stairs, Kieran rested his hand on the small of my back, sending tingles up my spine.

"After you," he murmured in my ear.

The dining room was at the back of the house behind the living room. Two of the walls were floor-to-ceiling windows. Although I couldn't see the cove from this height, I knew it was below us. During the day, this room would have a specular view of the ocean.

Half of the long table was set with china plates, crystal glasses, and gleaming candlesticks. The candlelight reflected off the windows, making the room glow in an inviting way. A large arrangement of white roses was the centerpiece. Their sweet, floral fragrance filled the air.

Ken stood behind the chair at the head of the table. He gestured for Evan to sit to his right. I sat next to Evan, and Kieran sat across from me, next to Ted.

"We're so thrilled you could join us tonight," Ken said as he sat down. "It isn't often that we entertain guests, and I do like to entertain."

"Thank you for having us," I said to be polite. With Evan staring at his plate and not speaking to me, this could prove to be one awkward dinner party.

As if on cue, Stonewall entered with a female servant. Both carried trays with salad plates and dressing. Strips of grayish meat and small, black eggs covered the bed of lettuce.

Caviar, Kieran said. *It's good. Try it.*

I took a small bite and resisted the urge to spit it in my napkin. It was salty and slimy. Quickly swallowing, I washed it down with wine. I pushed the rest to the side of my plate, along with the gray meat. I wasn't even going to try that.

Don't like it? I heard the laughter in Kieran's voice. *Maybe it's an acquired taste.*

Kieran was very good at conversing this way. He gave no outward indication with his poker face. I struggled just to keep from looking at him every time I heard his voice.

"What do you do for a living, Kieran?" Ken asked. "Are you still in school?"

"I just graduated," Kieran said smoothly. "I'm looking for a job."

"Your accent," Ted said. "It's not Scottish."

"It's not," Kieran agreed. "I'm from California."

"Aren't you American, too, Meara?" Ted asked.

"Yes," I said. "I'm from Wisconsin, although Mom and I moved to Nova Scotia last year."

The words brought painful memories of the last year. I missed Mom so much. I thought Evan might show me some sympathy, but he was looking at Ken. The conversation lulled as the second course was served.

Ken sat back. Stonewall removed his salad plate and served a steaming bowl of soup. Leaning forward and breathing in the steam, Ken smiled broadly. "Stonewall makes the best seafood chowder. You'll love it."

I was used to chowder being white, but this was a deep red. The broth was thick and spicy. I tasted shrimp, scallops, lobster, and whitefish. It was delicious.

"How did you two meet?" Ken motioned to Kieran and me with his free hand.

"Our fathers are friends," Kieran said. "I'm just visiting for the summer."

"And, what does your father do, Meara?" Ken asked.

"He's a fisherman." I said the first thing that came to mind.

"Ah, yes. A popular trade in this area."

Evan glanced between us, but didn't say anything. He went back to eating his stew. If Ken or Ted found his behavior odd, they didn't say anything. Ken did most of the talking. He told us how his father had been a commercial fisherman and built his trade to several fleets. Eventually, he owned most of the marina in Aberdeen. Ken inherited it, but he preferred to let others manage the docks.

"My love is science and art," he said. "Some may find that a contradiction. Not me."

"Ken has financed several of my projects," Ted added. "He's a wonderful benefactor."

"I like to think of myself as a partner, Ted," Ken said warmly. "We're in this together."

They appeared to be good friends. Ted was uncomfortable and shy. Ken was gregarious and direct. Maybe they balanced each other out.

"Shall we have another glass of wine with the main course?" Ken held a bottle out to us. The label was old and peeling. "I've been saving this for a special occasion."

This was a special occasion? What was so special about us coming to dinner?

"We're flattered," Kieran said. He held the glass to his nose and breathed in. "Bordeaux?"

"You know wines?" Ken asked, impressed. "It's Château Lafleur, 1970."

Kieran took a small sip, rolling the wine around in his mouth. Ken waited for his approval. "Delicious," Kieran murmured.

It's laced. Kieran's voice rang in my head. *Don't drink it. Excuse yourself to the bathroom, and then go out front. I'll meet you there.* When I didn't move, he yelled in my head, *Meara, go now!*

I pushed my chair back and stood, struggling to appear nonchalant while my heart raced. "Excuse me, Ken, but where is the bathroom?"

"Second door on the right," he said. "Would you like Evan to show you?"

Evan made no move to stand. I shook my head.

"I can find it. I'll be right back."

I stepped in the hall and almost ran into Stonewall. He and the female server stood by the dinner cart, waiting for Ken to request their entrance. I couldn't walk to the front door now. They'd see me and wonder. I headed to the bathroom, closed the door, and locked it before turning the water on low. Then, I transported to the front porch. If anyone came to check on me, they'd assume I was washing my hands.

I almost yelped when Kieran grabbed my hand. Before I could say anything, he transported us back to Ronac. He didn't speak. I was getting a fuzzy vibe from him. We landed at the cove, half in the water. Kieran collapsed face forward into the surf.

"Kieran!" I screamed. I scooped my arms under his and dragged him to the shore, rolling him over onto his back. His eyes were closed and his face was pale. He was breathing, but not responsive. I lifted his eyelids and jumped back. All that showed were the whites.

I did the only thing I could think of. I held onto him and transported us to Angus' room. The amount of energy required to transport us made my head pound. I rubbed my temples, and after a moment, observed the details around me. The television was on and paused. The shower was running. I moved Kieran to the couch and ran to the bathroom door. Pounding on it, I shouted for Uncle Angus.

The water stopped. My uncle threw open the door. Dripping with water, he clutched a towel around his waist.

"Uncle Angus, something is wrong with Kieran!" I said before he could say anything.

"Where is he?" he asked.

"In your living room," I said. "Come quick."

"I'll be right there, child." He closed the door, and I ran back by Kieran. His breathing was shallow and fast. Every few seconds, his body shook with racking coughs. He remained unresponsive.

Uncle Angus came out in a thick robe. He sat next to Kieran and took his pulse. His face was grim. "You better tell me what happened."

"We went to dinner at Ken's where Evan—"

"Your boyfriend? You left the island?" His voice vibrated with fury.

"Uncle Angus, please." I glanced at Kieran, and Uncle Angus' face softened slightly.

"Continue," he ordered gruffly.

"It was fine, and then Ken served wine before the main course. He poured for Kieran first. Kieran took a sip and told me it was poisoned. He had me meet him out front and transported us back here. When we arrived, he collapsed."

"Poison." Angus sounded surprised. "Why would this human poison you?"

"I don't know, Uncle Angus, but how can we help Kieran?"

His brows drew together in thought. "I need to determine what they gave him." He went into his kitchen and grabbed a spoon and a glass. Opening Kieran's mouth, he ran the spoon along his cheek and gathered saliva. He placed the spoon in the glass and straightened. "I'm going to analyze this. You stay with him. Call me if he gets worse."

"Call you?"

Uncle Angus tapped his temple in reply. Oh right, telepathy. I chalked my stupidity up to fear for Kieran. I sat next to him and held his hand. It was clammy.

"Hurry back," I called as my uncle closed the door.

Kieran started to shiver, his teeth chattering. I took the throw from the back of the couch and covered us both. I hoped my body heat would warm him up. It worked. He stopped shivering within minutes. I rubbed his hand nervously, chanting in my head, *Please wake up. Please don't die, Kieran. Please wake up. I'll never forgive myself.*

Meara, where are you?

Evan's voice sent a chill down my spine. I'd forgotten about the necklace. *Oh, now you're going to talk to me?* I cried. *What did Ken do to Kieran?*

What are you talking about? Evan sounded angry.

He poisoned Kieran. The wine was poisoned.

You're crazy, Evan said. *I had two glasses, and I'm fine. No, the two of you just left, probably to go make out somewhere. Are you an item now?*

Standing, I started to pace. Was Evan serious? *What? No! How absurd. I love you, Evan, although you'd never know it by the way you're treating me.*

I haven't changed, Meara. Evan sounded sad. *You have. I don't think we should see each other anymore.*

You're breaking up with me? I had trouble swallowing. Kieran could be dying right now, and Evan was breaking up with me? I'd done nothing wrong. If I changed, I couldn't help it. He used to be understanding. Lately, everything I did seemed to annoy him.

You know what? I said angrily. *Fine.*

Great, he said. *Oh, and don't worry about Ken. I'll apologize for you both. You missed some fabulous swordfish, by the way.*

Tears filled my eyes, more out of anger and disbelief than sadness. For the moment, I was so done with Evan. I told him Kieran was poisoned, and he didn't even listen. He cared more about stupid Ken who he just met a few weeks ago. This was supposed to be our big summer romance. What a mess! In tears, I unhooked the necklace and flung it on the coffee table. I didn't want to be able to talk to him anymore. I sat on the edge of the couch next to Kieran just as Uncle Angus came back.

"Tetrodotoxin," he announced triumphantly.

"What?" I wiped my eyes, hoping he took the tears for worry.

"Pufferfish toxin," he said. "I'm not sure what it was doing in wine, but that's what I found. It can be toxic to humans. Luckily, the effects are temporary on Selkies."

"He'll be okay?" My body sagged with relief as the guilt lifted.

"He's going to have one hell of a hangover," Uncle Angus explained. "But in a day or two, he'll be fine." He opened a wardrobe and pulled out a blanket and pillow. "Help me get him comfortable. He can sleep on my couch tonight. I'll keep an eye on him."

I untied Kieran's shoes and tucked them under the coffee table. Angus removed his suit coat and his tie. I placed the pillow under Kieran's head while Angus straightened out his legs.

"He looks comfortable now," my uncle observed. "Why don't you get some rest? You can take over in the morning. I've got a meeting with your dad and your aunt."

"They're back?" My heart jumped in my chest. My dad was going to be furious.

"They will be tomorrow morning." He patted my shoulder. "I won't say anything, if you promise me not to go there again."

"I promise," I said. "Anyway, Evan broke up with me."

"Tonight?"

I heard the concern in my uncle's voice and swallowed my tears. I could break down in my own room. "While you were looking for the toxins," I said. I picked up the necklace from the end table and showed him. Recognition lit in his eyes before they filled with sympathy. My fist clenched, the necklace biting into my palm. The pain helped me focus, and I blinked rapidly.

"I'm sorry," he said.

"I'm not." My wavering voice betrayed me. I kissed his cheek and gave him a faltering smile. "Thank you for helping Kieran."

He pulled me close and hugged me. "It will be okay, Meara. Everything will work out."

His kindness broke through the fragile wall around my heart. As he held me, I cried.

Chapter 27

*A*gain. He did it again. He was an idiot the first time, so there was really no excuse. How could he break up with her? A month ago, hell, a week ago, she was his world, his everything. Now he couldn't look at her without disgust. Was it that other Selkie, Kieran? Evan didn't think so. Meara wasn't lying when she said that she loved him. She did, and he knew it. The question was— did he still love her? As he paced in his room and swore, he knew the answer. He did.

When he was alone, it all came flooding back. The first time he met her when she introduced herself in his backyard. The time he taught her how to sand and paint, and he almost kissed her on her grandfather's boat. Then there was their first kiss, slow and sweet, after the carnival in Halifax. She owned his heart then, she owned it now, and so what was the matter?

He couldn't think. When the headaches went away, so did his ability to reason. Only when he was alone were his thoughts his own. What were the voices that whispered poison? He rolled his neck and heard each vertebrae pop. Could he admit to Meara what he was experiencing? If he wanted to get her back, he'd have to. There was no excuse for how he treated her, but maybe if he explained.

Could she love him, even if he were going crazy? He shook his head and sighed. She did love him, and she would understand. Meara was a good person. She wouldn't abandon him because he was going through a difficult period. She'd remember how he stuck with her last year, how he helped her figure out what she was and what to do about it.

The worst was that he lied to her.

She hadn't changed. At least, not in any way that was bad or wrong. If she had changed, it was for the better. She was stronger, more confident. He was the one turning bad, going insane. She was better off without him, but he knew there was no way he would last without her.

Meara? He reached out through their connection. *Can you hear me?*

Silence.

He called her name a few more times with no reply. She could be ignoring him, or maybe she took the necklace off. His stomach twisted when he thought of that. Of course that was what she did. He broke up with her—why would she want to speak to him? He hoped that she would eventually put it back on.

He strode to the window and threw it open. The cool ocean air calmed him. Leaning on the windowsill, he wondered how he was going to win her back if he couldn't talk to her. What had she told him? Kieran was poisoned. Evan hadn't lied when he told Meara that he had two glasses of that wine, so had Ken. Only Ted passed on it. Was there any left?

He could check. The house was quiet. Odds were that everyone retired for the night. He could find the bottle. He threw on his sweatshirt and headed for his door. That was exactly what he could do... find the bottle and have it tested.

Yeah, right, he muttered to himself. He stopped with his hand on the doorframe. *Where would you take it?*

The voice hissed in a condescending way. Evan closed his eyes and concentrated. He put every effort into blocking the voice. He didn't open his eyes until the room was silent.

I'll bring it back to my room, he thought. *And when I reach Meara, I'll tell her that I have it.*

You'll lure her with a bottle? A dark glee echoed through his head when the voice giggled. *Oh yes, do that. It's perfect.*

Evan ignored the voice as best he could. It was getting hard to resist. He couldn't think of another plan. It would have to work. He climbed down the stairs quickly and quietly into the darkness of the lower level. The hall was wide and open, so he saw no need to turn on lights. He stayed toward the center and used his memory to navigate to the kitchen. Once there, he turned on the small light above the stove.

He hadn't used the kitchen before, so he didn't know where things were located. Most houses had the recycling somewhere near the sink. He noticed a narrow cabinet and pulled the door open. It was a sliding drawer, containing a bin for recyclables and one for trash. He found several empty bottles, but the Bordeaux was not there. He closed the cabinet and shut off the light. Perhaps the bottle was still in the dining room. It was worth looking at least.

He opened the dining room and stepped inside. The room glowed, the two outer walls of windows allowing for ample moonlight. On the buffet in the back corner, he found the candlesticks used at dinner, as well as the wine bottle and three empty glasses. The bottle had a little wine left in it. Hoping that no one would miss them, Evan took the bottle and the three glasses. What if the poison had only been in Kieran's cup? He couldn't rule it out. If he could talk to Meara, he would give them all to her.

Some men brought their lovers jewelry and roses when they needed to beg for forgiveness. He was giving his girlfriend potentially poisoned wine and three empty glasses, but he hoped she would see it for what it was. An apology.

Chapter 28

I couldn't sleep. Every time I tried, I dreamt of Evan. They weren't good dreams. Not the dreams I used to have, where we swam in the ocean or walked under a million stars stopping to kiss until we got dizzy. These dreams were scary. They left me in a cold sweat. I woke panting from exertion or screaming in fear. My eyelids drooped. I refused to close them, refused to see Evan with glowing eyes and sharp teeth again.

The necklace lay on the nightstand, the creamy pearl glistening in the moonlight. Should I put it back on? Was he trying to contact me? Was he having second thoughts?

My heart was broken, and yet, something wasn't right. The man I saw tonight was not the man I loved. In the year we dated, Evan never even raised his voice at me. He was kind and gentle. When we were together, I was a better person. He made me a better person. Something changed.

The headaches. It started with the headaches. He said they were gone now, but something else was happening. He'd been different since he saw that doctor. I didn't even know the man's name. Evan never mentioned it. I hadn't asked either, but could it be important?

The pearl felt cool and silky in my hand. I had picked it up without realizing it, but now, as I rubbed my thumb over the small jewel, I was comforted. Was it because it was my link to Evan? I set it back on the nightstand. I didn't want to think about it.

Kieran could've died tonight if he were human. Was Ken intending on poisoning me, too? Why would he poison us?

Dismayed, I realized I didn't even know Ken's last name. Evan told me very little about this internship. I did have his professor's name. Ted Nolan. I could start there and see if anything came up. Of course, it would require going to the mainland. I needed a computer and an internet connection.

If I were honest with myself, I'd admit that what I needed was my father. I had to tell him. I was endangering the entire island if I hid what happened. Maybe Ken was one of our enemies. He didn't fit any of the descriptions that Kieran shared with me. Then again, Kieran admitted he hadn't encountered every creature in the book. Not knowing who or what Ken was didn't make him any less of a threat. He tried to kill us. What would stop him from trying with someone else?

My mouth widened in a huge, involuntary yawn. Sleep was coming, whether I wanted it or not. Panicked, I swept the necklace up and gripped it in my hand. If I was going to dream of Evan as a monster, I could at least keep the necklace close so I could scream at him in my sleep. I tucked my hand under my pillow and closed my eyes.

Evan and I sat beside an in-ground pool. Our feet dangled in the water, which was pleasantly warm. We were alone, and when I looked around, I recognized the place. It was the apartment complex where some of his hockey buddies lived. He took me here for a party last year.

"I'm sorry I've been such a jerk." His shoulder bumped mine, and he entwined his left foot with my right. With a small pang, I remembered sitting this way before too.

He was a jerk. He hurt me. I stared ahead and watched the water ripple as our feet moved, the reflection of the parking lot lights dancing before us. Evan touched my chin and turned my face toward him. His eyes filled with sadness. "I can't lose you, Meara. I know it's my fault. I'll do anything to get you back."

"Why'd you break up with me in the first place?" The words were out before I could stop them. "You've been downright mean to me, Evan."

"I know, I know. Something's happening to me, Meara."

"What?"

When he said, "I don't know," I sighed and turned away. Another apology, an empty promise, and I'd give him back my heart only to have it trampled tomorrow. Once again, he turned me back with a gentle touch.

"I . . . I want to tell you." He paused. The look on his face was pure fear. What was Evan afraid of?

"You can tell me anything," I said.

He laughed bitterly. "Remember that later, okay?" He took my hand and held it in his lap between his own hands. His grip was gentle, but firm, almost as though he was afraid I would bolt. "So, those headaches I was having? I wasn't just having headaches; I was having horrible dreams, too. Death, destruction, screaming—I dreamed of you running from me, afraid of me. I couldn't make sense of it. I would never hurt you, you know that right?"

I could've told him there were more ways to hurt me than just physically. He'd certainly broken my heart. Instead, I said, "You were just dreaming, Evan."

"I know, but it seemed so real." He ran his hand through his hair, and the thick waves stuck out messily. "Anyway, the headaches got worse, and I passed out while diving."

"Evan, you never told me—"

"I know." He squeezed my hand. "That's when Ken called Dr. Tenuis. They took me to a clinic. A private clinic, not a hospital. My memories are hazy at best. They drugged me, ran some tests, and gave me medicine. When I left, the headaches were gone."

"That's good, right?" I tried to comfort him, but he was making me nervous. What kind of doctor drugged his patient without consent?

"At first, I thought so, but I started to have these crazy thoughts. I hear voices sometimes, Meara. They whisper to me, and I find myself listening, even when I don't want to. When I'm around you…" His voice trailed off.

"Yes?" I encouraged.

"When I'm around you," he started again, "I feel revulsion, anger, violence… and after, I hate myself. That's why I drove you away. You need to stay away from me. I'm going crazy, and I don't know why."

The timing with the doctor couldn't be a coincidence.

"What kind of clinic was it? Can you get a copy of your medical records? Maybe they did something to you that's causing this."

"Maybe." He didn't sound convinced. "I can try." He raised my hand to his lips and kissed it. I shivered at the electricity that traveled up my arm and down my spine. He smiled at my reaction. "You do still love me, don't you?"

"Of course I do." I swallowed the lump in my throat. "How can you even ask?"

"I love you, too," he whispered as he leaned closer. "Always."

He kissed me, soft at first, and then with growing intensity. I broke away, breathing fast. "Maybe we shouldn't do this."

"Why not? It's just a dream." He gave me a crooked smile. I melted when I saw his dimple. "We could swim, if you like."

"I don't have a suit…"

"It's me, Meara." He stood and pulled off his T-shirt. "I'll go first." He took off the rest of his clothes and dove in, his lean figure cutting the water gracefully. When he broke the surface, he shook the water from his head and laughed. "Come on, it's warm."

I hesitated another moment, and then gave in. One more memory with him, even a dream memory, was too tempting to resist. I stripped quickly and jumped, splashing him in the process.

"You did that on purpose!" Laughing, he reached for me when I surfaced. His hands went around my waist, pulling me back against his chest. My squeal of surprise turned to a soft moan when he lowered his head and kissed my neck. His lips traveled up, and he nuzzled my earlobe. "I've missed this," he murmured.

"I've missed you." I turned in his arms and wrapped mine around his neck. He kissed me, slow and deep. I was slipping, falling under his spell, when I realized something he'd said earlier. It was just a dream. It was a dream. How would he know that, unless...

I pulled back and looked up at him. "Evan?"

He cleared his throat. "Yes?"

"Are you dreaming?"

"If I am, don't wake me up."

That sounded like the Evan I knew and loved. He never missed an opportunity to use a cheesy line. He moved to kiss me again, but I placed my hands on his chest and held him back. "I'm serious. You said something earlier, 'It's just a dream.' What did you mean?"

Sighing, he placed his hands over mine. He lifted my left one and kissed my palm, causing my stomach to quiver. "We're dreaming, Meara, but we're dreaming together."

"How can you be sure?"

He shrugged. "I just am. Are you wearing the necklace again?"

Startled, I asked, "You knew I took it off?"

"I tried to call you." He frowned. "You didn't answer. I guessed that you took it off."

"I did. I'm not wearing it now—"

"Then, how?"

"I was holding it in my hand when I fell asleep," I said. I pulled my right hand free from his grasp and ran it along his collarbone. "You're not wearing yours either."

"Not in this dream," he said. "But I am wearing it."

Satisfied, I leaned in to kiss him, but this time he stopped me. "Wait. I need to tell you something before I forget or one of us wakes up.

I took the bottle and the wine glasses."

"You what?" It was the last thing I expected him to say.

"Before I fell asleep. I thought about what you said, and I found the glasses and the bottle. There's still a little in it. You can have it tested."

"You did that for me? You could've been caught." What would Ken do if he found out?

"Don't worry about me, but I don't want you coming back to the house. I'll hide them under the stairs by the pier. Come and get them tomorrow while we're out."

"Thank you," I said. "For believing me."

"Meara, I don't know what's going on. I don't like the person I'm becoming, and I'm scared." His voice cracked as he lowered his head to my shoulder. His body shook. "I'm so scared."

I wrapped my arms around him and held him tight. My tears mixed with his in the pool. I didn't know how to help him, but I would try. We needed answers, but right now, I needed to comfort and be comforted.

"We have tonight," I whispered in his ear. "Let's not waste it."

I smelled bacon. The savory fragrance beckoned to me before I opened my eyes.

"Wakey, wakey, sleepyhead."

Ula sat at the end of my bed in bell-bottom jeans and a green, smocked shirt. Her hair hung in braided pigtails, tame for once. I sat up against the headboard, and she slid the breakfast tray full of eggs, bacon, and orange juice toward me.

"What's the occasion?" I picked up a strip of bacon. Ula's cheeks turned rosy. She pulled on a stray thread on her pant hem, not meeting my eyes. "Ula?"

"I ran into Uncle Angus, and he sort of told me about Evan...

Don't be mad!"

"I'm not mad," I said. "I'm glad you're here."

"You are?" She brightened considerably.

"I am, and I'm not sure we are still broken up."

"What?" She wrinkled her brow in confusion.

I told her about the dream, Evan's fear that he was losing his mind, and the wine bottle. Of course, then I had to back up and tell her about dinner the night before. Her face grew redder and redder. I was going to tell her to breathe once I reached the end of my story. Luckily, she took a deep breath, and then, she exploded.

"You did *what*? Are you *insane*? You could've been killed. Do you have *any idea* what kind of stupid, ridiculous—?"

"I know, I know. I'm sorry. I'll never do it again." I spoke quickly, hoping to diffuse her anger. I didn't want my dad to find out this way. I needed to tell him myself.

"Well, okay then." She fanned her face, and it returned to a semblance of its normal pale, although her freckles stood out brighter than usual. "So the real question is—when are we going to retrieve that bottle?"

"We?"

"Of course, we. Who else are you going to take? You've already put Kieran in a precarious situation. One, he almost died for you. Two, if something had happened to you, my brother would've declared war on Kieran's clan."

"Oh. Um..."

"You had no idea what you were doing, did you?"

Her accusing tone made me angry. "How was I supposed to know that my boyfriend's host was going to poison us? Is that something I should just suspect now of everyone I don't know?" I pushed the tray to the side. I was no longer hungry. "Why do we have so many enemies anyway? What's wrong with being a Selkie?"

"Nothing's wrong with being a Selkie, and we don't have *so many* enemies," she said, emphasizing my words. "But the ones we have, well, they're pretty powerful."

"Why do they hate us?"

"I'd love to tell you, but it depends on which 'they' you're talking about. Most creatures who hate us also hate humans. They live to destroy, we live to protect, and so we mix like oil and water." She paused and looked at me. "You know, because they don't really mix."

"I get it, Ula."

"I used an analogy," she said proudly.

"Yes. Very well done." My tone was indulgent. If she heard my sarcasm, she ignored it.

"So, back to the bottle and glasses," she said. "When are we going to get them?"

"We need to go when the ship is out. Evan said that they head out to sea daily. They leave around nine and return by five."

"Are we going today?" Ula bounced a bit on the bed, sloshing orange juice onto the tray. I picked up the glass and drained it before she could spill any more.

"We should. The sooner we have them, the sooner we can get answers."

I didn't like the idea of taking her. My dad was going to be furious when he found out that I'd broken his rules not once, not twice, but several times, and here I was planning to break them again before I could confess to him. Better to ask for forgiveness later. Wasn't that how the saying went?

"Can you transport that far?" I asked.

Ula frowned. "I'm not sure. I've never tried. I usually swim to travel any long distance."

"I'll take us. I've been there enough." I wanted to tell her that it would be faster if I went myself, but that would hurt her feelings. She was already sensitive about her powers; I didn't need to rub it in.

"When?" she asked.

I glanced out the window. The sun was high in the sky. It was well after nine.

"Are you ready to go now?" I asked.

She grinned, more excited about this adventure than I was. "Okay."

I held her hands and pictured the pier so clearly that we arrived within seconds.

"Wow," Ula exclaimed. "You're fast."

"I've been here a few times."

The boat was gone. We were safe, for now. I quickly walked toward the stairs. He said he would hide the bottle at the base, so it had to be nearby. I stepped off the edge of the pier and crouched on the large boulder to look under the staircase. Sure enough, I caught the glimmer of glass. I reached in and pulled out the bottle first, handing it to Ula. I gave her a wine glass next, and then pulled out the last two for myself.

"Um... how are we getting back?" Ula asked. "Our hands are full."

"Wrap your arms around me," I said. "Like you're giving me a hug."

She stood close and placed her arms around me. I barely felt them. "A bear hug," I clarified.

"How do bears hug?" she asked.

"Tightly." I was trying not to lose patience, but with each second that passed, the risk increased that someone might see us.

"Oh!" She tightened her grip, and we disappeared.

We landed back in my room and grinned at each other.

"That's a rush!" Ula laughed. "Wish I was as good at transporting as you are."

A throat cleared, and we both jumped. My dad sat on the edge of my bed. I really needed to figure out how to keep Selkies out of my room. Between Ula, Kieran, and now my dad, this was getting ridiculous.

"Do you mind telling me where you've been?" Dad's voice was deceptively calm, but the tick in his cheek told me that he was angry.

"Dad!" I exclaimed. "You're back!"

He stood and crossed the room to me. "And so, apparently, are you. Why are you carrying wine and glasses? Were you having a party?"

"I can explain…" I glanced at Ula, but she just shrugged at me. Some help she was.

"Hand me your glasses, Meara," she said. "I'll take them to Angus."

"Angus?" My dad looked from Ula to me. "Does this have anything to do with Kieran?"

"You know?" Dad gave me a stern look. Damn, I was in trouble. I gave Ula the glasses. "Let me know what you find out."

"Of course." She nodded and left the room quickly.

Arms crossed, Dad tapped his foot impatiently. "Do you mind telling me what's going on?"

Where should I start? What did he know already? There was so much to tell him, though I deserved answers, too. "Can we go somewhere else to talk?" I asked. "I don't really feel like hanging out in my room."

"As you wish." Dad's hand wrapped around mine. A second later, we were in the study next to Angus' quarters. "Is this better?"

"Um, yeah."

It really wasn't. This close to Kieran, I wanted to check and see how he was feeling. Dad wouldn't understand, so I kept my mouth shut.

"So…" He sat in a chair and leaned back, gesturing for me to sit across from him. "What kind of trouble have you been up to?"

Although he was trying to appear calm, the edge of anger was there. That was fine, but I had a right to be angry, too. He brought me here and handed me off to his sister and Kieran. I barely saw him and had no idea what he was doing. I lost my mom, not my dad. Sometimes, it felt like I lost both.

"You first. What did you and Aunt Brigid discover?"

"I don't think you're in any position to make demands." He frowned at me. "What have you been doing while I was away?"

218

"If you'd been here, you wouldn't have to ask."

He hit the table and shouted, "Meara! Stop playing games! Tell me what's going on."

I jumped. I couldn't recall him ever yelling at me. Then again, Mom was there to play interference in the past. "Where would you like me to start?"

"Wherever you like, but tell me something." He sat back and took a deep breath. "Angus mentioned Kieran was poisoned yesterday. Seeing the bottle and goblets, I assume you were involved. Why don't you start there?"

"Did Angus say if Kieran's okay?" I hoped to check on him first thing this morning. My plans were altered by my two visitors.

Dad's expression softened with sympathy. "He's weak, but alert. He's still in Angus' room. You can see him when we're finished." He reached for my hand and squeezed it. "Tell me what happened, Meara."

I nodded and met his eyes. He might get angry, but he was right. He needed to know. Maybe he could even help with Evan's problem, if he was willing. He and Evan didn't always get along so well, especially last year when I was trying to figure out what I was. Evan made it clear that my dad was not helping me enough. "Last night we attended a dinner party. Kieran was poisoned by the man funding Evan's internship. His name is Ken. I don't know anything else about him."

I said it all quickly, knowing what was coming next.

"You left the island when I strictly forbade it?"

I pointed at him, and my finger shook. "You left. You're always gone. The rest of us are just supposed to sit here like beached whales. I was going crazy. I love Evan, and I have a right to see him."

"You have a right? How about you have a responsibility! You have a responsibility to keep yourself and our clan safe. Your recklessness could've gotten Kieran killed." He stared hard at me, his mouth a line of disappointment. "The glasses and bottle. You went back this morning with Ula, didn't you?"

"I had to." Before he could argue, I told him about Evan and the voices. "Evan admitted it to me in my dream last night. He started hearing them after he saw a doctor friend of Ken's. Dr. Tenoo, I think he said."

"You and Evan shared a dream with those necklaces?" When I nodded, he stood and paced. For a few seconds, he was lost in thought, and then he asked, "Besides the voices, what else has Evan noticed?"

"He said that when he's around me, he feels repulsed." I had a hard time saying it aloud. "He's been mean to me. He broke up with me yesterday."

"Strange," he murmured. "What about you? Have you noticed anything else unusual about him?"

I remembered the night I transported to his room after he returned from the clinic. I didn't want to admit I'd left the island numerous times, but this seemed like an important detail. "One time, I saw his eyes glow blue."

Dad stopped pacing. "Describe."

"They glowed turquoise in the dark. When the lights came on, they looked normal. I asked him to turn the lights off again, and the glowing was gone."

My dad resumed pacing, muttering under his breath. Twice he went to the bookshelf, pulled down a book, flipped through the pages, and put it back. Finally, he turned to me. "You can't leave the island, Meara. It's critical now more than before. Something is happening. The Icelandia clan lost six guards in the last moon cycle. The bodies were found in the same condition as ours."

"Could it be a coincidence?"

"No. We are under attack." While my heart leapt in fear, his face was hard and proud. For the first time, I saw him as the other Selkies must. He was a warrior, a leader, and a protector.

"Who's attacking us?"

"I don't know for sure. You've given me some ideas." His eyes lowered to my collar. "Are you wearing your necklace?"

"No. I wasn't wearing it last night either. I was holding it."

"The connection between you and Evan is strong. I know you love him and want to help him, but you shouldn't wear it anymore."

"Why? What do you know?"

"I don't know anything yet. I only have theories. It's too early to share. I need to go and research the area with Brigid. Angus told us about a wide area of destruction not far from here. You wouldn't know anything about that, would you?"

Once again, he gave me a hard look. I stared back evenly and didn't say anything. If he wasn't going to confide in me, I was done confessing to him.

"Can I come with you?" I asked instead.

"Absolutely not. Meara, you are not to set one fin in the water."

"That's not fair. You and Aunt Brigid are constantly going in it."

He came over and sat next to me, his hand on my shoulder. "And we are much older and more experienced than you. I know you want to help. The best thing you can do right now is stay here with Kieran and Ula so I know that you're safe."

"I'm not a little girl anymore."

"You'll always be my little girl, and I can't lose you now that I've found you." His voice quavered. I was stunned to see his eyes were full of tears. "Please, Meara."

"Geez, Dad. Okay." I couldn't stay angry with him when he obviously loved me enough to cry. He wanted to keep me safe. This time, I would do what he asked. If he thought I'd stop looking for answers, though, he was wrong. "When you confirm your theory, I want you to tell me. If I'm making you a promise, you must promise me, too."

"I promise I will tell you."

"And Evan. If you know how to help him?"

"Of course." He stood and pulled me up into a hug. "We're in this together from now on, okay?"

I hugged him tight and prayed he meant it. Now it was my turn to cry. I hadn't realized how much I missed my father. "I love you, Dad."

"I love you, too." He kissed the top of my head and rested his cheek there. His whiskers tickled and made me laugh.

"You need to shave," I said.

"I know it. I could use a shower, too." He sighed and kissed my head one more time before straightening up. "Now, go and see Kieran."

"Thanks, Dad."

I went next door and knocked on Angus' door. Kieran called out, "Come in!" and my pulse quickened at the sound of his voice. I opened the door and found him sitting on the couch in Nike track pants and a T-shirt. His bare feet were on the coffee table. He grinned when he saw me. "How's my partner in crime?"

"I'm fine." I crossed the room and sat next to him. "I should be asking how you're doing."

"Right as rain," he said, and then frowned. "I never understood that expression."

"You scared me last night," I said quietly. "I'm sorry for putting you in danger."

"You don't have to apologize." He took my hand and ran his thumb over the back of it. How could I welcome his touch and love Evan at the same time? "You didn't know it was poisoned."

"You warned me. You drank it anyway to give me time to escape." I swallowed painfully and looked down at our joined hands. "You saved my life."

"It wouldn't have killed you, Meara." His fingers lightly touched my chin and lifted it until our eyes met. It was a gesture uncomfortably similar to Evan's from the night before. Guilt made my cheeks burn. "You're dramatic today. What's going on?"

"You didn't know that at the time. You would've died for me. I was worried you were going to die." The tears flowed again.

Kieran frowned as he watched me cry. He gently wiped my

cheeks. "Hey... it's okay. I'm not dead, Meara. I'm right here." Holding me close, he stroked his hand gently through my hair and down my back. I tried to pull myself together, but all I could think about was how good his arms felt and how wonderful he smelled. He always smelled like a spring rain, clean and fresh. His arms tightened around me, and his fingers entwined in my hair. I realized that I wanted him to kiss me. I wanted to feel his lips on mine. I lifted my face, and that was all it took. He captured my mouth with his. I kissed him back in a rush of heat. He saved my life and almost died for me. He hadn't said it, but I knew he loved me. Did I love him, too?

I lost track of time. He maneuvered our bodies so that we stretched out on the couch. I could've kissed him forever, but a loud cough had us breaking apart and staring at each other in shock.

"You might want to find a more private spot for that kind of activity. You're going to give your old uncle a heart attack." Angus chuckled at his joke and settled into his recliner. "The look on your faces was priceless. I take it you're feeling better, Kieran?"

"Yes, sir. Thank you." Kieran tugged at the hem of his shirt before sitting up and moving to the far end of the couch. "How was the meeting?"

"Not much was discussed. Brigid and David left to check out those coordinates you gave me. We're regrouping this evening when they get back. You're welcome to join us, if you're free."

I knew that my uncle was referring to Kieran only and not me. I wouldn't be allowed to attend the elders' meeting.

"I'll be there."

"Did Ula give you the bottle and glasses?" I asked my uncle.

Kieran gave me a sharp look. "You went back?"

"Evan hid them near the pier for me. I didn't go back to the house."

"You spoke to the boy again last night?" Uncle Angus asked in surprised voice.

"Again?" Kieran looked confused.

223

"Yes," I said, not wanting to explain the break up or the dream.

Uncle Angus seemed to sense my predicament. He didn't push for details. "She gave them to me. They all contained the poison."

My stomach quivered. "Evan told me that he and Ken each had two glasses."

My uncle looked shocked. "Impossible. They'd be dead."

"Can humans build up a tolerance?" Kieran asked.

"Not that I've heard of," Angus answered. "Even a small dose of puffer venom is fatal."

"Then how could humans survive it?" I asked.

"Unless they're not human," Kieran said slowly. "How well do you know Evan, Meara?"

"I dated him for over a year," I said. "I know his mother and his father. They're both human, I swear it."

Was it possible that Evan wasn't human? If either Lydia or Darren were not his biological parents, he didn't know. I was sure of it. If he wasn't human, what was he?

Uncle Angus stroked his beard, staring at the television. "Perhaps they are, but something is amiss. I'll discuss it with your father."

My uncle gave us a pointed look. Clearly, he had enough of our company for one day. Kieran stood and stretched, offering me his hand. "Ready to go, Meara?"

I let him pull me up, then walked over and kissed my uncle's cheek. "Thank you for taking care of Kieran, Uncle Angus."

"Think nothing of it, my girl." He beamed at me and pulled me into a hug, whispering in my ear, "I'm glad to see you're feeling better, too." My cheeks burned, and he laughed again. Louder, he said, "Off with you two."

Following Kieran into the hall, guilt hit me full force. What business did I have making out with him when I didn't know where Evan and I stood? We broke up, but then we shared that dream... although he didn't ask me to go out with him again. In fact, he never really mentioned anything about our relationship at all.

Kieran closed Angus' door behind us. "You're lost in thought again. Are you okay?"

"I think so." My voice was small and made him frown.

"Are you worried about Evan?"

"Yes."

"Don't worry, we'll figure it out." He reached for my hand.

"Easy for you to say." No matter what was happening to Evan, I should be there for him. He was there for me last year. I certainly shouldn't have these feelings for someone else. Guilt heated my face. We walked in silence down the hall until Kieran cleared his throat.

"Should I apologize for earlier?" he asked slowly. I knew he meant kissing me on Angus' couch, and my heart raced at the mention of it.

"No. I had just as much to do with it as you did."

"Do you regret what happened?" He sounded worried. When I shook my head, he sighed in relief. "Good."

He stepped forward to kiss me again. I stopped him with a hand on his chest. "I don't regret it, and I want to kiss you, but I still love Evan, too."

"I know," he said. "Give me a chance to change that."

I touched his cheek and smiled sadly. "I'm confused. I need time."

"I understand." He hugged me. "Want to go for a walk? I need some fresh air."

"Sure."

Taking my hand, he transported us to the far end of the island. Shadowed by the cliffs, the ground was rocky, spotted with mossy, green patches. Instead of walking, Kieran sat on a large, flat boulder and motioned for me to sit next to him. We sat in silence for a while, but curiosity got the better of me.

"What do you make of everything that's going on?"

Kieran shrugged. "I don't think Ken's human. I don't think Evan is either."

"What about his parents?"

"What about them? Unless you do a blood test, you won't know for certain that, biologically, they're related. I know it's messed up, but it's the only thing that makes sense." He shifted on the rock until he was facing me. "If they were human, the poison would've killed them. Did Evan get sick?"

"Um… I don't think so."

"What happened yesterday while I unconscious? I know you don't want to tell me, but I saw the look Angus gave you. You can tell me. I'm your friend. I want to help."

"You want to be more than friends, too."

"I do, but that doesn't change this. I'm here for you." He took my hands in his. "Tell me or I can't help you."

I told him about the break up and my dream. When I finished, he looked worried. "Are you wearing the necklace?"

"My dad asked me the same thing. No, it's on my nightstand. Last night, I wasn't even wearing it. I was holding it."

"Will you let me keep it for you?" When I just stared at him, he added, "Please? I think you'll be tempted to use it. I'm not sure it's safe. If you want to reach Evan, come see me. I promise I'll let you, but I want to be there."

"Do you think he'd hurt me?"

He considered before saying, "Not intentionally."

I worried about that. Evan admitted that he lost control when the voices spoke to him. He admitted that he felt hatred toward me. That scared me more than anything did.

"I'll give it to you," I said. "Come back with me."

We transported to my room. I crossed to the nightstand and picked up the necklace. Sadness overwhelmed me. Why did it feel like I was saying goodbye to Evan? Tears slid down my face as I placed the necklace in Kieran's outstretched palm.

"Anytime, Meara. Just let me know, okay?" He slid the necklace into his pocket, and then hugged me. Wrapped in his arms, I was comforted and buzzing with electricity at the same time. Why was it so easy to be ruled by my heart? Where was my head in all of this?

"Do you want me to stop by after the meeting?"

"You have to ask?" I sniffed and wiped my eyes before poking him playfully in the stomach to lighten the mood. "I want to know everything."

"Okay." He kissed my nose. "Get some sleep. It sounds like you didn't get much last night."

With a grimace, he was gone.

Chapter 29

When Meara and Kieran disappeared in the middle of the dinner, Ken was furious. "Where did they go?" he demanded at breakfast.

"I have no idea." Evan couldn't tell Ken about Meara's accusation that Kieran was poisoned. First, Evan and Ken both drank several glasses of the same wine after they left. The only impact it had on him was a slight hangover. Second, he was embarrassed and confused. He broke up with her, but then they shared that dream. Now he wasn't sure who was right. He tried to sort through his thoughts. Ken's anger clouded the air and made it impossible to think about anything.

Ted was absent. Evan didn't know where he was, but apparently, Ken wasn't bothered. They spent most of the meal eating in silence. When the food and coffee were gone, they headed down to the docks together. Ted was already on the boat and ready to go.

Evan forced himself not to glance at the spot under the stairs were he hid the bottle and glasses. He wondered if Meara already picked them up. Hopefully, they'd give her whatever information she needed. He wished they could go back to when things were simpler between them, knowing that he was the one to create the rift. He doubted if that was even possible. The best thing he could give her right now was space while he sorted out whatever was going on with him.

The motor roaring to life brought Evan out of his reminiscing. It was time to work. He joined Ken at the wheel as he requested. He showed Evan how to steer the ship, and now he expected Evan to copilot their expeditions.

"Sorry... did you say something?" Evan asked. Ken had been muttering and talking under his breath for the past twenty minutes. When he paused and stared at him, Evan assumed he was waiting for a response to a question he didn't hear.

"What? Nothing, nothing. I wasn't talking to you." Ken patted his shoulder absentmindedly, although the pressure made Evan wince. "Just thinking, my boy."

They anchored at their usual coordinates. Evan prepared to leave the cabin and go suit up for the dive. Ken stopped him.

"Ted's going down alone today, Evan. I need your assistance here." Ken squeezed his shoulder and stepped past him into the doorway. "Wait for me. I'll just see Ted out."

While Evan waited, he watched Ken and Ted talking at the bow. He couldn't make out Ken's words, but he was clearly agitated. He waved his arms and raised his voice at Ted. In return, the other man cowered under the wrath. From what Evan knew, the project was successful so far. What was Ken upset about?

"Everything okay?" Evan asked when Ken returned.

"Fine." The man's face was unreadable. "It's the last week of our project, Evan. I have a lot of money invested in this research. I needed to make sure Ted understood the importance."

"Isn't everything going well?"

"It is," Ken admitted. "This is also the most critical part. It's no time to slack off."

The professor would never slack off. The man was a workaholic. It surprised Evan that Ken did not realize this. Weren't they supposed to be longtime friends and colleagues? Evan figured it out within a few weeks of school at King's College. It didn't take a rocket scientist to notice that the professor was in his office, or his lab, at least twelve hours out of every day.

Later that night, Evan wondered why Ken made him stay behind on the ship. He helped label plant and animal specimens. It was nothing that Ken couldn't have completed on his own. In fact, they were done an hour before Ted returned. He spent the extra time learning more about the ship's controls. Ken seemed adamant that he learn how to control it. He didn't know why, since he would be leaving soon anyway.

The evening hours stretched without Meara. He hoped she was okay. He missed her. Would she contact him once she had the results back on the wine? What could he possibly do with that information if she did? Accuse his host of poisoning his guests?

The next few days passed in a tidal wave of emotions, all of them rolling off Ken. His temper got the best of him, and meals were no longer a pleasant affair. He sulked and ordered the staff around, complaining loudly about their service and the quality of food. Evan thought the food tasted amazing, but he didn't say anything. He tried to be as quiet as possible. His mission was to eat and get the hell out of there.

The professor was smart. Most of the time, he gave a passable excuse and didn't join them. Evan couldn't do it. He felt obligated to visit with their host since room and board were free.

The one thing Ken's erratic behavior and stormy moods reinforced was that Evan made the right choice. Meara wasn't safe with him. He wasn't sure he was even safe anymore. Ken was acting stranger and stranger. While Ken raged, anger tore through Evan like a living thing, filling his head with violent thoughts. The blackness intrigued and fascinated him, but mostly left him scared. Where were these thoughts coming from and why couldn't he control them?

Evan tried to talk to Ted about Ken's behavior. The professor didn't know any more than Evan did. His theory was that Ken was anxious about completing the project before the two of them left. *Some way to motivate your employees*, Evan thought.

Wednesday evening, Evan entered the room and sighed at the two place settings—just him and Ken again. *A few more days, and I'll be on my way home*, he reminded himself.

"Good evening, Evan." Ken smiled as he strolled into the room. He made a ceremony out of unfolding his napkin and placing it across his lap as he sat. Snapping for Stonewall to fill his glass, he didn't even acknowledge that he was already by his side with a bottle of Chablis. He was merely waiting for Ken to sit back so he could pour. Stonewall rolled his eyes, which surprised Evan. He typically did not let emotions show. Ken's behavior must be getting to him, too.

Ken gulped down half the liquid in his glass before fixing Evan with a calculated look. Frosty cold replaced the warmth his expression held moments earlier. "Any word from the girl?"

Annoyance flared with Ken's refusal to use Meara's name, but Evan answered, "No, I haven't heard from her."

"You think she'd at least apologize for her behavior." Ken scoffed. "Who leaves a dinner party in the middle of dinner? No gratitude to the host and no apology."

"I can't explain it. As I told you, I only spoke with her briefly afterwards, and it was to break up with her."

"You're through with the girl then? No lingering emotions?"

"None," Evan lied. "I planned to break up with her anyway. Her actions simply sped the decision."

"And you plan to return to Halifax with Ted?" Ken focused on cutting the steak placed before him, but Evan was no fool. Although he acted nonchalant, Ken desperately wanted to know his answer.

"I do," Evan said. "I have two years of college left, sir. It's important that I finish."

"Of course, of course." Ken finished his wine and motioned to Stonewall, who stood discreetly in the corner, for a refill. "I hadn't meant to imply otherwise. I could use an apprentice, however, and you do seem to have the ideal skill set."

"What exactly is it that you do, Ken?" Evan asked before he lost his nerve. He wondered about that since he arrived here, but it seemed impolite to ask. It didn't seem rude now, or maybe, with so little time left here, he didn't care anymore.

"I'm an investor, Evan, and a collector. As you can see, I prefer to surround myself with beauty, quality, and knowledge. Priceless items are my specialty."

Evan considered the various collections of artwork displayed throughout the house. "You collect classic paintings?"

"Yes, among other things."

Ken was being purposefully vague. *Why?* Evan wondered. It didn't add up. "Why are you interested in the mantle plume?"

"It intrigues me. You intrigue me, Evan." Cobalt blue flickered through Ken's eyes before they dulled to their usual gray. He smiled widely. "Am I making you uncomfortable? It's not my intent."

Evan tried to laugh, but it sounded forced. "Uh... no. I'm fine." He turned his attention to his meal, hoping that Ken would change subjects. A chill settled in him, and it wasn't the room temperature. There was something off about the man before him. On the other hand, Professor Nolan knew Ken for years and worked with him on other projects. He wouldn't have brought Evan here if he thought Ken was dangerous, would he?

"I won't hurt you," Ken said softly. "You've become like a son to me, Evan. I'd like the opportunity to groom you in the family business."

"Collecting and investing?" Evan asked, having no idea what that actually meant.

"Exactly." Ken nodded with satisfaction. "You're a quick study. Please at least consider it."

"Okay," Evan agreed. Why would an investor want a marine biology student for an intern? Evan wasn't interested in art, but he would agree to almost anything to end this dinner. Luckily, Ken seemed content to finish the rest of the meal in silence.

Placing his napkin next to his empty plate, Evan stood. "Have a good evening."

"You, too, my boy, you too. I'll see you in the morning."

Evan stepped into the hall and practically ran into Ted. He opened his mouth to speak, but Ted silenced him with a quick shake of his head. He motioned for Evan to follow him. Ted led him through the kitchen and out of the house through a servant's door.

"Where are we going?" Evan asked. Ted didn't answer as they walked around the house. "Why didn't we just go out the front door?"

"Too obvious." Ted finally spoke, barely above a whisper. "I didn't want to be seen leaving together."

"Why?"

The hairs rose on the back of Evan's neck. Why was everyone acting so strange? A week ago, he thought he was losing his mind. Now, he thought they all might be. The weirdness factor had increased since the dinner party. Strange was becoming the norm.

"Let's go for a drive." Ted opened the driver's side door and waited for Evan. "Coming?"

"Okay." Evan got in and hoped he was making the right decision. Was Ted the safer of the two? Who was less crazy?

Ted buckled his seatbelt and backed out of the driveway. He flicked on the headlights once they were a safe distance from the house.

"What's going on, Professor?"

Ted's gaze flickered to Evan before turning back to the road. He pushed his glasses up on his nose, a nervous habit Evan noticed months ago.

"Why the spy-like maneuvers?" Evan asked. "Are we in trouble?"

"How are you feeling, Evan? How are the headaches?"

"Fine," Evan said cautiously. Ted never asked or cared about his health before. "Never felt better."

"Really? Any side effects? Strange thoughts? Voices?"

A lump formed in Evan's throat. He tried to control the tremor in his voice. "How'd you know?"

"Guessed, really. I wondered about that. Can you tell me more?"

The professor looked at him with fascination, the way he studied his specimens under a microscope. What was this about?

"Have you been experimenting on me?" A chill ran down Evan's spine when Ted's eyes widened. He guessed correctly. "What did you do?"

"I did nothing. Dr. Tenuis did the work, of course. He treated you. You're feeling better, so no harm done." Ted smiled at him in a reassuring way. Evan wasn't reassured.

"How did you know about the voices?"

"I hear them, too, Evan." Ted's voice changed to a deeper, gravely baritone. He guided the car to the side of the road and stopped, turning to face Evan. Popping and stretching noises filled the car. The sound made Evan's hair stand on end. Headlights from a passing car lit up the interior. Evan gasped. Ted's fingers lengthened on the steering wheel. Glancing from Ted's fingers to his face, Evan jerked back. The man sitting next to him wore the professor's clothes, but that was the only resemblance. His skin was the deep blue of berries, and his eyes lit from within—a bright turquoise blue.

"Don't be afraid." The professor spoke again in that strange, scratchy voice. Evan noticed how pointy his teeth were as he spoke. He remembered seeing a similar set on the doctor. At the time, he blamed it on the drugs. He couldn't do that now. He was completely sober.

"What are you?" Evan whispered. He slowly moved his hand toward the car door. Could he open it and get out before the professor noticed?

"The same thing you are," Ted said.

"No." Evan shook his head and pressed against the door. "No. I don't believe you."

Before Evan could flee, the professor grabbed his wrist. "There's nowhere for you to go, Evan." With his free hand, he reached up and lowered the car visor, opening the vanity mirror. "Look."

Evan stared in the mirror. His body tingled with a million pins and needles. His muscles tightened and pulled, rearranging his features.

He screamed in pain and disbelief at the monster staring back at him. His fingers rose to touch his face, and he screamed again. His skin was blue and his fingers elongated, the nails pointy and sharp.

"You are one of us, Evan, whether you like it or not."

"Why did you bring me here to tell me this? What have you done to me?"

"Get a grip on yourself," Ted snapped, flipping the visor closed. "I brought you here because I thought it was time you knew. Ken didn't want to tell you yet."

"Ken is like this?" Evan's voice quavered while he tried to control it. What kind of monster had they turned him into?

"Yes. There are more of us, too."

"Dr. Tenuis?"

"Yes."

"He made me a monster!" Evan yelled.

Ted shook him. "He didn't, Evan. None of us did. We saved you. Your body was fighting the change. If we hadn't stepped in, you would've died."

"I don't understand. I'm human. Why would I change?"

"Your fa—"

A blue light exploded in front of the car, hitting them with a shock of paralyzing cold. The last thing Evan heard was Ken shouting, "I told you not to tell him!"

Chapter 30

My aunt stalked in circles around me. Dressed in head-to-toe leather, she looked like an assassin. "I'm impressed, niece. Your skills have grown."

"Thank you, Aunt Brigid." I bent and tried to catch my breath. We'd been training for hours. Sweat rolled off my body, and she didn't even look winded. What was it like to have that kind of power?

You'll have it too one day, she spoke in my head before I raised my shield and blocked her. She laughed. "Haven't been shielding much, have you?"

"Not really," I admitted.

"You and Kieran have grown close. He's a powerful ally."

"He's a good friend," I retorted without thinking.

"Friend." Her lips twisted as if the words left a bad taste in her mouth. "Emotions make you soft."

"Really?" I went to a nearby rock and sat. I was tired, and it seemed, at least temporarily, she was giving me a break. "Don't you care for the people of Ronac? Your family?"

"I would die for them," she spat. "Yet, I never let emotions get in my way."

"Never? There was never anyone special for you, Aunt Brigid?" It was bold to ask. Curiosity won. I knew so little about her.

"Hmpf." She turned and started picking up her gear, but not before I noticed the sadness that passed through her eyes. There had been someone in her life. Someone she loved.

"Can you tell me?" I coaxed. "Please?"

Though her back was to me, I saw her shoulders sag. "Why do you want to know?"

"I'd like to know you better," I said. "In many ways, you're a stranger to me."

"I prefer to keep my distance." She straightened. I thought she was going to walk away. She surprised me by joining me on the rock. "I was young." Her eyes flicked to me, assessing. "Not as young as you are, but young by Selkie standards. My father let me accompany my mother to her former clan. She liked to visit on occasion. We were to stay for one moon cycle."

"Like Uncle Ren's family?"

"Exactly. It's the way of Selkies. We travel by moon. Anyway..." Her eyebrows rose while she waited to see if I'd interrupt. I smiled sweetly at her, and her lips twitched. "We weren't the only visitors. My uncle Fiero came from the Aleutian Islands. He ruled there after he married my aunt Catherine. They brought several of their guard with them. Amongst them was Talus." Her eyes grew soft as she remembered. Her lips turned up slightly, and she looked... she looked pretty. "He was the head of my uncle's guard, fierce and strong. He ignored me at first, but I'm not easily ignored." She smirked at me. "Once I got him talking, it didn't take long for us to fall in love. He was amazing. Handsome. Strong."

I tried to imagine my aunt, who was always poised and distant, as young and flirty. No image came to mind. To me, she was the Brigid before me, beautiful, but cold. "Did you break up at the end of the moon cycle when you had to go back home?"

"What? No, of course not." Some of her cool exterior returned. She sat taller and tugged her leather jacket straight. "By the end of that moon cycle, we were promised. My parents approved of the union. I was to join him at the end of the next moon cycle on his island." She stood and crossed to her gear. Picking up her bag, she stared at me. Her eyes filled with tears, which she brushed away impatiently. "It was not meant to be. Their clan was attacked. Only a handful survived. Talus was not among them."

I gasped. "Who attacked them?"

"Water demons. We could tell by the stench." She blinked, and her expression hardened. "I learned a tough lesson. Love is a weakness I cannot afford." Hiding once again behind a cool mask of indifference, she gave me a curt nod. "Good day to you, niece."

After she vanished, the sadness lingered. My aunt lost much more than her love. She lost her hope, her soul. My father said we were under attack. There would be casualties. I would lose friends, people I loved. Would I lose myself like my aunt or was I stronger than that?

No, I would be stronger. Without love, without hope, what was there worth living for? I would be strong enough to protect those I loved. I had to be stronger. I conjured my dagger. The cold metal grew warm in my hand and comforted me. It was time for my next training session.

Angus lunged forward. I anticipated his move, spun, and locked his sword arm. He cursed and raised his other arm in surrender, so I released him.

"You're better with that thing than my mother ever was." He collapsed in his chair and pointed his sword at my dagger. "I'm not sure there is much else I can teach you."

"That's it?" I sank into the couch. The dagger was an extension of my arm now, and I parried with it easily. Yet, if our enemies were plotting to attack, it didn't feel like enough. "Is anyone else good with weapons?"

"Your father." Angus considered. "And Ren. Your uncle Ren's a master with a club."

I wasn't sure that my uncle's club handling would help me much with a dagger. "What does Dad have?"

"A sword. Similar to my own. Your great-great-great-grandfather made them both." Angus sword was finely crafted, the engraved blade elegant and deadly.

"Do you think he could teach me anything new?"

"Ask him," Angus urged. "It's about time that boy did something, leaving you to fend by yourself, not telling you what's at stake."

"What *is* at stake?" I leaned closer to my uncle. He mentioned it, so maybe he was willing to talk. Kieran didn't share much after their meeting the other night. He seemed as frustrated as I did about what we were facing, and he had been very tired. The poison was still leaving his system. After a few minutes, I sent him to his room to recover. I asked my uncle again, "What kind of battle are we preparing for?"

"I wish I knew." Angus shook his head sadly. "Your dad and aunt are speculating. So far, nothing seems to fit with our usual enemies."

"Which are?" I prompted, impatient. Was anyone going to tell me anything?

"Eh. A kelpie or Mer. They travel alone. Our guard can typically take them down without a problem. Few of our enemies work in unison. Water demons and the Blue Men are about the only ones I can think of."

Water demons or Blue Men, both scared me. "Dad told me that the Blue Men killed my grandparents, and Aunt Brigid said water demons killed Talus."

Bushy, white eyebrows rising, Angus sat up. "She told you about that?"

I nodded. "It's true, then?"

"Seems likely," Angus admitted. "And they very well could be behind these attacks."

"What do they want?" I asked. "Can we defeat them?"

"I don't know on either account." My uncle's voice sounded heavy. "They are powerful enemies. Sometimes, I think they know more about us than we do about them."

His words chilled me. Were we that vulnerable? Were they that powerful? There had to be a way to stop them. Nothing was invincible. I would have to figure it out, before it was too late.

I was tired when I left my uncle's room. Mental, physical, and emotional exhaustion hit me on all angles, which explains why I sighed heavily when my father called my name before I reached the staircase.

"Meara, do you have a moment?"

He stood in his doorway, dressed much like the first night I met him, faded blue jeans and a white dress shirt with loosely rolled sleeves. His hair was mussed, his feet bare. He looked as tired as I felt.

"Sure, Dad. What's up?"

He held the door as I walked past him. I plopped on his couch and realized Angus' was much more comfortable.

"Can I get you something? Milk? Soda?"

"Do you have anything stronger?" If we were gearing up for a major battle, I think I deserved a real drink.

He laughed and conjured two glasses. Handing me one, he gently clinked his against mine. "Here's to us."

"To us," I agreed and took a sip. The warmth slid down my throat and left the lingering taste of melted butterscotch.

"Butterscotch schnapps." He stared at his glass wistfully. "Your mother liked it."

"It's good." I sipped some more, enjoying the gentle heat. "You wanted to talk to me?"

He sat next to me and placed his drink on the coffee table. "I haven't been a very good father."

It was so unexpected. I didn't know what to say, so I said the first thing that came to mind, "What makes you say that?"

"I haven't been here for you. I don't know what to tell you and what to shelter you from. I wish your mom were still here. She'd know what to do."

"You're doing okay, Dad, but I'm not a young child. I can handle a little truth." I thought about what I knew so far about our enemies and shivered. "Or a lot of truth. I'm stronger than you think."

"I know you're strong. If I doubted it, I only have to listen to Kieran and Brigid sing your praises." He continued while I stared at him, "Were you coming from Angus' room?"

"Yes, he's been training me."

"Training you? On what?"

I finished the drink and set my glass next to his. My head buzzed pleasantly, and I grinned at him as I held out my hand and produced the knife. "Weaponry."

"His mother's dagger." My dad looked from the knife to me. "He's teaching you to use it?"

"I know how to use it," I said proudly. "Tonight, he told me that our lessons are done. He's taught me all that he can."

Dad gestured for the knife. "May I?"

I handed it to him and watched him turn it over in his hand. "It's a formidable weapon. I saw her use it in battle just once."

"Did she survive?"

"She saved my life." He handed me back the knife. "I'm impressed, Meara. Perhaps tomorrow you can show me what you know?"

"I'd like that. Do you think you might be able to teach me more?"

"I can try." Before I could protest, he ruffled my hair. "Let me see what you know first, and then I can judge how much more I can show you."

I picked up his glass and finished off its contents. He clucked his tongue, but he didn't say anything. I gave him a sticky kiss on his cheek before standing up. "Hoping it will help me sleep tonight," I mumbled.

He stood and walked me to the door, pulling me into a tight hug.

"We'll figure it out, Meara. I won't let anything happen to you."

"I know, Dad." I pulled back and looked into his eyes. "But you can't shelter me, either. This is my family, too. My people. You have to let me help."

He started to protest, and then shook his head. "You're right, Meara. Get a good night's rest. Tomorrow, you can show me what you've learned."

I walked down the hall, slightly unsteady on my feet. My head swam in a pleasant way, and I hummed a little under my breath. My cares, for the time being, took a backseat to the lovely buzzing. I stepped into the semi-darkness of the stairwell and heard my dad close his door softly behind me.

The only thought on my mind was crawling into my soft bed and falling asleep. I couldn't remember the last time I'd slept uninterrupted through the night. My eyelids drooped heavily just thinking about my fluffy pillows and warm blankets. I reached my door and pushed it open, the torchlight from the hall illuminating the dark room. I frowned at the lump on my bed. Someone was already in it, stretched across it, and from the looks of things, quite comfortable. Kieran.

I cleared my throat. He didn't budge. I poked him lightly in his shoulder. Nothing. I called his name. Still no answer. I placed my hand on his forehead. It was cool. At least he wasn't sick, although he was apparently a deep sleeper. A monsoon could tear through and he wouldn't notice. With a sigh, I lay down next to him. I needed sleep, and it would take too much effort to move him. Plus, if I did manage to wake him, he'd probably want to talk. Or something else. Something I wasn't prepared to deal with at the moment.

I crawled under the covers. Heat radiated off his body and relaxed mine. Within moments, I was asleep.

"Morning."

I woke to a muscular arm around my waist and a warm, wet kiss on my ear. It was disorienting. I jumped out of bed, and then shrieked when my feet hit the cold, stone floor.

"Kieran! What are you doing here?"

He gave me puppy dog eyes. "I couldn't sleep. I wanted to talk to you, and you weren't here. I fell asleep waiting for you. Why didn't you wake me?"

"I tried. You sleep like the dead."

"That's not very nice." He lifted the covers and patted the spot next to him on the bed. "Why don't you get off that cold floor and come back where it's warm?"

"You promise not to try anything?" I asked. He grinned. "Kieran—"

"I promise. Jeez, you're stubborn." He jumped when I crawled back in next to him and brushed his shin with my foot. "And your feet are like ice. Ever hear of slippers, woman?"

"What did you want to talk about?" I leaned back against the headboard and smoothed the covers over my legs. Kieran lay on his side, looking comfortable on my pillow and cuter than anyone should when first waking up.

"I was thinking about Evan."

"That's an interesting twist."

"Shut up, Meara." His smirk softened his words. "What do you know about this Ken or the professor?"

"Not much. Only what Evan told me, and when we talked, we didn't really talk about his work." I looked down at Kieran. He was staring off with a frown on his face.

"What are you thinking?"

He met my eyes with an intense look. "You told David that you saw Evan's eyes glow. You've seen my eyes glow. Were they like that?"

I shook my head. "They were brighter, like they were lit from within. The color was an icy turquoise." I shivered. "It was eerie."

"Did you notice anything else?"

"He was sweaty, feverish. It took a while to wake him." The shock... that was when he woke. "I tried to bring his fever down, heal him like Dad healed Mom."

"Meara! That's dangerous magic."

"It didn't work," I said. "At first, I thought it was working. I could feel it, but then, something pushed my magic back at me, like an electrical shock."

"Did it hurt?"

"It stung, like a burn." He reached for my hand, but I pulled it back. "There's no mark. The pain is gone."

"Fair enough." Kieran sat up and faced me. "If he were fully human, he couldn't have resisted your magic."

"How do you know that's what he did?"

"Because I've felt something similar. It's a defense mechanism."

Cold seeped into my chest. I didn't want to hear that Evan was not human. What if he was part of something that hated us? He said he still loved me, but would it endure?

"I'm telling the truth. Do you want me to show you?" He obviously mistook my silence for disbelief.

"No thanks. I'm not up for shock therapy today. I believe you." I slipped out of bed again and stood up. This time, I visualized shoes. Kieran sat back and watched me. "Well, you're welcome to stay as long as you like, but I need to get going."

He frowned. "Where are you off to? Don't we have a lesson this morning?"

"Not today," I sang. "My dad's giving me my lesson today."

"Really? On what?"

I produced my dagger and waved it in front of him. "Paring."

"Where'd you get that?" Kieran reached for it, but I jumped back. "Angus gave it to me. It belonged to his mother."

"Be careful with it." His eyes followed the blade, and his eyes filled with worry. Did he think I was clueless?

"I know how to use it. I'm not helpless!"

"Angus taught you?"

"Yes," I admitted.

Kieran seemed to consider the weapon again. His eyes moved between the knife and me. A slow smile grew on his face. "Can I watch you and your dad?"

Would my dad mind? I didn't think so. "Sure, why not?"

He jumped up. "Great. Let's go."

I took his arm and pulled him toward the door. "No, you can go. I am in desperate need of a shower, and I want to change."

"I can wait—"

"You can go." I gave him a firm shove. "I'll meet you and my dad in the cavern in a half hour."

I closed the door and pushed a chair in front of it. Okay, so a determined Selkie would laugh at my attempts at privacy, but I thought Kieran would get the hint. I lingered in the shower a minute longer than necessary, enjoying the hot stream of water on my achy muscles. This was my chance to show my dad I was ready to fight alongside him. I couldn't complain, and I couldn't let a few muscle pains get in my way. I had to be in top form.

Chapter 31

"You ruined everything." Ken's voice dripped with hatred and accusation. Evan rubbed his temple. So much for not having headaches, he had a hell of a one now. He blinked and tried to focus. He heard Ken's voice, but no one else was in the room. Where was he anyhow? Were those bars?

Fully alert, Evan sat up and looked around. He was on a cot in a cell. Was he in jail? The last thing he remembered was the blinding light. Before that...

His hands!

He raised them. They looked normal. Blunt nails, pale skin. Had it all been a dream? It seemed so real...

"*Now* what are we going to do?" Ken's voice rose again. Though someone murmured a reply, Evan couldn't make out the words. Was that the professor? The voice was so low, it was impossible to distinguish.

Why was he in a cell? Had he done something wrong? He followed Ken's orders, and the professor's, too. The weird experience with the professor, had he dreamed it? What the hell happened? He'd lost Meara, he was possibly a monster, and now, they locked him up. Was he dangerous?

He crossed to the bars and checked for a padlock. He didn't see one. Maybe they put him here to rest until he woke up. He was probably reading more into the situation than he should. He wrapped his hand around the metal bars and pulled. Nothing.

The sweet stench of burning flesh hit him before the pain. He cried out at the sight of his blistered hands, the throbbing pain matching the one in his head. Panting, he staggered back to the cot and collapsed. Resting his hands palms up on his legs, he looked around for something to cool the burn. The cell held nothing except the cot, not even a sink.

"You're awake."

Ken came into the room from a doorway Evan hadn't noticed. His voice and expression were pleasant, calm. Quite different from the angry conversation Evan heard moments earlier. "And from the smell of things, you've tried to escape."

"Escape? Why is it locked? What did it burn me? Am I in trouble?" The questions tumbled out as the panic rose. Bile burned his throat.

"Trouble? No. We just want to keep you safe, my boy." Ken unlocked the door and slid it open. Thick gloves encased his hands. After shutting the metal gate behind him, he peeled the gloves off. "Let me see your hands."

Evan held out his palms, wincing at the pain. No flesh was visible, only angry, red welts and blistering boils.

"Tsk, tsk. The bars are electrified. It won't kill you, of course, but it does leave a nasty impression." Ken blew across Evan's hands, and icy cold replaced the stinging heat. The pain died instantly. His hands were healed. "Take better care in the future, please."

"Thank you," Evan said. "Who were you talking to?"

"Ted, of course." Ken's face twisted in rage. "The meddling imbecile. I should kill him for what he did."

"It really happened then? What he told me? It's real?" With mounting fear, Evan shrank away from the man before him.

"Why wouldn't it be?" Seemingly unaware of Evan's growing hysteria, Ken sat next to him on the cot and beamed. "You are the first success. We've tried for decades, all failures, until you, my boy."

Evan stared at the man. What was he? What kind of creature could cool and heal a burn by mere breath? In all the books he studied, he hadn't found any power like that. What did Ken want from him?

247

Was he expecting gratitude? Of all the questions circling in his head, he asked the ones that bothered him the most, "What did you do to me? What am I?"

"I did nothing *to* you, my boy. I created you. You are one of us."

"You created me...?" Evan shook his head. What was Ken saying?

"In part. Your mother had a role, too." His eyes lit up merrily. On Ken, it was rather creepy.

The accusation made Evan's blood boil. "My mother would never cheat on my father," he said. His parents loved each other. There was no way.

"What if she didn't know she was cheating?"

"What are you saying?" Evan watched Ken closely. He looked smug. The air shimmered around him. His features melted and reformed. Within moments, Darren Mitchell was sitting next to him.

"No..." Evan moaned as dread wiped out any thought in his mind.

"I'm afraid it's true," Ken said. "I am your real father."

"What about my sister?" Evan asked. "Katie."

Ken chuckled, a deep rumble low in his chest. It was creepy considering he still looked like Evan's dad. "I'm not Darren, my boy. I just made myself look like him. Darren is Katie's father. I suppose you could say she is your half sister."

"You tricked my mother? That's rape!"

Ken's eyes lit in pleasure. "She was more than willing and none the wiser for it. No harm came to her. She's perfectly safe as long as you cooperate."

Now Ken was threatening his family? Evan lay down on the cot and covered his eyes with his arm. This was too much to take in. Maybe Ken would leave if he ignored him. Minutes passed, and silence ensued. Breathing a sigh of relief, Evan uncovered his eyes and found Ken staring at him in amusement.

"I am immortal, Evan, a few minutes or a few months, it's all the same to me. To humans, existence is so brief. To us, well, I'll just say that

I'm very patient."

"What are you?" Evan asked again. He was relieved, at least, that Ken looked like himself again and not like his dad.

Ken stood and faced him. As Evan watched, he grew three feet, the top of his head stopping just inches below the ceiling. His fingers were long and pointed, his teeth sharp. He gave Evan a razor-filled smile. "I am Kennaught, king of the Blue Men of the Minch. As my son, you are the prince."

Prince? Was he supposed to be impressed? Everything he read about the Blue Men spoke to death, destruction, and despair. It didn't sound like a kingdom he wanted to be a part of. "Don't you have other children?"

"I told you... you are the first success. We are immortal and finite in number. We tried for centuries to reproduce with various species and could not. Until now."

"What makes me different?"

"Ah. Now, that is an intelligent question." Ken shrunk back down into his human form and sat on the cot again. "We're not sure, but we're going to find out." Something about that didn't reassure Evan. Ken must have noticed his nervousness, because he added, "We will not harm you, Evan. I told you, you are one of us. We don't hurt our family."

Evan sat up and leaned against the wall. "And my family?"

"Will be safe as long as you cooperate."

"I have your word?" Evan glared at Ken.

"Of course." Ken sounded insulted. "My oath is sacred. I will not break it."

Meara wasn't safe. There was no doubt that Ken did try to poison her. "Why did you try to poison my girlfriend?"

Ken's eyebrow rose. "Ex-girlfriend?"

"Whatever. You know what I meant. Why did you try to poison Meara?"

Ken shrugged and brushed a few wrinkles out of his pants. "I had my suspicions that she was not human. If she was, she died. If she wasn't, well... let me ask. Is her friend Kieran alive?"

Evan reluctantly answered, "Yes." He didn't want to give Ken any more information on Meara and her world than he had to.

"As I thought. They are Selkie, of course." When Evan's eyes widened, Ken chuckled again. "Our kind has loathed Selkies for lifetimes. You were wise to break up with her."

"Why? What have they done to you?"

"Let me tell you a story." Ken scooted back on the cot, making himself comfortable. "It starts as many fairy tales do, 'There once was a beautiful queen...' She was breathtakingly beautiful and kind. Her kingdom was isolated from most of the world, but peaceful. When strangers entered her realm, they were welcomed and assisted if they needed it. She had many children, all sons. They were happy."

A sucker for fairy tales, the story already captured Evan's imagination. Ken's deep, flowing voice was hypnotic to his ears.

"One day, she was swimming in a secluded cove and realized she wasn't alone. Another humanlike creature was there. She saw a seal, but felt the presence of an intelligent mind."

"A Selkie." Evan hadn't meant to speak the words out loud, but Ken seemed pleased by his interruption.

"Yes. She swam to the shore and sat on a large rock, watching him cut through the water with speed and strength. Eventually, he noticed her as well, or maybe he knew she was there all along and was showing off." Ken stared off in the distance, lost in his memories.

"What happened next?" Evan asked.

Ken waved an impatient hand and snapped, "What always happens when Selkies are involved? He seduced the queen, broke her heart, and left her to die."

"He killed her?" Evan was confused. The story didn't add up in his mind. How did they jump from seduction to death?

"He might as well have. When he abandoned her, as all Selkies eventually do to their lovers, she was so heartbroken that she killed herself. Her kingdom suffered with her death."

It was sad. A tragic love story, but Evan still didn't understand. Then Ken faced him with eyes full of tears and his face filled with hatred. He spit, "She was my mother. Our Mother. *The* mother. Mother to all Blue Men. When the Selkie seduced her, he cursed us all."

Evan didn't know what to say. He could see Ken's pain, but the story was missing too many details. Had the Selkie meant to seduce her? How long did their relationship last? Was the Selkie truly at fault for her suicide? Lots of questions and not enough answers. Wisely, he kept his mouth shut. Ken would not offer an unbiased opinion.

Ken stood abruptly and pulled on his gloves. "Get some rest. I'll have Stonewall bring you something to eat later."

"Wait! You're keeping me here?" Evan couldn't hide the shock in his voice. Ken was leaving him locked up like a prisoner.

"For now," Ken said. "I wouldn't want you to escape."

"I gave you my word," Evan said.

"Did you? Hmm... I did not hear it. It was I who gave you mine. Good night, Evan." He flipped the switch on the way out and threw the room into darkness.

Evan realized Ken was right. At the same time, he couldn't bring himself to make any promises. He didn't know what Ken's intentions were, and he needed to find out. For his sake, for his family's sake, and for Meara.

Lying down on the cot, Evan clasped his hands behind his head, lost in thought. Ken told more than just a story. As he talked, images formed in Evan's mind. Without Ken knowing it, Evan saw what Ken was thinking. Could all Blue Men do that? Something told him they couldn't, and asking Ken or anyone else would be a very bad idea.

In the cold dark, Evan smiled. He had a secret weapon.

Chapter 32

*K*ieran waited in the hall outside my father's suite. He clearly took a shower since his hair was damp, and he smelled like soap. I was grateful he wore jeans and a T-shirt. I didn't need his muscles distracting me.

"Is he in there?" I asked.

"Don't know. Didn't knock. I was waiting for you."

"How sweet," I said. He moved out of the way, so I could knock.

My dad opened the door, a cheery greeting on his lips. His brows rose when he spotted Kieran next to me. "Kieran, I didn't realize that you were coming along."

"I invited myself, sir. I hope that's okay. After training with Meara all summer, I'd like to see how she handles a weapon."

My dad shrugged and stood back so we could enter. "It's okay with me if it's okay with her. Can I get you anything? Coffee? Diet Coke?"

"I'm fine," Kieran said.

At the same time, I asked, "You have Diet Coke?"

"I keep some for you. Would you like one?"

"Please."

My dad opened the fridge and handed me a Diet Coke. I opened it and drank deeply. The sugary sweetness bubbled in my mouth.

Kieran watched me, his mouth turned down with distaste. "Wouldn't water be better for training?"

"Shut your mouth," I said in a playful tone. "I haven't had one of these in ages."

Kieran laughed. "Was it worth the wait?"

"What do you think?"

"The best things always are," he said, soft enough that only I heard him. His words made my face flame hot. Luckily, my dad was rinsing out the coffee pot and didn't notice.

"Where are we going, Dad?"

"We'll start in the cove," he said. "And go from there."

I finished the soda and handed him the empty can. "Let's go."

I transported to the cove first. Kieran and my dad arrived a second later. Kieran sat on a boulder to watch. Far enough away that he wouldn't distract us.

My dad and I circled on the sand, getting a feel for each other's motions. I wasn't sure if he'd give me a warning or some sign that we were starting. When he thrust his sword toward my chest, I ducked, spun, and poked his side with the tip of my dagger.

"Point," I called.

"Not bad." He caught the sole of my shoe and knocked me off balance. Before I fell, I vanished, transporting behind him, my knife at his throat.

"You fight dirty," I complained.

He locked his hand on my arm holding the dagger and flipped me over his head. I landed on my back, the breath knocked out of me. He leaned over me, smiling. I saw something in his eyes I couldn't read. Was it amusement? Pride? Once again, he lunged at me with his sword. I rolled to the side and jumped to my feet. We began to circle again.

"You are skilled, Meara. Your reactions are quick. You use your Selkie powers to your advantage." As he spoke, I listened to his thoughts. I knew his next move.

When he charged toward me, I caught his sword arm in an upward block and sent the sword flying. Before he could react, the sword was in my other hand. I pointed both weapons at his chest. "Do you surrender?"

His face blanked in shock before he laughed and held up his hands. "Well played."

Did you know I was in your mind? I asked him.

He shook his head. *I'm getting rusty in my old age.*

I knew Kieran was listening. I felt him on the peripheral. His presence was familiar to me now.

"Perhaps I should engage Meara in combat," Kieran said. "To show you what I've taught her. After all, you commissioned me."

My dad looked thoughtful as he took back his sword. "Very well. I would like to see what she's learned."

You ready? Kieran's smile was indulgent.

Are you? I challenged in reply. My duel with my dad was surprisingly easy. He misjudged me. The next time we fought, he would be more prepared.

Kieran knew my moves, and the further I got in my training with him, the less he held back. He was a formidable partner. Still, I was confident that I knew his moves, too. Blocking him from my mind was the bigger obstacle. I was used to him being there.

With a deep breath, I focused and brought up my shield. When he frowned slightly, I knew he felt it. My lips twitched as I held back a smile. He wasn't used to the silence either.

We faced each other, waiting. When we dueled, it was never predictable who would go first. Typically, the one who lost patience went first. Neither of us was very patient. He moved slightly, an almost unnoticeable shift to the left. I took the opening and attacked, catching him in the side with my foot, hard enough to make impact, but not to hurt. He reached for my foot and missed. I was already out of his reach.

With a grunt of frustration, Kieran struck at my shoulder. I flipped back and spun into a kick. This time, I caught him in the small of his back. I didn't pull back quick enough. He caught my foot and pushed to knock me off balance. As I fell, I reached forward and locked my hands on his wrists. I flipped him over my head and onto his back. We both rolled onto our stomachs and jumped up. Breathing hard, we circled again.

Kieran attacked. I blocked both fists, spun past him, and got him between the shoulder blades. He turned and caught my hand, preparing to flip me over his shoulder. Before he could, I stomped on his instep, making him wince in pain. While he hesitated, I punched him in the stomach. Not hard, but effective enough. He let me go.

My dad stood and clapped. "Excellent, excellent. Meara, you've made amazing progress."

I was happy and disappointed at the same time. "Does that mean you can't teach me anything?"

"I didn't say that. You are never too young or too old to learn new things." He rubbed his chin thoughtfully. "I'm not sure combat is what I need to teach you, though."

"Then what?" I asked.

"You need to learn about our enemies. Their weaknesses. In battle, your cunningness will serve you well. You must be prepared." My dad glanced at Kieran. "You're welcome to participate in the training, too."

"Thank you, sir." Kieran appeared to bow in response, which seemed over the top. Then I noticed he was just wiping the sweat off his face with the bottom of his shirt, exposing a strip of tanned, muscled flesh in the process. He lifted his head and caught me staring. A slow smile crept over his face.

I turned away. "Are we done for now?"

Another shower would be nice. While the fight with my dad barely warmed me up, the one with Kieran left me dripping with sweat.

"Go ahead and clean up," my dad said. "Then we'll have lunch in my suite."

We transported our own ways. I stood in the shower and let the hot water loosen my muscles. I did well. My dad was proud of me. I stood my ground against Kieran, who not only taught me, but also was quite a bit older than I was in Selkie years. Human years, too. He was older than my grandparents were. He was old. I didn't like to think about it.

I turned off the water and stepped out of the shower, wrapping a thick, white towel around me. The finger trick to dry my hair was fabulous. Before the mirror was completely unfogged, my hair was dried and styled. Smiling in satisfaction, I stepped into my bedroom and froze.

"Kieran, you've got to stop coming into my room."

My heart raced at the site of him in a pair of basketball shorts, casually lying on my bed. His hair was damp from the shower, his chest and feet bare.

I tilted my head and asked, "Is that how you're dressing for lunch with my dad? Kind of casual, isn't it?"

He eyed me greedily, and I remembered I was standing in a towel. With a sigh, I visualized shorts and a tank top. It was comical how his face fell in disappointment. He recovered quickly, pulling me next to him on the bed. "You were amazing today."

I gave him a suspicious look. "Were you holding back?"

"You know I didn't." He ran his finger down my arm from shoulder to wrist, leaving a trail of gooseflesh in its wake. "I don't have to. You're strong." His finger made its slow passage back up my arm, where he ran it teasingly under the strap of my tank top. "So powerful."

"Kieran—"

I wasn't exactly sure what I was going to say. Maybe, "We should get going," or "We shouldn't do this." Whatever thought I had, it was lost when his lips crushed mine, demanding to be kissed. His hand slid down my arm, moving to caress my hip. Unable to resist, my hands slid across his muscled torso, up his chest, until they wrapped behind his neck to pull him closer. I breathed in his clean scent. Where his skin touched mine, I was on fire. It scared me, this passion. At the same time, I wanted more.

He rolled until I was lying on top of him. His hands roamed

freely, leaving a trail of heat where they touched. A knock at the door made me scramble to the other side of the bed and tug my top straight.

"Meara, are you almost ready?" My dad spoke from behind the closed door. "Padraic just brought lunch."

"I'll be right there."

"I'll go let Kieran know," he said. "See you soon."

I relaxed when I could no longer hear Dad's footsteps. Kieran reached for me. I slid off the bed and out of his reach. Talking to my dad was like a cold shower. I could think clearly again.

"You heard him," I said. "We need to get going."

Chapter 33

Stonewall brought a plate of fish and a bottle of wine. He held up the bottle with a wry grin. "What else are you going to do in here?" It was the first time Stonewall showed any real kindness.

"May I use the bathroom?" Evan asked. It had been hours since Ken spoke to him. There was no place in the cell to relieve himself.

Stonewall frowned. "I was strictly ordered not to let you out, but I can bring you something." He left quickly, locking the gate behind him.

Fighting the discomfort of a full bladder meant that Evan couldn't eat right now, no matter how delicious the food smelled or how hungry he was. Why didn't they lock him in a room with plumbing?

Stonewall returned with a bucket, a jug of water, and a towel. "It's the best I can do," he apologized as he opened the cell, placed the items inside, and locked it again.

"It's better than nothing," Evan said. "Thank you."

Stonewall stared at him for a moment. He looked like he wanted to say something else. Uncertainty flitted across his features before the polite mask returned. "I'll leave you to your business," he mumbled and departed.

Embarrassed to use a bucket where anyone could walk in and see him, Evan was quick about his business. He washed his hands with the water. Feeling better, he ate everything on the plate and drank half the wine.

With a mildly fuzzy head, he stretched out on the cot. How was he going to get out of this mess? He was part Blue Man. What did that mean? The voices in his head had been quiet since he learned his true nature. Everything was quiet, yet he felt sick inside. What he read about the Blue Men, he didn't like. Ken's story at least partially explained why they were so angry. They wanted revenge. Would he grow to be like that, too? Would he hate Meara? Was that why he felt such a strong repulsion around her lately?

He fingered the chain on his neck. He could contact her. She said she would help him. After enduring his mood swings, she still professed to love him. It was worth a shot. Closing his eyes, his breath slowed in concentration.

Meara, I need help. He waited for a response. Something wasn't right. The space felt empty, like he was speaking into a cave. She told him in the dream that she was holding the necklace, not wearing it. Did she stop wearing it all together?

Meara, if you can hear me, say something.

Silence. She wasn't there. The blackness of despair settled on his soul. She was his only hope. If he couldn't reach her, no one would know he was captive. He chanted in his thoughts until he fell asleep.

Please hear me.

Please hear me

Please hear me.

No one answered his plea.

Chapter 34

The water turned from gold to fiery red as the sun sunk low on the horizon. The cool, Scottish air dipped a few degrees cooler. I conjured a blanket and wrapped it around myself. When it wasn't enough, I started a campfire and lost myself in the dancing flames.

Lunch with Kieran and my dad was pleasant, especially since Kieran kept his distance. He confused me. When he got too close, I lost all sense of reason. There was no excuse. I needed to be stronger. Until I figured things out with Evan, I couldn't get into another relationship.

After lunch, we spent the afternoon in the strategy room. I had to feign surprise so Dad wouldn't know Kieran brought me there before. It wasn't hard. Within minutes, I was horrified when he confirmed what Kieran already told me about the array of creatures that we must guard against. Kieran may have prepared me for the discussion, but I wasn't going to sleep any better. The nightmares were true. Monsters existed.

"Do you want some company?"

Ula sat next to me and tugged until I gave her the edge of the blanket. She scooted closer and pulled it around herself. "Sure is chilly tonight."

I didn't say anything. Evan would be leaving soon, heading back to Nova Scotia. I didn't know when I'd see him again, or even if he'd want to see me.

Ula tilted her head and studied me. "You okay?"

"I'm tired from training." I shrugged and gazed back at the fire. It was easier to watch the dancing flames than the concern on Ula's face. "I spent the day with my dad and Kieran."

"That's good, right?"

"It was nice to see Dad," I relented.

"I know what will cheer you up!" She waved her hand and put out the fire. Irritated, I tried not to show it. The fire felt wonderful, easing my aches, soothing my heart. The ashy embers almost seemed sad to me.

Ula squeezed my hand to get my attention. She was smiling broadly. "I have exciting news."

"What is it?"

"First, let's go and get some hot cocoa to warm up."

She transported us to the kitchen, and we almost landed on Uncle Padraic, who was carrying a tray of ginger snap cookies. He caught me with his free arm when I stumbled toward the hot oven.

"Whoa, ladies. Perhaps next time, you'd like to arrive in the entranceway."

"Thanks, Uncle Padraic." I hugged him before stepping back.

"Sorry, brother. My doing." Ula didn't sound sorry at all, and her eyes danced merrily. "Looks like we arrived just in time. My favorite cookies!" She reached for one and jerked her fingers back.

"I just took them out, dear sister." Paddy chuckled as he piled cookies on a plate. "Take these with you and be gone. I have work to do here."

"Why are you baking tonight?" I asked. Dinner was long over. Didn't he ever go to his room and just relax?

"A feast does not cook itself," he chastised. "Now, off with you."

He put a hand on each of our backs and gently pushed. Giggling, we abided.

"Feast?" I asked Ula once we were in the hallway and walking toward the tower. We agreed to go back to her room with our treats.

"That's the news I wanted to share. Ren, Atiya, and Nico leave in two days' time. We're having a celebration the night before."

261

"They're leaving in two days?" I couldn't believe that much time had passed. That meant Evan would be leaving in less than a week. I needed to get the necklace from Kieran and try to contact him again. Surely, I would be able to say goodbye. I hoped that it wouldn't be for good.

"You're missing the point, Meara. Another celebration. Another chance to get dressed up. We had so much fun last time." She pouted and sunk into a beanbag chair. "I thought you'd be excited to go with me again."

"Of course I'll go to the party with you." I took a cookie off the plate and sat across from her. "But you know this means that Evan's going home soon."

"Maybe it's for the best." Her voice was gentle. "His visit has not done much for your relationship."

"You mean besides end it?" I laughed bitterly.

She ate the rest of her cookie and conjured up two mugs of cocoa, handing one to me. "I think you need this." Her eyes grew sympathetic. "Have you spoken to him at all?"

"Not since I gave Kieran the necklace."

Hot chocolate sloshed dangerously close to the rim as Ula straightened in surprise. "You did what?"

"He thought the necklace would be too much of a temptation, so he offered to take it and hold it for me. He said I could talk to Evan whenever I wanted, but he wanted to be there to make sure nothing happened."

"That was generous of him." Ula sounded doubtful. "Are you going to try to contact Evan again?"

I nodded. "If nothing else, I want to say goodbye."

"You still love him." It wasn't a question. Ula patted my knee.

"Of course I do," I said. "I don't know if he loves me, though."

"From what you described of your dream, I'd say he does." She looked at me thoughtfully. "Something else is going on. It sounds like

Evan is a victim in it."

"Do you think that doctor did something to him? Besides knocking him out, I mean? He told me they injected him with something. Could the drug cause him to hallucinate?"

"Possibly." She shook her head in confusion. "And you shared all of this with David?"

"I did." The three of us also searched stacks of books in the strategy room library. It took most of the afternoon, and we found nothing. None of the symptoms Evan exhibited. Maybe he was experiencing something else. Maybe his glowing eyes were a trick of the light. I hoped they were. I didn't want to think about him becoming one of those monsters. With any luck, he found answers in the time we've been apart.

"When you contact Evan, you'll have to ask him what he knows."

"That's what I was thinking, too," I said.

We drank the rest of our cocoa in silence. While the mood was peaceful, my mind was not. If I didn't stop worrying about Evan, I was going to drive myself crazy. I needed a distraction.

"Tell me about this party," I asked. Perking up, she grinned and began to describe what the clan planned for Ren, Atiya, and Nico's departure. I laughed when she told me about Arren and his friends. After I spoke with them at the last feast, they sought out and discovered rock music. What they lacked in wisdom, they made up for in enthusiasm. The group started a band. Not a very good one according to Ula.

"My ears bled." She winced. "Literally."

They insisted on debuting at the party. The elders wanted to give them something to focus on, since the current high-alert status meant they couldn't swim. Realizing the band would be a nice distraction, they agreed to let them play.

"I can't wait to see it." I smiled, a real smile. Ula never failed to lift my spirits. Then my thoughts returned to Evan, and my happiness faded.

No matter what, I hoped he was okay.

Chapter 35

"I'm dressing myself this time," I warned Ula and tried to look stern. I failed when I met her eyes in the mirror and smiled. She shrugged a slim, naked shoulder.

"Let's see it then." She tapped her foot as if impatient. I knew she was only teasing.

"You look amazing," I said. Her dress was simple, yet beautiful. The asymmetrical emerald gown complemented her shape, and the color flattered her copper ringlets. "Are you sure everyone is dressing up?"

She moved next to me, smoothing a wrinkle in her dress. Leaning in for a quick inspection of her flawless makeup, she asked, "How often do we get to dress up?"

I didn't bother pointing out that this would be the third time in my life I dressed this fancy, and two of those events occurred this summer. The other event was my parents' wedding. At the time, I was embarrassed watching my parents act so lovey-dovey. Looking back, I was glad they rediscovered each other and sealed their love with vows. I blinked and brushed the tears away. If Ula noticed, she didn't comment. Before I could get too melancholy, I closed my eyes and concentrated. When we were dress shopping for my mom's wedding gown, I saw the most amazing dress. It fit snugly from chest to hips. With a plunging, sweetheart neckline, it gave the wearer an hourglass shape, and then flared into frothy waves of fabric. It reminded me of the sea.

I imagined that dress, adding a few adjustments of my own.

Midnight blue, flecks of silver woven throughout like a starry sky or the reflection on a wave. When I heard Ula gasp, my eyes flew open.

"It's gorgeous!" she squealed.

Seeing my reflection, I took a step back. It couldn't possibly be me. Without realizing it, I'd visualized makeup to match, deep, smoky eyes and gorgeous, red lips. The reflection in the mirror was sophisticated and confident. No trace of a girl, this was a woman.

"You look like a mermaid," Ula commented and touched one of the waves. "It's really sexy."

A slow smile spread on my face. I couldn't wait to see Kieran's reaction. To complete the look, I twisted my hair in a complex style, threading pearls throughout.

Ula snapped her compact closed. No longer needed, it vanished. She offered me her arm. "Ready?"

Unafraid, confident, and full of anticipation, for the first time in a long time, I was.

When we arrived, the hall was full of laughter and conversation. Not everyone was dressed up, but I was relieved to see that many were. My dad, Brigid, and Angus sat at the head table, deep in conversation. Uncle Ren's family hadn't arrived yet.

"Meara!" My dad's eyes widened in surprise when he saw me. I watched with amusement as a myriad of emotions crossed his face. Clearly, he found the dress too revealing for his daughter. He let it go. Pulling me close, he kissed my cheek and whispered, "You look beautiful. Your mother would be so proud."

I blinked rapidly as I hugged him. "Thanks, Dad."

I stepped back and into a little person.

"Whee!"

The ruffles on my dress rose and fell as Nico played with the hem.

I spun and picked him up. "What do you think you're doing, rascal?" When I kissed his cheek, he laughed and squirmed in my arms. I was really going to miss the little cutie.

Horrified that my eyes were once again filling with tears—why did I bother with makeup?—I placed Nico in his mother's outstretched arms. Her gentle smile comforted me. "You're always welcome to visit, Meara. This is not a goodbye, but an 'until we meet again.'"

We took our seats as the first course was served. The meal was long, but pleasant. Thankfully, my dad and the other elders kept the conversation light. They reminisced about their childhood, which was fun for me to hear. My dad was a precocious child who apparently loved to play pranks on his siblings. The vision was so different from the man before me, the man burdened with the responsibility of leading. He was a good leader, a good man. He had some things to learn about being a father, but he was trying. I was proud.

The music started once dessert was served. It wasn't Arren's band, but the adults who played the more traditional dance music. Standing, I stretched. I reached my limit after the main course. There was no room for dessert. The tempo picked up, and the floor filled with dancing Selkies. How could they move like that after such a large meal? I wasn't ready to dance, though walking sounded doable.

"Want me to come with you?" Ula asked when I passed her chair. Her expression told me she didn't want to, so I appreciated her offer all the more. She was trying to make up for ditching me the last time.

I patted her shoulder and smiled. "I'm good. Stay and visit with your brother."

Kieran wasn't here, I realized with disappointment. Or if he was, I didn't see him. I laughed when my eyes did settle on some familiar faces—Arren and his friends. They wore rock star costumes. Well, their impression of what rock stars wore. They apparently couldn't distinguish decades. They looked like a mashup of early Beatles, Megadeath, Madonna, Run DMC, and Lady GaGa. I was almost afraid to hear their songs.

"Hi Arren," I said. His mouth dropped open when he eyed my dress. He quickly recovered, giving me an aloof stare so often seen on celebrities in photographs. Where had they been getting their information? Did they uncover a stash of *People* and *Rolling Stone* magazines?

"Hey, Meara. What's up?"

I fought the urge to shake my head or roll my eyes. "Are you guys playing soon?"

"We're up next," Madonna said. I couldn't remember any of the other bandmate's real names. She really looked like Madonna, so the name fit.

"Are you going to watch?" Like an eager puppy dog, Arren bounced in front of me.

"Of course," I said. "Can't wait."

Looking past Arren, my heart lept. Kieran strode across the room. Eyes burning, he locked me in his gaze. I had been wondering about his reaction. Seeing him, I melted into a pool of want. No one wore a tuxedo like Kieran did.

A slow, sexy smile spread across his face. He noticed my reaction. Damn, now he had the advantage. I tried to cool my thoughts and put on a poker face. I was fairly certain that I wasn't successful.

He didn't stop a respectable distance away. Toe to toe, he leaned in and whispered in a deep, throaty voice, "You're breathtaking."

The light brush of his lips on my ear sent shivers down my spine. His hands soon followed, pulling me against him and onto the dance floor. "Why do you do this to me?" he murmured into my hair. "You drive me crazy."

I hid my smile against his chest. His heart was beating fast, too. A voice cut through my emotional haze.

"It's not a slow song, you know."

Arren and his friends laughed. Kieran didn't acknowledge them.

To me, he said, "I'm not even hearing the music. You block everything else in the room."

My eyes sought his. Was he serious? He was if the shell-shocked expression on his face was any indication. I never meant to make him fall in love with me. I stepped back, afraid. I never meant to fall in love with him. Finally admitting it to myself, I fled.

"Meara, wait!"

Kieran caught me at the top of the stairs. I was mere steps away from the safety of my room, yet his arms tightened around my waist.

I waited, refusing to turn and see his face.

He stepped closer to me, the heat from his body erasing a bone-deep chill. His chin lighted on my head, and he sighed. "I scared you."

I collapsed in his arms, the fight gone. "I scared myself."

With a gentle touch, he turned me around and raised my chin until I met his gaze. His eyes searched mine, and then he smiled. "You have feelings for me, too."

"Kieran... I... Evan." Words tumbled as my mouth tried to speak for my frazzled brain.

"It's okay, Meara. I know. You love him." His voice was soft and understanding.

He puzzled me. "You're okay with that?" I asked, searching his eyes.

"It's enough," he answered. "For now. Knowing that you care for me, too."

He held my gaze as he lowered his head. When his lips met mine, all the emotions swirling in my head narrowed to one singular focus. Right then, right there, there was no one else but Kieran.

Reluctantly, he broke the kiss and stepped back. "I better go."

His absence left my body cold. He was leaving?

He laughed softly. "When we finally get together, Meara, I don't want you to wake up with regrets. I'm not sharing you with another man."

My face heated as I grew angry. I wasn't planning to sleep with him. How dare he think that! I immediately calmed when I realized he was teasing. He smiled with confidence. The expression I once thought arrogant was now endearing.

"Sweet dreams, beautiful."

Chapter 36

Water dripped nearby. Evan shivered in the dampness. Stonewall removed the dishes several hours ago. That was the last time he'd seen anyone.

With nothing to do, Evan took to counting the drops as they hit the cement floor. Three thousand, seven hundred and eighty-three, three thousand seven hundred and eighty-four, the pace never wavered. Plop, plop. How long were they going to keep him here?

His thin T-shirt did little to insulate his clammy skin. He pulled his arms into the shirt against his stomach and did his best to stay warm. Would it kill them to give him a blanket? He could do without a pillow, but he hated being cold.

Evan rubbed his hands up and down his biceps, trying to generate heat. His skin prickled lightly. Was it his imagination or were his arms getting warm?

He pulled his hands back through his shirt's armholes. His fingertips were a deep blue. The color worked its way slowly up his arms. As the blue spread, so did the heat. Fascinated, he watched his body change. If it brought comfort, there was no reason to fight it.

The heat spread up his torso and flowed down his legs. Dimly, he was aware that his feet now hung off the end of the cot. The cot fit his length moments ago. What would happen when the change was complete? Floating in warmth and comfort, Evan realized he didn't care.

A flame burst inside him. Fury, a fierce beast, uncoiled in his belly. If it weren't for her, he'd be home safe. If it weren't for *her*, he'd never have taken this internship. A growl, low and terrifying, rose in his throat. One name tore from his mouth.

Meara.

Chapter 37

He called my name. The hatred in his voice left me shivering in the dark. How could he reach me? How was it possible? Kieran had the necklace.

Evan?

My voice was tentative, weak. Alone in the dark, I waited.

Chapter 38

Her voice slid, silk in his mind. The fog lessened, and Evan saw her lying on her bed, hopeful and afraid at the same time. Meara.

Are you okay? Please be okay.

Her lips formed the words, but he heard no voice in his head. She worried about him. Through everything, she loved him. The anger dissipated the moment he heard her voice. Where had it even come from?

I'm okay, he said. *They've imprisoned me.*

What? Where? She jerked up now, her back against the headboard. Her eyes searched the dark, not focusing on anything. She couldn't see him. He wasn't sure how he could see her.

In the basement, he said. *I'm in a cell.*

I'll come get you. She jumped out of bed.

No! Evan shouted. *It's not safe. That's exactly what Ken wants.*

She settled on the edge of the bed, unsure, blinking in the dark. *Tell me what you want me to do.*

Wait for me to contact you again. Voices in the stairwell made him rush to add, *I love you. Be safe.*

Chapter 39

I tore through the hall, a million questions in my mind. Why was Ken holding Evan hostage? Where was Professor Nolan? Was he in on it? The thought made my heart jump. Would they hurt him?

I wasn't thinking about my destination until I arrived at Kieran's door. It was unlocked. It was always unlocked. I crossed to his bed and clasped his bare shoulder, shaking him out of sleep. This time, he woke easily.

"What is it?" He sat up, instantly alert.

"Ken's holding Evan hostage." I paced the length of his room, rubbing my arms in agitation. "He's locked in a cell."

Kieran's sharp eyes met mine. "How do you know?"

"He spoke to me. " I pointed to my head. A year ago, I would've thought it was crazy. After so many mental conversations, I didn't even question it. Kieran did.

"How do you know it wasn't a dream?"

"I was awake, Kieran. It was no dream." My pace slowed as I considered our conversation. "Somehow, he can reach me without the necklace. He must have powers now." I glanced at Kieran for confirmation. He tilted his head and frowned.

"Could be," he finally conceded. "Wish we knew what those powers were."

He crossed to his dresser. Opening the top drawer, he pulled out a small box and handed it to me. "You might as well take this back now.

If he can contact you either way, then my holding the necklace affords you no security."

I chilled at his words. Was I in danger from Evan? No. I dismissed the thought and secured the necklace around my neck. It fell into place and righted my world.

Kieran glanced at it for a moment, sighed, and then reached for the shirt at the end of his bed. Pulling it over his head, he asked, "Did he happen to tell you what species he is?"

"No."

"You didn't ask?"

"It didn't come up in our conversation. You know, when he was telling me that he's being held *prisoner*." Kieran's attitude irritated me. I wasn't playing twenty questions with him.

"I need to tell my dad." I huffed out a breath and moved toward the door. "Are you coming?"

"Don't I always?" he mumbled, closing the door behind us.

Chapter 40

"Did you sleep well?"

Ken's smooth voice grated on Evan's nerves. He sat up and cracked his neck. "It's great. Downright cozy down here."

Evan's sarcasm knocked the grin off Ken's face. The man infuriated him. While he waited to see what Ken wanted, he massaged the knot on his right shoulder. Last night was miserable. He barely slept. There was no need for Ken to know.

"Stonewall!" Ken hollered. "Where are you?"

The servant hurried across the room and into the cell, with a tray of food in his hands. He set it before Evan and made a hasty retreat.

"Finish the preparations!" Ken yelled after him. Evan doubted Stonewall heard. As fast as that man hustled, he was halfway to China by now.

Not waiting for an invitation, Evan dug into the food. Eggs, bacon, and toast. Black coffee, steaming hot. He ate fast, worried that Ken might take it away. Who knew what that man would do next?

Ken watched him eat, drumming his fingers impatiently on his thighs. Evan wondered if Ken was aware of his jumpy movements. "I suppose you're wondering if I'm going to let you out of here."

Evan shrugged since his mouth was full of food. Ken took it as an invitation to continue. "We're leaving today. Before the Selkies return. I prefer to be on the offense, not defense."

Swallowing quickly, Evan asked, "Where will we go?"

"Not for you to know." Ken wagged a finger at him. "I can't have you telling your girlfriend. How have you been communicating with her anyway?"

Evan squirmed under Ken's assessing gaze. "I'm not," he said. "I broke up with her."

Ken made a noncommittal sound and stared at Evan a moment longer before waving his hand in dismissal. "No matter," he said. "She won't find you. Not where we're going."

"I thought you had a plan," Evan said. "Does it include running and hiding?" He hoped to goad an answer out of Ken. It didn't work. Ken laughed. It was a low, evil sound.

"Oh, I do, son. I do." He stretched and smiled. "As I told you, I'm very patient. I have no doubt I'll win."

He strolled out of cell and left the door open. Evan tensed and waited. He held no pretense that he could escape. At the base of the stairs, Ken turned and confirmed as much. "Pack your things. We leave in one hour." He smirked at Evan. "Don't run. Don't do anything stupid. I'll know, and you'll pay."

The warning barely off his lips, he left without a backwards glance. Evan knew he needed to act quickly. He moved to stand and knocked over the dinner tray. The food was gone, but plates and utensils flew. His eyes caught on a steak knife. Was that on the tray?

Picking up the knife, he pressed his finger against the tip. It drew blood. Praying that Stonewall wasn't returning soon for the tray, he picked up the white, cloth napkin and began to write. Satisfied, he unclasped the necklace and wrapped it in the cloth. Now, where should he hide it? The cot was just that. A canvas cot. No mattress. No sheet or blanket. That wouldn't work.   He shoved the package in his pocket. He'd find a spot in his room. Turning his attention to the cell, it appeared that the door was no longer electrified. Evan had no desire to repeat the experience. He steered clear of the bars as he exited. With an inward sigh of relief, he was glad to be rid of that prison. Then again, he might be trading one set of bars for another one. He hoped not.

He passed through the doorway, not exactly sure where to go to find the stairs, but heading the way he saw Ken go. A hand snagged out of the shadows and grabbed his arm. Before he could react, the other hand covered his mouth.

Eyes widening in panic, Evan tensed to fight until the figure stepped out of the shadows. Professor Nolan pulled him close and frantically whispered, "We need to talk. There's not much time." His eyes flitted to another doorway across the room. "He may return to see what's taking you so long."

"What happened to you?" Evan asked. The professor looked terrible. His lips, swollen and bloody, cracked when he talked, displaying a mouth with several teeth missing. His eyes, mere slits between black and blue lumps, fought to stay open. Someone or something attacked him with no mercy.

"No time for that. Be careful, Evan. You do not realize how powerful Ken is." He squeezed Evan's arm almost painfully. "Watch your back at all times."

"You're not coming with us?"

Ted chuckled. It turned to a painful cough. When he wiped his mouth with his sleeve, it left a bloody smear. "I'm no use to him now. He'll leave me here."

Evan thought fast. Could he trust Ted? He needed to. He wasn't sure he'd have time to get Meara a message. "Meara will be coming for me," he said.

Ted's eyebrows lifted. It looked excruciating on his broken face. "Does she have a death wish?"

Smiling wistfully, Evan said, "No, just misplaced bravery. I need you to give her something." He took the folded napkin from his pocket and placed it in the professor's malformed hand. Was no bone left unbroken?

Ted didn't ask what it was. He placed it in his pocket. "Consider it done."

278

Footsteps sounded in the distance, making him flinch. "Go. Don't tell anyone you spoke with me." He placed a shaking hand on Evan's shoulder. "I'm sorry you're involved in this."

Evan didn't know what else to say besides, "Me, too."

He hurried up the stairs and into a flurry of activity on the main floor. People he'd never seen were running to and fro, mainly carrying paintings or other pieces of art. Ken wasn't lying. They really were leaving.

He climbed the stairs to the second floor, wondering why they were leaving now. Ken poisoned Kieran almost two weeks ago. If the Selkies were going to attack, wouldn't they have done it by now?

His room was untouched. That was a relief. His suitcase and duffel bag were still under the bed. He pulled them out and began to throw his things inside. As he packed, a million questions flew through his mind. Where were they going? Would they take the boat or car? Who was all going? Ted wasn't, but what about Stonewall and Dr. Tenuis?

Lost in thought, Evan didn't hear the footsteps approaching until it was too late. When the cloth covered his face, he tried to fight. It was a wasted effort. Everything went black.

Chapter 41

"I'll check it out in the morning."

My dad stood and crossed to the door, dismissing us. Too bad I wasn't ready to go.

"*You'll* check it out?" I said. "What about me? Evan's my boyfriend. I have a right to come along."

Behind my dad, Kieran had been shaking his head frantically. He winced at the end of my outburst. A glance at my dad's face told me I'd taken it too far. He was furious.

"You will stay here and do as I say. You've been a Selkie for less than three months. What qualifies you to go on a mission against an enemy we haven't even identified yet?"

"But—"

"You're staying. That's final!" He grabbed my arm in one hand and pulled me to the door. "Kieran, you're to keep an eye on her."

"David—"

Whatever Kieran was going to say, he stopped when he saw my dad's face. Sighing, he took hold of my other arm. I moved from Dad's grasp to his. Was I just a pawn? A possession? When would I be taken seriously and allowed to fight?

I yanked my arm from Kieran's grip. Lifting my chin, I stepped into the hall. "I can walk on my own two feet. I don't need an escort."

"Meara, wait!"

I stopped at my dad's voice. Those two words were full of remorse. Blinking back tears of frustration and anger, I gave in, looked over my shoulder, and met his eyes. "Yes?"

"I'll do everything I can to rescue Evan," he said. "I'll send two of our best guards to scope things out."

It wasn't enough, but it was something. "Thank you," I said.

He nodded and closed the door behind us.

My heart beat frantically in my chest as I moved down the hall. Kieran followed close behind. I knew that without turning.

You're going. His voice was smug, his words a statement, not a question.

I hurried down the steps. *Wouldn't you?*

I would, and I will. His hand fell on my shoulder and squeezed. *Promise to your father or not, I won't let you go alone.*

I reached up and squeezed his hand.

He continued, *Aren't you worried about what we'll run into?*

I'm more worried about running into my dad, I responded automatically. My dad would never forgive me if I let myself get hurt. If I died, well, it was no longer my concern then, was it?

When are we leaving?

Midnight, I decided. *Dad will be watching me for the next couple of hours.*

You're right. Kieran chuckled.

We'll meet at the cove. I continued to mindspeak. There was no telling who might be listening in the halls. Kieran knew it, too. *I don't want to draw unnecessary attention by meeting in one of our rooms.*

Afraid of the rumors, he teased. *Poor Arren's heart will be broken.*

Arren. The concert. Did he realize I missed it? Sure, Arren and his friends were teens like me, but they slipped from my mind with ease. We were so different, and well, I was a little preoccupied. I rolled my eyes as Kieran continued to laugh.

"Midnight," I said, slipping into my room.

The next few hours felt like torture. Lying still in the dark room, I tried to appear to be sleeping while adrenaline coursed through my veins. I wanted to run, swim, and fight. Do anything but lay on my bed with my eyes closed. I noted the clicks every time my door opened and closed, fighting the curiosity to open my eyes and see who was there, checking on me. Instead, I willed every muscle to relax and took slow, deep breaths.

Between the door checks, I monitored the lighting. The moon was near full, just days away, and my room was washed in moonlight. Now that I could track the cycle and the time, I wondered how it was so difficult for me before. The Selkie ways were coming easier to me with each passing day.

The subtle shift of the light told me it was close to midnight, and I hadn't been checked on in at least an hour. My dad must have finally decided I was asleep and not going anywhere.

Stretching my arms and legs, I listened. The halls were quiet. This was my moment. With no time to waste, I moved my pillows to look like a body, pulled the blankets into place, and transported to the beach.

Kieran faced the sea, the moonlight bleaching his blond hair to silver white. "You're sure you want to do this?" he asked without turning around.

I didn't hesitate. "Positive."

He gave a curt nod, and the air shifted. In seal form, he slid into the water. I followed quickly behind, transforming in motion. The waves glided over my back. We dove deep into the cool calm.

What's your plan? he asked.

I used the hours in bed to consider my options. Only one made any sense. After all, there were only two of us. Reconnaissance.

We'll scope the grounds and go from there.

He didn't speak, but I knew he was pleased. What did he think I would do? Confront them? That would be suicide.

As we neared the shore, I warned. *Watch for our guards. I don't know if they're still here.*

On it. He slid out of the water into an area of the cove shadowed by the cliff. He disappeared from view. I waited in the water for his report. I didn't have to wait long.

The cove's clear. He motioned to the staircase. *I'm heading up.*

I changed form, adding a black shirt and pants, along with black running shoes. Better to be prepared. As a last precaution, I conjured my dagger and slid it into my back pocket.

I climbed hurriedly. Kieran was almost at the top. While I was certain he could defend himself, I wanted to be there to back him up. It was my responsibility to ensure his safety. He came on this expedition because of me.

Just below the landing, Kieran turned and looked down. He pointed to the pier, and I looked. The moon lit the landscape, and one thing was clear. Their boat was gone.

I ran up the last couple of steps to his side. If the boat was missing, the odds were that they were gone already, too. We couldn't make any risky moves, yet I felt braver than I had minutes ago. Bravery mixed with disappointment. The chances of finding Evan here were slim at best.

We crossed the yard, crouching low to avoid any motion lights or cameras. Most of the yard lights were off. A few security lights cast a glow to certain areas. We avoided them and hung in the shadows.

Kieran tried the back door. The handled turned and, with a noiseless shove, he opened it. We looked at each other in surprise. Was it a trap? It seemed too easy.

He wanted to scope things out first, but I wouldn't let him. I entered on his heels, closing the door behind me. The house was dark, but Selkie eyes adjusted fast. Within seconds, I could see everything in detail.

We passed the kitchen on the right. The room was untouched, the counters clean and uncluttered. Pans hung from the ceiling, and a fresh vase of flowers sat on the counter. The dining room was next on the left. Like the kitchen, it was in pristine condition. If they left, they didn't take the time to pack up the house.

Kieran entered the living room and stopped. I wondered why until I noticed the fireplace. The large oil painting was missing. Only the nails hung on the wall.

Some things had been packed. The precious ones, apparently.

Where do you suppose the basement is? I continued to talk to Kieran through telepathy. Someone could be in the house. It was too soon to throw away precautions.

There was another hall past the kitchen, Kieran noted. *I say we try there first.*

Good thinking. I went to move ahead. He stopped me with his hand, gave me a look, and took the lead. With a sigh, I followed him back down the hall, through the kitchen, and into the back hallway. There was a door on either end of the short hallway.

You try that one. I pointed to the door on the left. *I'll try the other.*

Kieran grimaced, but he moved to the door. I pulled mine open and smiled. The steps lead down. Without waiting, I took the lead.

I moved fast with little noise. The area around the base of the stairs was dark, but light flickered beneath a closed door.

Meara, please. Kieran's voice held reproach. *Let me go first.*

I stepped to the side and waited for him to open the door. I was dying to know what was in that room. My heart hammered in my chest, nerves causing the blood in my ears to pound like waves. Was Evan still here in the cell?

The lit room held one desk covered in oddly shaped tools. A wooden chair rested in the middle of the room, the seat and rungs stained black. The floor surrounding the chair was painted a deep crimson. My head swam when I put it all together. Torture. Did they torture Evan?

Kieran stilled. Then I heard it, too. Rattled breaths drifting from the room next door.

"I can hear you," the voice whispered. Weak and filled with pain, I didn't recognize it. "I can't and won't hurt you. Show yourselves."

What's your decision? Kieran's eyes bore into mine.

I could be leading us to our deaths, but I needed answers. *We go in.*

The room was large, most of the space taken up by a four-sided cell. The bars hummed, warning us that it was electrified. The cell was sparse—a bucket and a cot covered in bloody rags. The rags moved, and I gasped. It was a man, beaten almost beyond recognition. My eyes filled with tears. Almost beyond recognition. I knew him. It was Evan's professor, Ted Nolan.

"Where's Evan?" I cried.

"He said you would come. Brave and foolish is a dangerous combination." Ted sat up on shaky arms. He grinned. Someone who was missing several prominent teeth should not grin. It was creepy. Bloody spittle dripped from the corner of his mouth. He gently dabbed a sleeve to his chin. "Excuse my appearance. It's been a rough week."

I felt Kieran at my side. He'd yet to say or do anything, but he was on full alert.

"Your bravery is admirable." Ted's swollen eyes locked on mine. "You must love Evan very much to risk your life."

"Do you know where he is?"

Ted coughed, bending at the waist. When he quieted, he said, "I was not privy to the information. Ken considers me a traitor."

Kieran spoke up. "Are you?"

A deep growl rumbled in Ted's throat. It could've been from pain or anger. I wasn't sure. "I wasn't." He sighed and motioned to his body. "Until he did this to me, locked Evan in a cell, and showed me what kind of monster he truly is."

"What is he?" Kieran asked. Like Ping-Pong, my eyes bounced between the two of them, both men sizing each other up.

"The same as me." With a wail, Ted rose. He swayed on his feet, clearly in extreme pain. "I'll show you."

We watched as his body elongated. Muscles and bones popped with the sudden growth. His nails turned long and sharp, as did his teeth. When the transformation was complete, he was inches from the ceiling, his skin and eyes a vivid blue. The red blood streaming down his arms appeared black against his skin.

Blue Men of Minch, Kieran confirmed in my head.

Ted bent down toward us, grunting as he went. We jumped back, but he shook his head. "I won't hurt you. I never meant to hurt anyone." He sighed and fell back from his hunched position, a dazed expression on his face. "I don't have much longer."

Struggling with his pocket, he pulled out a poorly wrapped package and handed it to me through the bars. The package was light, but flexible. It wasn't paper, rather, smooth, white fabric. A dinner napkin, I realized. Unfolded, the bundle revealed Evan's necklace. He'd left it for me. Why?

Wait. Something was on the fabric, writing in reddish-brown ink. Ink or blood? Stretching the napkin between my hands, I read the message clearly. There was one word carefully printed with thick and jagged lines in the center of the napkin. One word that seared itself into my brain.

Azuria.

Kieran read over my shoulder. When I looked back at him, he shook his head in confusion. He didn't know.

"What's Azuria?" I asked.

Professor Nolan didn't respond. He was already dead.

THE END

Acknowledgements

In a blink of an eye, I've gone from being an unpublished author to having not one, but two books under my name. I have the amazing women at Clean Teen Publishing to thank for that. Thank you for believing in me and giving me beautiful books with captivating covers and lovely typography. A special thanks to Cynthia, the editing guru, for your sharp eye and wise advice, and to Melanie for promoting my stories to the world. You are all so good at what you do, and I'm thrilled to be a part of it.

Once again, I also want to thank the staff and students at AllWriters' Workplace and Workshop. Your critiques and discussions of Current Impressions helped to make the story what it is today. Thank you to Katie, Stephanie, and Ceci who kindly beta read the story and gave me solid feedback, asking questions about the things that needed questioning.

A big shout out to my husband, John; my daughter, Dori; and my son, Nate; who put up with my crabbiness when the words weren't coming right and my isolation when I was in "writer mode."

Finally, to my other friends and family who provide encouraging words, celebrate my successes, and allow me to always dream a little bigger. This one's for you!

About the Author

*K*elly Risser knew at a young age what she wanted to be when she grew up. Unfortunately, Fairytale Princess was not a lucrative career. Leaving the castle and wand behind, she entered the world of creative business writing where she worked in advertising, marketing, and training at various companies.

She's often found lamenting, "It's hard to write when there's so many good books to read!" So, when she's not immersed in the middle of someone else's fantasy world, she's busy creating one of her own. This world is introduced in her first novel, Never Forgotten. Never Forgotten, a YA/NA Fantasy, was released by Clean Teen Publishing in the Summer of 2014.

Kelly lives in Wisconsin with her husband and two children. They share their home with Clyde the Whoodle and a school of fish.

CPSIA information can be obtained at www.ICGtesting.com
Printed in the USA
BVOW11s2107080814

362232BV00022B/265/P